The Necromancer's Child

FELICIA JEDLICKA

For those who wish they could change the past.

SISTER WITCHES
THE DEVIL'S SHADOW
THE DEVIL'S SOUL

DESTINY REJECTED
DESTINY RECLAIMED
DESTINY RAZED
DESTINY RESTORED

DÉJÀ VU

SAVE THE HUMANS

THE NECROMANCER'S CHILD

<u>THE NEBRASKA APOCALYPSE NOVELS</u>
CORN COWS AND THE APOCALYPSE
COW TIPPING AFTER THE APOCALYPSE
CORN HUSKING AFTER THE APOCALYPSE

<u>THE WARDEN SERIES</u>
SUCCESSORS
RIVALS
LOVERS AND LIARS
BAD BLOOD
TENANTS AND TYRANTS
THE RING BEARER
GODS AND MONSTERS
BEASTS AND BURDENS
MAGIC AND MAYHEM
FORK IN THE ROAD
DETAILS AND DEADLINES
*CURSES AND SACRIFICES**
*WITCHES AND WOLVES**
*SAINTS AND SERPENTS**
*ENEMIES AND ALLIES**

*MARRIED TO DEATH**

The Necromancer's Child

FELICIA JEDLICKA

The House

I stepped up onto the old porch, disregarding the realtor's suggestion that I "watch my step." Had she clarified that the porch was rotted out and I might find myself knee-deep in splintered wood two steps later, I would have been a little more mindful of her warning.

"Oh, wait, wait!" The stout forty-something feathered blonde hurried up the steps behind me to help me out of the painful predicament. "I got you." The woman looped her arm undermine and assisted my rise. She hissed on my behalf as the split boards scraped my calf for the second time on the way out. "I'm so sorry, Tori. I should have taken you in the back door—although that one isn't much better."

"It's all right, Mrs. Hanson. It's only a few scratches." I disentangled myself from her grip and dusted the dirt off my leg. The stinging cuts were already puffing up, but they weren't technically bleeding.

Mrs. Hanson sighed and shook her head at the broken wood by her feet. "I just wish you would let me sell you a proper home. A young woman doesn't belong in a place this old and desolate." She looked out over the property that was covered in water-starved grass and an endless crop of sticker patches. Even the gravel road leading up to the house was almost completely overgrown. The only redeeming feature of the property was the view. From high on the bluff, I could see the whole town below. The downside, of course, was that they could also see me, and it gave the abandoned property a very *House-on-Haunted-Hill* feel. "Well..." Mrs. Hanson turned back to me and smiled. "I'll let you decide." She scooted around the hole in the porch, moving as nimbly as she could in her A-line red skirt and jacket.

"Don't worry, Mrs. Hanson, my lawyer has warned me the place needs work."

"Work?" She scoffed as she typed her code into the key box. "It needs a wrecking ball. The town was going to burn it down, you know. It was even gifted to the fire department, but I guess they never got around to it."

"Their loss, my gain," I said cheerfully.

"I don't understand why you don't buy a new home. You'll spend as much money on renovating this one. I have five properties that would be perfect for you. This place doesn't even have central air. And good luck trying to get cable service out this far."

"Then I'll get a satellite...And a fan." I smiled, trying to impress upon the woman as nicely as possible that I was not as naïve as she suspected me to be. I may have been a little wet behind the ears, but I was educated, independently wealthy, and terribly stubborn when it came to getting my own way. I hadn't come back to my hometown fourteen years after my parents' tragic and untimely death simply to stare from afar at the home that rightfully belonged to me. I wanted to embrace my past and hopefully get some answers about it. Answers that had unfortunately been eluding my memory since the day of the accident.

Mrs. Hanson sighed, giving up on the feat of convincing me to buy a condominium. She pushed open the door with some effort, liberating the hinges of a long-held groan. She stepped into the dimly lit home and disappeared, muttering about the basement and the breaker box.

I cautiously stepped to the entrance. Like the rest of the house, the front door desperately needed a fresh coat of paint. At one time, a decoratively etched window may have adorned it, but someone had broken it out long ago and now the space was covered with plywood. Fortunately, the rest of the home's windows were intact, but if I expected to stay warm through the winter, I would need to have them replaced.

As I passed over the threshold, the stagnant air of a lifeless house hit me—a mixture of dust, wood, mildew, and the droppings of the current squatters. I had hoped to have an epiphany, a sudden and complete anamnesis to join my disjointed childhood memories. However, that wasn't the case. There were a few lazy recollections, but nothing substantial.

I had only been eight when my parents died, so there weren't a lot of significant memories to weed through. Birthday cakes, Christmas presents, bedtime stories, and the tormented screams of two fiery deaths. That was all I remembered prior to being placed with my foster parents.

I passed by the open staircase, letting my fingers drag across the spindles. Did I peek out between these bars? Did I spy Santa putting presents under the tree on Christmas Eve? Did I see my parents fighting from here?

I shook away the unpleasant memory and turned left into the front room. There was a piano in the center of the room, draped in sheet cloth. There had been music in this house. In the beginning, anyway.

Next to the piano was a small settee, also covered. My lawyer had warned me not to have high expectations for the furnishings. He even went so far as to give me a business card for a local furniture store. I reached down and pulled the fabric off to check out the hideous floral design I would be subjected to. I exposed a bed of yellow daisies—surrounding a burrowed nest of fresh pink baby mice. I groaned and put the sheet back over them. There were a good number of cards Ed should have given me, but the furniture store was probably not where I would need to start.

Off the front room, behind unhinged pocket doors, was the family room. It still held a bubble television and a traditional puffy couch. I didn't bother checking whether anything had nested under the brown corduroy cushions. I now considered every piece of fabric in the house to be a loss.

Through a set of glass parlor doors, was the dining room. There was something vaguely familiar about the mahogany-colored table and chairs, but it was the blue striped wallpaper that brought back the most memories. Nothing firm, just familiar. Like a dream, fleeting even as you try to remember it.

Beyond a swinging door to the right, I found a small kitchen, complete with a fridge, oven, sink, the tiniest island ever, and one standing pantry cabinet. The back door was to my left, and on the right was another swinging door leading to the hallway straight off the foyer.

I jumped as the hideous grinding of the garbage disposal came on with the overhead light. I rushed over to the sink and found the switch on the wall to shut it off. "Guess she found the power," I mumbled to myself, pretending I hadn't almost peed my pants.

I pushed through the swinging door that led to the hall just as Mrs. Hanson came up from the basement. I passed by a rather large storage closet and the smallest half bath to ever exist, to meet up with her.

"There are more bugs than floor space down there. I hope you didn't expect to turn the basement into living space because it's hardly more than a root cellar." The woman dusted off her hands. "I'm surprised it isn't growing mold." She sniffed her fingers.

"How's the roof?" I asked.

"Ah." Mrs. Hanson sputtered her lips as she pulled her paperwork from her red leather briefcase purse. "Okay, yes, the roof was replaced five years ago. That was authorized by the executor of the estate, Mr. Ladner."

I nodded. Ed Ladner was my father's best friend and our family lawyer. After my parents' death, he was charged with the task of managing their estate. In many ways, he was as much a guardian to me as my foster family. More so, perhaps. "What else did he authorize?"

"Let's see...Lawn maintenance, exterior electrical plugs were added, and okay, it looks like they put in a new garage door last spring. It was damaged by a tree during a storm, so the insurance took care of that. Aaaaand...They converted the oven to electric so they could get rid of the propane tank. They put in a high-efficiency boiler. It will still be radiant heat, but at least it won't cost you a fortune to stay warm. Staying cool, however..." She grimaced and walked away rather than go into her concerns about the lacking accommodations.

"Let's take a look at the upstairs." Mrs. Hanson climbed the carpet-trimmed staircase.

I followed her up, taking care to watch my footing, just in case. At the top of the stairs, the banister continued to hook around, providing an open balcony to the main foyer from the bedrooms. The setup mimicked the downstairs, almost room for room. There were three bedrooms; the third one, which was closest to the back of the house, was dubbed the master bedroom because it shared a door with the upstairs bath, but it was actually the smallest room in the house.

The bathroom wasn't much bigger than the kitchen, but someone remodeled it within the last thirty years, so it had clean, white subway tiles on the walls, black-and-white checkered floor tiles, and the necessities of a sink, toilet, and claw-foot tub. The tub had an added shower extension and a curtain rod for stand-up showering, but the curtain looked as yellow as the daisy couch downstairs.

"Well?" Mrs. Hanson leaned on the door frame from the bedroom side. Someone was thoughtful enough to make that door swing out so the two doors didn't bang into each other when people opened them. "Are you really going to live here?"

"Why not?" I asked.

Mrs. Hanson pinched her lips. "Listen, I know I'm nobody to you, and honestly, it's my job to talk people into buying houses, but money pit aside...why are you doing this?"

I narrowed my eyes in confusion. "This is my home. My parents' home."

"I get that, but Harold is a small town. With your money, you could live anywhere in the world."

I bit back my annoyance. I was used to people making assumptions about my income. No one ever took into consideration that my monthly allowance wasn't much more than a middle-class citizen. People also never considered that I didn't want to blow my inheritance like a winning lottery ticket. I still didn't know what I wanted to do with my life, and until I did, there was nothing to replenish what I spent.

"I think Harold is a lovely town. It was good enough for my parents. Besides, I'm not really interested in a fast-paced lifestyle, so this should be fine."

"It won't bring them back, you know," the realtor whispered.

My feigned smile dropped, and my eyes widened; I wondered whether I had heard the woman correctly. I wasn't sure if I considered the statement rude, presumptuous, or downright stupid. "I don't need to be reminded that my parents are dead, Mrs. Hanson. I was there when they were killed."

She blinked at me for a moment. "I just mean, it's only a house. You don't have to hold on to it to hold on to them." She shriveled before me and backed away. No doubt the enraged look on my face had signaled her immediate dismissal. "I'll leave the keys and the forms on the dresser in here. The garage and shed are on the back side of the property. The keys are marked. I turned the water on, but I would advise draining the pipes out for a good ten minutes. They haven't been turned on since..." She neglected the remainder of the statement since I was well aware of when the house had been put out of commission. "Anyway, good luck. Let me know if you have any questions." She scurried away, dropping the intended items on the dresser before leaving.

I waited for the front door to slam and moved to sit on the edge of the tub. I turned on the tub faucet as well as the sink and listened to the rattling and groaning of the plumbing. An echoing moan started from the depths of the basement and crept up the pipes. Rust-colored water sputtered from both faucets. Years of residue poured out into the sink and tub basin. For a moment, it almost looked as if blood was gushing forth, but it soon turned orange, and after three minutes the water finally turned clear. I wished I could clean out the rest of the house as easily.

I moved into the adjacent bedroom and looked over the cracked plaster walls. Someone had painted them pink for me. Like most young girls, I'd had a princess phase. It was a time in my life I'd believed the world circled around me. It was partly true, I suppose, since I had been the center of my parents' lives.

I moved to the window overlooking the backyard. I stared down at the rocky terrain and half-dead lawn. There were no longer any remnants of the destruction that had taken place there over a decade ago. No evidence of a fire or the death it had brought.

Standing inside this house should have brought back memories, but it didn't. My mind was a black hole, resistant to releasing even the smallest recollections from my childhood. Fortunately, I no longer had to rely on my memory to solve this mystery. The entire town of Harold had witnessed my parents' so-called accident, and one of them was bound to have the key to unlocking this mystery.

One of them might know who murdered my parents.

The Lawyer

"What do you want me to do?" Ed Ladner yelled into the phone as he waved me into his office. I sneaked in with my pile of papers and a tube full of blueprints. "No, I don't think that's the right course of action. If I did, I would have done it years ago." I sat down in front of his desk and waited patiently for him to finish his phone call.

I had always had a sort of fatherly crush on him. Since I had been away at college, he had grayed something awful. Silver speckled his once sleek brown hair. His heavy brow looked creased, and his nose looked bigger than I remembered. He was a good deal taller than me and unobtrusively muscular. He smelled of pipe tobacco even though I had never seen him smoke.

"No." His eyes caught on mine, and he looked me over. He smiled despite the unfriendly tone he was offering his phone conversation. "I don't want to do that. You'll have to find another way. I have to go. An old friend just walked in." Ed hung up the phone and leaned back in his chair. He looked me over again. His eyes paused on the paperwork in my hands and narrowed.

His feigned irritation made me smile, which made me blush, which made me smile more, which made me blush more. I chuckled and looked down. I bit my cheek and forced myself to look up at him again. I was not a bashful sixteen-year-old girl anymore. I was an adult, or at least that was what I wanted to be. Unfortunately, Edward Ladner had been with me from the very beginning. He had seen me at my worst. I was more intimately involved with him than even some of my closest friends.

"You look amazing," he said sweetly, like a proud father rather than a man. His compliments always pleased me, but every time I saw him they meant something different to me. His acceptance was always important to me, but as a child, I'd wanted his love; as a teenager, I'd wanted his guidance; as a young adult I'd wanted his attention; and now as a full-fledged adult, I wanted all of it. Add in some latent female hormones, and I was liable to make a fool of myself at any moment.

"Thank you." I cleared my throat. "I...missed you." I raised my gaze to meet his. His smile faded.

"I usually don't hug my clients, but it's kind of killing me not to. Do you mind?" He smirked.

"I'd be insulted if you didn't." I stood and set down my stuff as he came around the desk. He wrapped his arms around me and held me tightly against him. It was a good hug, the best I'd had in a while, but even as I relaxed my head onto his shoulder, he pulled away. He held me at arm's length to look at me.

"Did you seriously grow two more inches?" he asked.

"It's the heels." I pointed down and made a point of pulling up the length of my sundress to show off my freshly shaven legs. He smiled and looked over my face.

"You cut your hair too." He reached around and tugged at the sloppy layered waves tightly hugging my head. My black/brown hair had always been my best feature, but it had also drawn the wrong attention during college. When I'd cut it all off, I had expected to draw the attention of a more cultured group of men. However, it had only resulted in my obscurity behind the veil of busty blondes and vibrant outgoing redheads. As a result, I'd never really dated.

"Do you like it?" I asked, trying to hide my eagerness for his answer.

"I love it. You look so...grown up." He smiled and moved his hand to my shoulder. He gave it a tight squeeze and returned to his chair—business as usual. "So, Pauline tells me you've moved into the house."

"Pauline?"

"Mrs. Hanson."

"Oh, right. Sort of. The upstairs is in good shape, but..." I paused, not sure how personally he might take my assessment of the property.

"Go on, Tori. I already know you're here for money."

I dipped my brow and shook my head. "I didn't just come for money." I nearly broke into tears hearing those words. I hated how he made me feel ten years old again, and fifteen, and seventeen.

"I don't mean it like that, honey. I just mean I know the place is in disrepair, and I'm prepared to help you in any way I can. Why don't you tell me what you are proposing for renovations, and we can crunch some numbers." He nodded at the tube I had laid on his desk.

I opened the tube and rolled out the plan for my remodel in front of him. He laughed in awe of my preparation. "I'm going to break out the wall to the storage closet and expand the kitchen this way. Then open the wall up here for a pass-through so I can have a breakfast bar in the dining room. I'm going to open up the ceiling in the master bedroom and bathroom, so I can have vaulted ceilings, and a skylight in the bathroom. And of course, new appliances, new fixtures. The electrical needs updating. I'm going to need a new water heater. All the windows need to be updated. The floors need to be sanded and resealed upstairs and down. The basement steps need to be redone, and both porches are dangerously rotted. New siding, a sidewalk to the garage, fencing, landscaping, and all new furniture."

"Oh, is that all?" Ed asked, losing the amusement on his face.

"No, but I've already gone over budget this week on exterminators and chimney sweeps."

"You needed the chimney swept in June?" He raised an eyebrow.

"Bats were living in it," I grumbled, and he pinched his lips together. "Don't look at me like that. How much would a new house cost?"

"A new house would be a monthly mortgage we could account for. All these repairs call for upfront money. You know what a pain in the ass that is."

"I know you can do it."

"Tori, why don't you just finish school and then you can do whatever you want with the money?"

I frowned at him. This wasn't the first time we had had this discussion. Granted, it was the first time I had looked in his eyes since I had told him I had dropped out of college a semester before completing my degree. Technically, I already had my associate's degree, but the will had demanded a bachelor's degree. Short of that, I had to wait until my twenty-fifth birthday to get access to my money, and even then I could only get half. I didn't get full access until I was thirty.

"I don't want to have this argument again." I pulled the blueprint away. He touched my hand.

"We never finished this argument. You hung up on me, remember? Are you going to storm out this time?"

"No." I clenched my jaw defiantly, but I still couldn't look him in the eye.

"Look, I know losing your foster parents must have reminded you of what happened to your mom and dad, but that's no reason to—"

"This isn't about that," I snapped.

He gripped my hand incrementally tighter. "Of course it is." I finally looked at him. I felt guilty that I was making him worry about me, but seeing the worry plastered on his face made me feel good. "I know we aren't that close, at least not the way we used to be, but you can tell me anything. Money problems, life problems, I'm here for you. What happened? Why are you giving up?"

I took a deep breath and resigned myself to the truth. Not the whole truth, though, because admitting I didn't want to get access to my money because I didn't want to lose him as a mentor was not really the type of revelation I wanted to make today. Especially since—according to him—*we weren't that close.*

"Nothing happened. I just got burned out. I'll finish up online. Besides, what are three more years? I've waited for fourteen to get you off my back; I can make it three more." I chuckled, and he smiled.

"Well, I can't complain from my end. I'll see about getting you a home equity loan. The house isn't worth much as is, but after you update it, I'm sure we can get more for you," he conceded.

"Thank you, Ed."

He tilted his head. "I think that's the first time you've called me by my first name."

"I'm an adult now, aren't I?" I said silkily and smiled.

He nodded and glanced over me again. "You certainly are." He took a breath. "Listen, I know you value your solitude, but I'd love for you to come over for dinner sometime."

My smile broadened. "Sure, I'd like that."

"Darcie is dying to meet you."

"Darcie?" I tipped my head trying to place a face to the name.

"Darcie, my wife." He paused, looking over my befuddled face. "Didn't I tell you I got remarried?"

I felt my heart seize in preparation of being broken, but I smiled anyway. "No, I don't think I would have forgotten that."

"Oh, I'm sorry. It was a small wedding last fall. It's her second marriage as well, so neither of us wanted a big to-do."

"How nice. I can't wait to meet her." My voice pitched with insincerity, but I couldn't help it. I was dying inside, and there was no one I could turn to for comfort. The only constant in my life had happily remarried a woman of appropriate age. My lifelong crush had finally succeeded in crushing me. "Just let me know when."

I finished rolling up my blueprints and carefully choreographed my steps to the door so I wouldn't look like I was fleeing the scene. "Tori," Ed said softly, and I turned back. He shook his head and sighed. "I know I give you grief, but...they would be so proud of you."

Tears sprang to my eyes, and I passed them off as an honest reaction to his statement. Once I slipped out of his office and made it past his receptionist, the rest of them came. They had nothing to do with my parents—two people I barely remembered. They were tears for a man who had never, nor ever would, see me as anything but a child.

The Firehouse

As I strolled around town collecting my rabid emotions and drying my tears, I stumbled across the fire station. I had been meaning to stop there since it was the most logical place to start my investigation, and there was no time like the present.

I pulled a rumpled old newspaper article from my purse. It had been in my possession for years; the only evidence I had that the fire had really happened—besides a few nightmares that might have been memories. I headed into the fire station through one of the open bay doors. I walked alongside a bright red fire truck in search of the voices I could hear conversing deeper inside. Peals of laughter echoed off the cement and I finally reached the source of the gaiety.

At the tail end of the firetruck, four firemen—tall, brawny, and wearing tight-fitting white t-shirts—turned to look at me. It was like looking at Mr. June, July, August, and September on a firemen calendar, although in the calendar they would have been shirtless.

The one nearest me looked me up and down and gave me a sideways smirk. "Well, hello there." He raised his thumb and pressed the edge of his mustache. "What can we do for you?"

I looked at each of them in turn: tall, taller, big, and biggest. My throat closed up, and I took a step backward. They were all giving me the same sort of smile, like I was a hen in the doghouse. I wasn't sure I had ever been in the presence of so many men who could bench press me. It was intimidating enough to make me consider running back outside.

"Do you need some help, miss?" the largest of the muscle men asked.

"I have some questions," I croaked out.

"The answer is yes to all the above, sweetheart," Mr. Mustachio answered, and two of his friends laughed at him.

"Knock it off," the largest man said with a deep rumble in his voice. "Who are you lookin' to talk to?"

I lifted my newspaper clipping and read the name in the article. "Captain Louis Bradford."

The large man shook his head. "I'm the captain of this station now. Mitch Hughes." Captain Hughes stepped forward and put his hand out. I shook it, doing a double take on his mammoth hands. "What sort of information are you looking for?"

"I had some questions about a fire. He was the lead firefighter at the time. Do you know how I can reach him?"

"With a Ouija board," Mr. Mustachio mumbled.

"Start washing the trucks," Captain Hughes barked at the men.

"We just got done washing them," Mustachio said.

"Then do it again." Captain Hughes wrapped his arm around my back and pointed me toward the back of the station. "My office is this way," he said when I glanced back toward the open bay doors.

I maneuvered around several folding chairs and stepped through the door with a glass window labeled "Chief." The office was small but had a large desk and two tall file cabinets. Hughes brought in a folding chair with him and set it in front of the desk for me. Once I was situated, he shut the door and sat down behind the desk. "Captain Bradford retired about five years back. He's since passed away."

"Oh." I slumped in my chair. "I'm sorry to hear that."

Captain Hughes tipped his head. "Did you know him?"

"No." I glanced at the article clutched in my hand. "I just had some questions my research couldn't answer. Did he have a wife or any children?"

"Yes, but she moved down to Florida, and his son is in D.C."

"Oh." My enthusiasm for my investigation died. "Thank you for your time, Captain." I stood up to leave.

"I'm not sure if you are aware of this, but firemen write reports on the fires they are called to put out. It's one of our least favorite parts of the job, but one of the most important, secondary to saving lives, of course." Hughes leaned forward and extended his hand. "May I?"

I handed him the yellow scrap of newspaper and sat back down as he read it. His expression changed slightly when he reached the end. He looked up at me from beneath his brow, his eyes tracing over my features, then back to the article. The newspaper had superimposed my old school photo over the burned metal wreckage. The heading on the article read: *Miracle Girl Is Unharmed.* "Are you the miracle girl?" he asked.

I shrugged. "I'm a survivor. I don't know if it was a miracle."

He glanced at the article once more before handing it back to me. "I moved here about ten years ago. Started on the crew with Bradford as my captain. I had heard rumors about that fire. I never bought the miracle stories. Fire does strange things sometimes. It can crawl. It can jump. It can hide. It can even put itself out without warning and start back up again with less warning. That was always my interpretation of things. Then Bradford gave me his report. It was a bit embellished, but all the facts were there, and every guy there that day wrote a similar report, backing up his statements. The pictures were pretty convincing too. It was obvious the fire never reached you. It was everywhere except right where you were sitting."

"And that was your proof it was a miracle?" I smiled.

"No, like I said, fire does strange things." He paused and took a breath. "But heat...Now that's another story. I don't know how close you can stand to a bonfire, but I find a good 900-degree fire is enough to back me up several feet. That fire..." Hughes pointed to the article in my hand. "...was hot enough to melt the steel frame and the windows of the car."

"How hot is that?"

"Around 2800 degrees." He paused to let me imagine how hot it must have been inside the car. "Say what you will about the movement of the fire, but you were in that car for nearly eighteen minutes by Bradford's estimate. The heat should have killed you. And if the heat didn't kill you, the smoke should have suffocated you." Captain Hughes stared at me. "By all imaginable natural scenarios, you should have died in that car with your parents."

I frowned and shifted back in my chair. "The thing is, Captain, I didn't come here to find out why I survived the fire. I'm willing to take that on faith if necessary. What I'm actually more interested in is the report you were just speaking about. The mystery to me isn't how I survived, but why I was in danger to begin with. How did the car start on fire? What was fueling it? Why couldn't my parents get out of the car the minute it started? Who dies in a car fire unless they've been pinned somehow? The car hadn't even run into anything."

Captain Hughes nodded and tented his fingers together. "If you'd like a copy of the report, I can get you one, but I don't think you'll get your answers there."

"Why is that?"

"Because Bradford never found a reason for the fire. The gas contributed to the fire, but there was never any explosion, and there simply wasn't enough fuel to get the fire as hot as it got."

"You're not mistaken about the temperature?"

"Metal and glass melt at very specific temperatures. That's a scientific fact."

"But you just said there wasn't enough fuel to reach that temperature."

"And that is the question Bradford spent 14 years asking himself. What was fueling that fire?"

I frowned. "So it wasn't just a miraculous event that I survived. It was miraculous that I was in danger to begin with."

"I'm not sure *miraculous* is the right word for that fire. What happened that day wasn't heaven-sent." I stared at the captain, waiting for him to start throwing out phrases like "hell's fire" and "eternal damnation." He was staring back at me with a question in his eyes, but it wasn't the type of question he could ask without sounding crazy.

Had it been the 1600s, he might have strung me up in the town square and accused me of being a witch, maybe even given the fire another chance to take me out, but we lived in civilized times now. Times when angels and demons were not discussed outside of the walls of a church. "I suppose we will never really know what happened that day," the captain said, shifting his gaze from mine.

"I suppose not," I agreed and stood up. "Thank you for your time." He gave me a nod, and I turned to leave. When I reached the door, I turned back. "I'm curious about something else, and you might be the person to ask."

"What's that?"

"I was told the house—my parents' house—was donated to the fire department for use in fire practice. It obviously hasn't been burned down. Do you know why?"

The captain scoffed and shook his head. "We tried. The whole department went out for a practice burn on it three times. It should have gone up like a forest in the wind, but every single time we tried, the fire tamped out and wouldn't take off. We went out for a fourth time to evaluate. See if we could start a fire upstairs. Unfortunately, two of our men took a spill down the steps. One broke his leg; the other, his arm. The strange thing was, they both claimed to feel a force pushing on their chests, like a hand pushing them down the stairs. After that, the department was reluctant to make it a priority."

"Ghost stories, Captain?" I smiled.

"I take it you're not a believer in the paranormal."

"No, I think old houses creak and moan, but with a little love they can be a good real estate choice."

"If you say so, but that house is gonna need a lot more than love. If I were you, I would follow your parents' lead and bulldoze the place."

I gave him a half-smile and left. I wondered if he was right about the house. My parents had obviously had something against the place if they were willing to donate it to be burned rather than sell it. Maybe it was better to hire a wrecking ball instead of an electrician.

The Dead and Gone

A decade's worth of dust had layered itself onto the kitchen countertops, making the process of food preparation closer to harvesting penicillin than gourmet cooking. Thankfully, since the kitchen hadn't endured years of use during that time, all it needed was a good washing and a proper oil treatment.

Twenty minutes later, both counters in the galley-style kitchen space were back to the shimmering gold they were meant to be. Give or take the line of oil across my shirt where I'd leaned over to reach the back of the counter, I was none the worse for wear. Although I was resigned to letting most of my clothing go the way of the dodo for the sake of a better house, I was running out of unstained clothing. Short of reducing myself to grubby t-shirts for my trips into town, I needed to get more aggressive with my laundry efforts.

I headed downstairs into my dank, dark basement to find my pre-wash stain remover stick. As I clunked down the old wooden steps, taking my life into my hands, I debated the option of moving my washer and dryer upstairs. I had the budget for it, but I wasn't sure I wanted to sacrifice the upstairs floor plan. The bedrooms were rather dinky as it was.

At the foot of the stairs, I pulled on the chain light above me. Three lights flipped on, lighting my way to the laundry area and scaring the bejeebers out of every cockroach, mouse, and spider making its home in my cellar. Even with the three high-watt bulbs, the basement still had dark crevices and corners to hide in. As always, I glanced around searching for immediate threats: cobwebs, dead things, and especially living things. So far, the bulk of those threats had already been cleaned up. However, after a replenished supply of rat poison and an armada of bug bombs, there was bound to be creepy-crawly creatures belly-up all over the place.

I headed over to the washer and found my stain stick. I pulled off my shirt and treated the long smear of oil. The prospects for survival were not good, especially with an oil stain, but I gave it a heavy dose and tossed it in the washer with the rest of my colored clothes waiting to be run when I had a full load.

I yanked the light off and headed back upstairs, happy to be exiting the basement. Though I was certain no bogeymen were waiting for me, I still felt the urgency of danger pushing on my back as I climbed the slender stairwell, putting wings on my feet.

I closed the door to the basement and considered grabbing a fresh shirt. However, since I had so few left to risk, I decided my sports bra was adequate coverage for cleaning. I grabbed my bucket of soapy and now sooty water from the hall and headed to the kitchen to dump it.

As the water sloshed in the bucket, I heard a gravelly sound, like my brush was dragging behind me. I looked down and saw the long-stem dish brush was still hanging from the bucket's edge.

I heard it again and looked for the source of the sound. It was almost a growl, and for a moment I thought perhaps a dog had gotten in the back door.

I put down the bucket gently and continued to seek the noise. I couldn't tell if it was coming from the kitchen or the foyer. I moved toward the kitchen, listening between my steps.

A buzzing bee? Too loud. A lawnmower? Stopping and going?

I reached the kitchen and looked for an appliance that might cause the rumbling noise, but nothing was on. I turned into the dining room to check the living room.

At the head of the table, I peered through the wide entryway into the living room, where the sound was clearly coming from. Something was off, but my eyes couldn't immediately detect it. It was the hair on the back of my neck that was screaming with agitation, demanding I run, but from what?

Then I saw it.

Feet.

Propped up on a footstool—that I didn't own. The rest of the body was just out of my view behind the short wall. The long rumbling interludes were snores. A strange man was sleeping in my house.

I shifted back, not sure what to do. I wanted to run and scream for help, but my car keys were in my purse on the piano bench—in full view of the stranger. It would be a long trip for help on foot. I was well over three miles from town. Even the closest neighbor was almost that far. I was alone in my home with a stranger.

I tiptoed backward and grabbed the phone hanging on the wall in the kitchen. I picked up the receiver and painstakingly slowly dialed 911 into the rotary dial. After a moment, the operator came on the line. "What is your emergency?"

"Someone is in my house," I whispered.

"Can you tell me your address?" she immediately asked, and I gave her the street address. "Can you get out of the house?"

I looked at the back door, but I knew the screen would make an awful squawk when I opened it. I looked at the front door. It was farther to walk, but I was certain that it was a quieter option. "I think so."

"I want you to hang up and get out of the house quickly and quietly. Run as far as you can and don't go back until the police arrive."

I lifted the receiver and placed it back on the hanging base. I once again debated front or back. The snoring man snorted and coughed. After a second, I heard his chair creak with his movement. A groan signaled his rise. I took a step back, wondering which direction he would go. Around to his left would bring him to the foyer, and to his right would bring him to the kitchen.

I heard the floorboards in the dining room squawk with his heavy footsteps, and I took several gliding steps back toward the front entrance. I reached the door, but I didn't have time to open it before he emerged from the dining room. I stepped out of sight behind the stairway as he stepped into the kitchen. Just as I disappeared from view, I glimpsed his tall frame and rounded belly.

His hacking cough announced his arrival into the kitchen. I heard the faucet turn on. Whoever this thug was, he was more than comfortable helping himself to a glass of water. I waited for him to finish gulping and return to the living room, but when he finally moved again, the footsteps were echoing down the hall. Closer each time.

I looked upstairs, wanting so much to flee from view, but I knew that wasn't the smart choice. The smart choice was to get out as fast as I could, regardless of whether he saw me leave.

I reached for the doorknob, putting myself in full view, but I didn't dare look or I'd lose my nerve. I twisted it and yanked, but the door caught on the jamb. I pulled with all my weight, and it released.

I spun around, putting myself outside the door as fast as I could get there. I finally glanced up to see if it was my pumping heart or his pounding footsteps that had me ready for a marathon.

His face was inches from mine, peering out the door I was peering back through. Sallow skin, puffy cheeks, and bloodshot eyes stared back at me. "Can't breathe," his voice rasped.

I screamed and fell back. I dropped to the porch and, in a frantic effort to get away, rolled down the steps. I got to my feet at the bottom and ran out into the darkness toward the flashing red and blue lights in the distance.

The Police

Halfway down the hill, I met up with three squad cars. The first one stopped to check on me while the other two continued up the hill to my house. An officer about my height with a medium build stepped out of his car and rushed to my side. I was trembling and panting, but I attempted to describe the man I'd seen inside the house. "Are you hurt?" the officer interrupted my babbling. I noticed his name tag read *Higgs*.

"No."

"Okay, get in." Higgs opened the back door to his car, and I jumped inside. He shut the door and climbed back into the driver's seat. He raced to catch up with his fellow officers at the top of the hill. While en route, he reported to the station that he had found the resident and that I wasn't hurt.

As we pulled up to my house, I saw one of the officers standing on the porch, back to the house, gun pointed upward. He was poised to pounce on my trespasser. Higgs opened his door, pulled his firearm and ducked behind his door. I was fairly certain the stranger was unarmed, but I instinctively ducked lower in my seat just in case.

The officer on the porch announced his arrival loudly and demanded that anyone inside lay down their weapons and come out with their hands visible. No one came out. He turned his head and spoke into the radio perched on his shoulder. Through Higgs's radio, I heard him report that he was going in. The third officer chimed in as well. He was going in the back door.

After the officer disappeared inside, I waited for more shouting, slamming doors, or gunfire, but no other noises escaped the front door. Only the occasional "clear" sounded over the radio.

"Did this guy try to detain you or threaten you?" Higgs glanced back at me, but maintained his position guarding the front door.

"No," I said. "He just said he couldn't breathe."

"He said he couldn't breathe?"

"I think he was having an asthma attack. He didn't look well."

Higgs spoke into his radio. "Be advised, the intruder may need medical attention."

A few minutes later, the third policeman popped out from around the back of the house. He shook his head and Higgs holstered his gun.

"I'll be right back. Stay right here," Higgs said, leaving me in the car while he spoke privately with the other officer. He occasionally glanced back at me. The worried expression on his face didn't look promising.

A civilian car came up the drive and skidded to a stop behind the police cars, sending a plume of dust forward. With the headlights glaring in the back window, I couldn't see who it was yet. Higgs raised his hands as someone exited the car. "Easy now," he warned them.

"What's going on here?" Ed Ladner's voice sounded like heaven to my ears. "Why is she being detained?" He pointed to my face peering out at him from the backseat of a police car.

"Who are you?"

"I'm her lawyer." Higgs scoffed and propped his hands on his hips. He glanced back it me, and I noted his obvious disapproval.

Ed pulled out his wallet. He didn't even notice the sudden movement had made Higgs reach for his gun. When the only weapon being retrieved turned out to be a business card, he relaxed. Higgs took the card from him and frowned at it.

"Did she call you?" I was once again gifted with a harsh glower. Officer Higgs was obviously not a fan of the paperwork side of the legal system.

"No. I was on my way home, and I saw the police lights up here. I came to check on my client."

Higgs puffed out his chest and propped his hands on his hips. "Do you normally do that for your clients?"

Ed stared at Higgs for a moment. His bemusement was short-lived, replaced by narrowed eyes and a contrived smile. "I do for this one." Ed snatched back his business card and slipped it into his wallet. "Now what's going on here?"

"There was a disturbance at the house. She called—"

"Disturbance?"

"An intruder."

"Intruder! Jesus, Tori, are you okay?" Ed shouted to me. I gave him a solemn nod. I wasn't okay. I was scared shitless. But that wasn't what he was asking. His first thoughts were the same as Officer Higgs: single woman, alone in a house, male intruder. It definitely could have been a worse scenario. Not that I could convince my shaking hands of that.

Ed turned to Higgs. "Is there any reason you are confining her to your police car?"

"She's not confined. She was safer there."

"Then let her out."

Higgs all but rolled his eyes at Ed, but he came back to the car and released me. Before I could get clear of the door, Ed rushed over and pulled me into a big hug. I welcomed every bit of it, slumping against him like a proper lady in peril.

Just when I was feeling safe again, he pushed me away to look at me. He glanced at the officer, giving him a hearty glare as he pulled off his suit jacket and wrapped it around my shoulders. The remaining heat of the fabric warmed me. The scent of slightly sweet cologne made my heart melt, and I began to cry.

Ed pulled me close again and rubbed my back. "It's all right, Tori, I'm here now." And he was. He was always there for me. Sometimes only by phone, but he was there.

The second officer finally returned from searching the house.

"What did you find?" Higgs asked.

"Nothing." He shook his head. "There's no one inside."

I slid out of Ed's arms to confront the officer. "What do you mean there's no one there?"

"He must have slipped out the back door and disappeared."

"No, the back side of the property is a ravine." I looked between the officers. "He was over 300 pounds and having an asthma attack. There's no way we could've missed him." I looked around, surveying the terrain of my desolate property. I was certain the man I had seen could not handle the steep decline, or the rocky, pitted ground with ease. There was nowhere for him to go but down the road the officers had just driven up.

"And you think I missed a 300-pound man hiding in your house," the third officer said snidely. "There's no one in there. The only intruders in that house are the mice."

I opened my mouth to insist on another check, but Higgs put his arm in front of me and urged me to walk away. "What were you doing right before you saw this guy?"

"I was cleaning, why?"

"Sometimes a bad mixture of household cleaners can cause a person to pass out or get extremely dizzy. Perhaps you had a reaction and misinterpreted what you were seeing."

"You think she hallucinated an intruder?" Ed asked, obviously perturbed by his suggestion of temporary insanity.

"I didn't imagine this. He was there. He was wheezing. I could even smell him."

Higgs nodded. "Whoever you saw, they're gone. The house is empty. For now, I'll write up the report as a courtesy call. I wouldn't want you to get a bad reputation so soon after moving to town."

"Excuse me?"

"What sort of reputation are you talking about, Officer?" Ed crossed his arms.

Higgs looked him over, and a slight smirk tipped the corner of his mouth as if he found Ed's defense of me amusing. "Look, Tori was it?" Higgs turned to me, pointedly putting himself between Ed and me. "Old houses like this have lots of creaks and groans. It's easy to misinterpret these things as footsteps or moaning ghosts. This house in particular has always had a Halloween vibe. I just don't want you to help perpetuate that imagery."

"This wasn't a hoax," I defended.

"Reputations can get tarnished pretty easily in this town. The last thing you want to be known for is being the crazy lady on the hill who calls the police for every little bump in the night."

I shook my head. "It wasn't a bump in the night. I *saw* him."

"I don't doubt you did. But what I'm telling you is I can't arrest a ghost." Higgs gave me a grim look and walked away. I couldn't tell if he was being callous or literal. Did he really believe I'd seen a ghost?

I didn't have much experience with paranormal phenomena. Like anyone else , I enjoyed a good ghost story, something to get your heart racing a little. Something to put your senses into overdrive. It was no different from other forms of entertainment. Ghost stories were designed to stimulate, but in a different way than romance books or action-adventure movies.

The question was, did I believe it? Did I believe in ghosts?

For the time being, I would have to allow myself to consider the possibility of a supernatural justification, if for no other reason than avoiding the alternative, which was still far scarier to me than ghosts and goblins.

The Furniture Store

I flipped through the endless books of fabric trying to discern which pattern was more likely to hide chocolate milk stains. I had been at it for nearly an hour and decided I might be willing to share the lumpy green sofa with the rodent population of the house, so long as I could stop looking at samples of upholstery and faux leather.

"Any luck?" A young man around my age bounded over cheerfully. His name was Lane, and he was all sorts of personality balled up in one body. He snapped his fingers and slapped his hands together before sitting on the edge of the table I was sitting at. "You looking for something wild? Cause we got wild. I like this zig-zag pattern: fun, but artsy. You know?"

I nodded, but I didn't know. I just wanted a couch. I pointed to one of the floor models, but apparently cash and carry was not their policy. Slow torture in the design school from hell was apparently their motto.

"I need something soft and stain-resistant."

"Just a couch, or do you want a set? Cause you should start with the accent chair first, then match with a basic color."

"Lane, was it?" He nodded. "I will buy anything you want to sell me. How about that? You choose the set, the color, the fabric. You can even pick out some end tables and lamps."

"Really? Right on! What's your budget?"

"No budget, whatever you want."

Lane paused and looked me over. His eyes widened slightly, and his mouth gaped as if Christmas had arrived early. "Whoa, wait! You're the one who moved into that old house on the hill, right? I heard your dad was loaded."

"I guess."

"Cool, so..." he leaned in. "How rich are you?"

My mouth dropped, and I flipped through my brain for an appropriate response. I was never good at conversations involving myself, and I never understood why people insisted on asking me questions that would be considered rude of me to ask them.

"Lane." Another man approached and stopped behind me. I glanced up at him and found him to bear a striking resemblance to the buzz-cut teenager in front of me, except he had a full head of messy brown waves and thick eyebrows. "Go help Dad." His brown eyes bored into Lane, discreetly telling him to go away.

Lane plodded off without objection, snapping his fingers and popping his mouth on the way. His *brother* stepped around the table, holding tightly to the clipboard in his hand. His name tag introduced him as Brant and declared that he was the floor manager. "Sorry about my little brother. He isn't as well versed in conversation etiquette as I would prefer."

"Yeah, I forgot how small-minded small-town folk can be."

"How's that?" Brant tipped his head to the side. "Sounds like your conversation etiquette needs some improvement as well."

I gawked at the severity in his tone and face. Did he just scold me? He couldn't have been more than a few years older than me. "I only meant everyone is in everyone else's business," I clarified, trying to simmer the insult down to observation.

"That's a pretty stereotypical attitude for someone who's lived here all of a few weeks."

"Well, it's none of your business how long I've lived here, so I guess it's somewhat accurate," I retorted snappishly.

"It's my business to know my neighbors."

"No, it really isn't. It isn't your business to know my name, my bank account balance, or my comings and goings. Frankly," I stood from my chair, which didn't help my authority since the man was still six inches taller than me. I hated tall people. "The borrow-a-cup-of-sugar approach to neighborly civility is outdated. You want some sugar, go to the damn store." I huffed, satisfied I had finally said my piece for once in my life.

I should have stormed out, but I still needed to get some furniture, and this was the only place in town, so I stood there stupidly staring at Brant. He was glaring at me, but he didn't retaliate. I could tell by the look on his face that he wanted to say several scathing things to me, but he either couldn't think of any, or he was concerned about his sale. I was usually on that side of the argument, biting my tongue to stay polite, or too flabbergasted to even respond.

My shoulders dropped, and I exhaled. "I'm sorry." The instant I said the words, I knew I meant them. "I don't know why I said all that. Of course, everyone knows who I am. Of course they're curious. It's just...I don't feel welcome here. I feel...watched." His glare relaxed into mild interest. He was listening to me, and for some reason I was still talking. "Which is normal for a town this size, but I don't have any friends. Here, I mean. Obviously I have friends—elsewhere. I'm not a pariah." Why was I still talking? "But my friends don't know much about my past. I don't share my personal life with them, so it's weird when strangers know so much about me."

"You don't share your personal life with your friends?" he asked suspiciously. "How are they your friends then?"

I stared into his inquisitive eyes, which I realized now were a little more green than brown. Unlike his brother's lackluster hair, Brandt's had reddish highlights. He was gorgeous. Damn it. "That's not really my point."

He was right, of course. I kept so much of my history a secret that I could hardly consider anyone I socialized with a close friend. Which was probably why it had been easy to leave them all behind and move here.

The only people outside of this town who knew about my parents' tragic death had been my foster parents. And now that they were gone, I was truly alone.

"What is your point? Because it sounds to me like you moved back to a town where you are basically famous and expected everyone to just pretend like they don't know who you are so you can feel more comfortable."

My mouth gaped as I tried to recover from the dizzying turn of the tables. The entire conversation was well beyond my comfort level. I felt exposed and humiliated.

Instead of running from my past, like most people do—immersing themselves in a new, contrary lifestyle—I was colliding with it. There was no way to maintain my privacy and get the answers I wanted. I'd told myself I was prepared for the invasive interactions I would be subjected to, but clearly I wasn't.

I shook my head and looked down at the book of fabric. "I don't remember where we got off track here, but I would like to buy some furniture." I took a step back from him, pointing vaguely at the surrounding furniture. "I gave Lane the room dimensions. Could you guys just pick something out for me and deliver it as soon as possible?" I turned around ready to sprint, but bumped into an ottoman and toppled over it. I gracelessly bounced off it and landed on the floor beside it. I rolled over as Brant closed the space between us to provide his assistance.

"Are you okay?" he asked, his face a mixture of confusion and annoyance as he reached down to me.

"I'm fine." I tried to wave away his proffered hand, but he grabbed me anyway and pulled me upright. "Thank you."

"Here, let's talk about options." He ushered me forward, still holding my hand. The addition of his hand pressing against my back made it impossible for me to excuse myself politely.

"No," I said curtly, causing him to freeze. He slowly released his grip on me and took a step back.

"Okay," he said in a soothing tone, as if he needed to calm the crazy lady.

"I'm sorry. I'm not trying to be difficult. I just can't look at any more samples or I'll have to gouge out my eyes. I need something to sit on. I don't care what it looks like, as long as it's comfortable." I reached into my purse and pulled out Ed's business card and a pen. "This is my phone number." I scribbled my number on it and extended it to him. He reached for it tentatively, as if he were baffled as to why he would need it. "Just pick out something and deliver it to me. I assume you already know where I live." I clenched my jaw.

Brant nodded and looked down at the card, glancing at the name on the back. "Do you have a cost in mind, Miss Blake?"

I shrugged. "You work on commission?" A slight smile tipped the edge of his lips, and he nodded. "Well, then I guess it depends on how much you want to make this week."

"All right." He flicked the card I had given him. "I'll take care of it." He leaned forward to speak conspiratorially. "I'll even throw in a cup of sugar for free." He winked and walked away. I stood there a moment, trying to decide if he was being playful or prickish, and how I felt about either.

The Police Report

"**A**re you sure you want to look at these?" Higgs asked as he held up a manila envelope that contained photos from my parent's *accident*. I had stopped by the police station to take advantage of the officer who had shown so much sympathy for me the other night. I had a hunch his concern for my reputation as the crazy lady on the hill might work to my advantage during my investigation. Not that requesting crime scene photos was a completely sane thing to do, but he seemed to understand the idea of "closure," as I had put it.

"I'm sure, Officer Higgs," I said.

"Call me Danny, everyone does." Higgs gave me a genuine hometown-friendly smile, which made me smile. With his hat off, I could see his short locks were ginger-colored. He had a rounded face that looked boyish, but he was well into his thirties. I got the sense he used his adolescent charm as an asset in his job. After all, someone has to be the "good cop."

"Thank you, Danny." He handed me the envelope. Our fingers touched in the exchange, which my brain immediately categorized under new and different—and therefore exciting. I noticed the ring on his left hand and I dialed back my smile. This wasn't anything new or exciting; this was just me, once again, seeing romance in congeniality.

I started spreading out the photos across his desk to look at them. I tried not to flinch when I got to the pictures of the bodies. Charred flesh with an underbelly of red. I was no longer emotionally connected to these people, but that didn't mean I wanted to see them like this. I didn't want to see *anyone* like this. It was a horrible way to die, and despite Ed assuring me my parents had died before the flames reached them due to smoke inhalation, I knew it wasn't true. I knew it because the one memory I had left from my youth was the sound of my mother's blood-curdling screams and my father's yowls of agony. The memory of their pain was always accompanied by a vision of them thrashing violently in the front seats of their car. It sent chills down to my very core, making me physically cold. Just looking at these pictures brought on a shiver.

Rather than leave, Higgs sat down in the chair beside the desk. "You mind if I ask you a personal question?" he asked quietly.

I looked up from the photos and waited for the inevitable list of questions I had braced myself for before I came back to Harold. Questions about the fire. What happened that day? How did it start? Did the fire hurt? Do I have any scars?

"Are you and Ed Ladner...close?" Higgs posed the question carefully.

"What?" I stared at him, surprised by this change of direction.

"The other night," he continued just as carefully. "His arrival seemed a little coincidental."

"He said he saw the lights from your police cars."

"So he wasn't planning to visit you that night?"

"No. Not that I know of. Why?" I felt like I was being tested—unfortunately, I had studied for the wrong subject.

"You two seemed...close."

I knew what he was implying. My reddening face was probably portraying me as guilty, but I couldn't help feeling that way. Technically, my feelings for Ed would now have to be listed under the category of adulteress.

"I've known Ed all my life. He's taken care of me from afar. I don't see anything wrong with the two of us being friends." Higgs continued to stare at me. "Is there?" I asked, now unsure of myself. I was certainly not an expert on relationships. Perhaps I hadn't read the fine print on marriage vows. *I will love, honor, and remove all other female friendships from my life.*

Higgs seemed to recognize the fear on my face, and his smile returned. "No, of course not. I just wanted to make sure he wasn't taking advantage of your reliance on him. Some men do that, you know."

"I know," I said in a haughty tone.

Higgs leaned over the desk, hiding his smile behind his fist as he looked at the photos. "What exactly are you looking for?"

"Answers," I said simply.

"What answers?"

"Answers about how they died."

Higgs stared at me for a moment. "I think it's pretty obvious how they died."

"But why?" I looked up from my analysis. "How did the fire start? Who did this?"

He frowned. "Nobody did this to them. This was a freak accident."

There was that word again—*accident*. Apparently, I had a different definition of it than everyone else. How could a 2800-degree fire be an accident when there are no viable ignition sources and no fuel to feed it? And why were my parents trapped in that car? Why couldn't they open the doors and get out?

"Did anyone perform autopsies on my parents' bodies?"

Higgs's concerned face faded into a sort of disappointment. "There was barely anything left of them."

"So, no?"

"No, I don't believe they did autopsies."

"How would I go about getting that done?"

"Excuse me?"

"I mean dig them up—what's that called?"

"Exhume?"

"Yes. How do I get permission to exhume the bodies and do the autopsies now?"

"There's paperwork for it. You'll have to get a judge's order, but I can't guarantee he'll give you permission. There has to be a substantial reason."

"Like murder? Maybe they were drugged. Why else would they just sit in that car and burn to death?"

Higgs cleared his throat. "Look, I know you want answers, but you won't find them in a grave. Any evidence of foul play would have been destroyed in the fire." He glanced around as if he were concerned someone would overhear me. "Maybe you should go talk to the town historian."

"Who's that?"

"Maggie Plinth. I know she has photos of the fire. Plus, she knows everyone in town. Maybe she can help you find the answers you really need." Higgs scribbled down her name and a phone number on the back of one of his business cards and handed it to me.

"What do you mean by the answers I really need?"

"People in this town don't like talking about the bad stuff. They pretend everything bad happens in other places, but not here. Maggie knows all the gossip. If you want answers about anyone in this town, including your parents, she'll have them."

The Visitor

I sneezed again as I swept away the last of the cobwebs from the upstairs ceilings. The old furniture had been removed from the house, except for one bed that had proven to be rat-free, the dining room set and the grand piano, which were both easily dusted and polished. The piano would likely need tuning as well. Had I learned more than Chopsticks, I might have been in more of a hurry to do it. I loved the sound of piano music, but until I met someone who could play, there was no point.

The doorbell rang downstairs, so I gratefully put down my broom and blew my nose into one of the emergency tissues I had stuffed in my back pocket. Free of dust bunnies and boogies, I opened the front door to let my delivery men in.

Unfortunately, the porch was vacant.

I stepped out and double-checked the drive, but there was no one around. No signs of life at all, and that included my beige lawn.

The doorbell rang again, and I realized it had come from the back door. They were both on the same ringer, so there was no way to tell the difference between them. I shut the front door and jogged through the hall to the kitchen. It rang again. "Coming," I hollered as I reached the door. I opened it up and pushed through the screen.

The back porch was empty.

I peeked around the grounds outside, but it was just more dry, desolate grass, give or take a few more thistles. The bell rang again, and I glared back at the front door. Someone was playing a trick on me. No doubt some stupid kids. Well, two can play at that game.

I shut the screen door and propped the swinging kitchen door open with a doorstop. The front door was still boarded up, so I would have to stay closer to that one so I could catch the brats running off the porch.

I backed myself toward the front door, keeping a careful eye on the kitchen as I did. I listened for the creak of footsteps on the front porch and watched for movement on the back porch. I waited, but nothing happened. Perhaps they were satisfied with only two rounds of hide and seek. Not very devoted to their prank, but I was glad to be rid of them either way.

A little too eager to avoid my housework, I waited a little longer.

I saw movement on the back porch and I froze, trying to make out the shape I had glimpsed. It looked taller than I had expected. This wasn't a child. The figure flickered into view, and I was certain it was an adult, but a man or a woman was still in debate.

The doorbell rang again.

Satisfied I was actually going to see who was out there, I started to move back through the house to the kitchen. The figure shifted again, stepping fully into view in front of the screen door. At first, my only surprise was that I could see a clear outline of a man wearing a hat. It was not a modern style like a fedora, but rather like a wide-brimmed felt hat.

My feet slowed as I reached the midpoint of the house. I stopped short of the kitchen because something was wrong. I was only a few meters from the man on my back porch, but I couldn't see him yet. The sun was bright outside, beating down the way summer intended it to, but not an ounce of that light had bothered to wrap around to reveal my visitor's identity.

I should have been able to distinguish a skin tone or basic facial features, but everything was nondescript. He had no mouth, nose, or eyes. He was just a shadow.

A shadow standing in the sunlight.

A heavy knock on the front door startled me. I yelped and turned to face the potential attacker. I saw blurred movement behind the lace curtains next to the door and heard the murmur of conversation.

I turned back to face the man at the back door, but he was gone. "Who's there?" I tentatively asked, demanding the figure to reveal his identity.

"Furniture delivery," a voice announced on the other side of the front door.

"Just a minute," I yelled and ran to peek out the back door. I even looked under the tiny porch and on the roof. Just in case.

I ran back to the front door and opened it. A large, bearded man with a clipboard was waiting on the porch. The ballpoint pen in his hand rapped repetitively against the metal clamp. Behind him was his lanky sidekick, who I could only assume would be capable of carrying as much as the large man. "Did you send someone around back?" I asked almost hopefully.

"No." He shook his head, baffled by the strange question. "Were we supposed to?" He looked down at his work order.

"No, I just thought I saw..." I trailed off as I noticed Brant, my *favorite* salesman, lurking behind the second man. He was holding a table lamp in each hand. "What are you doing here?" I asked, not realizing how rude it sounded until his eyes narrowed. "I mean, I thought you were a salesman."

"Family business. I'm whatever I need to be."

"Oh." I waffled a moment longer, searching my mind for another shred of conversation. Something that didn't make me sound like such a jerk.

"Do you want us to bring the stuff in or what?" the bearded mover asked.

"Oh, yeah, sorry." I cleared a path to let the men in. "You can put everything through here." I directed them to the main living room and vaguely outlined how I thought the couch should be positioned.

"Can we move this piano?" The thinner mover pulled out a measuring tape to confirm his suspicions that they would need more room to make the turn from the front room into the living room. Even before I answered, the two movers started rolling the piano further back into the corner.

"Yeah, go for it," I murmured, my unnecessary permission.

"Don't worry, they'll put it back for you." Brant said as he placed the lamps on the floor before shuffling back outside with the other men.

Ten minutes later, the furniture was inside and positioned with no time to spare for lemonade or idle chit-chat. I heard the moving van rumble away, and I saw a streak of dust as it disappeared down the hill. I was glad to have them in and out so fast, but I also felt bad that I was now going to be labeled the town's rich bitch because of one weirdly intrusive conversation in a furniture store.

"What do you think?" Brant asked.

I jumped and turned around, surprised he hadn't left with the other two men. "I...oh crap... I'm supposed to tip or something, aren't I?"

"That's not necessary; we charge for delivery." He picked up one of the lamps he had set on the floor and put it into position on an end table. He even plugged it in and turned it on.

"I thought the delivery was free.""In town is free. You're technically outside of town."

"Oh."

"What do you think of the set?" He grabbed the other lamp and did the same to it.

I stepped closer to look over the textured brown suede. As Lane had suggested, the accent chair was a beautiful artistic floral design with blue, green, and brown. It provided visual interest to the set while allowing the couch pillows to be green and blue without questioning the blend.

"Lane chose well."

"I chose it," he said flatly.

"Oh." I glanced at him. "I'm surprised you didn't choose something hideous."

"I happen to be very good at my job," he snapped.

"No, that's not what I..." I huffed and rubbed my face. "I meant because I was such a bitch to you." A moment of silence passed, and I turned to him and stuck out my hand. "I'm Tori Blake." For a moment he just stared at my hand.

"I'm Brant Hart." He closed his hand around mine and squeezed gently rather than actually shaking it. "Nice to meet you officially." The same sensation ran through me as when Higgs had touched my hand. My brain was reminding me I was making contact with someone new. This time, however, there was no ring to tamp out my blooming interest.

Even this small contact revealed so much about Brant. His hand was rough. He had working hands—unlike Ed, who had well-manicured, soft hands. His grip was tight. A sign of authority—or something like that. Perhaps this contact wasn't revealing as much about Brant's personality as it was mine.

His thumb slid along the cleft of my hand. It was a small movement, nothing that could be discerned as sensual, but it brought to mind other contact I would like to have with him—which was new for me. The only man I had fantasized about, besides Hollywood hotties, was Ed. I was beginning to think Brant might be a contender for that spot.

"You should try it out," Brant said. "See how it feels."

"What?" With visions of unbridled, unprotected, unplanned-pregnancy sex in my mind, I pulled my hand away a little too suddenly.

"The couch." Brant motioned to it. "It's really comfortable. I believe that was a prerequisite."

"Oh, right." I moved over to the sofa and fell onto it. "Oh, yeah, that does feel good. I might have to sleep down here tonight."

Brant chuckled and sat down on the other end of the couch and bounced around a bit as if he were checking the springs. "I have one similar to this. I frequently use it as a bed." He propped his arm on the back of the sofa and looked over the room. "Is that your only TV? We sell electronics too, you know."

"I'm not very tech-savvy."

"I'll pick one out for you." He pulled out a tiny notebook from his shirt pocket and scribbled down a note. "I'll get you a center rug too." He looked over the bare wood floor as if he were imagining his inventory options.

It took me a moment to realize his generosity was simply adding to his commission. It seemed less generous after that. "Are they coming back for you?"

Brant didn't look up from his notebook. "Who?"

"The movers. They already left, didn't they?"

He looked up at me, confused, but then his face dawned with understanding. "No, I drove my own car. I wanted to make sure you liked the set." I smiled, thinking about how thoughtful he was. "I was on my way home anyway." Maybe it wasn't that thoughtful. "I'll get out of your way and let you enjoy your couch." He jumped up and headed to the door.

I followed him out, more than a little disappointed the interaction was over. I was never good at reading men, but I was certain Brant was harder than the average man. Still, he was attractive, single, and age-appropriate. So far, he was a better catch than my usual obsession.

"Where's my cup of sugar?" I asked as his feet hit the front steps. He turned back to look at me. I leaned against the door frame and crossed my arms, feigning annoyance at the missing delivery.

A small smile flitted across his lips. "I actually considered bringing you a baggie full of sugar, but I wasn't sure if you would find it as funny as me."

"Well, now I'm definitely not tipping you." I stepped out onto the porch and propped my hands on my hips. "How about *I* give *you* the sugar?" I asked.

The amusement on his face melted into shock. He shifted uncomfortably and glanced around as if someone might be watching us. "Um, I really don't need a tip. Certainly not that kind of tip."

I gasped, suddenly realizing what he thought I was implying. I clamped my hand over my mouth. "Ooo-mo-mo-mo," I ranted through my muffling hand before lowering it again. "Lemonade!" I put up my hands to halt his words as well as any thoughts he might be having. "I was offering a glass of sweet lemonade. I was doing the whole neighborly thing." I motioned between us. "I didn't mean... *That.*"

Brant finally started blinking again and closed his mouth. "Oh." He let out a breathy chuckle. "That's a relief."

"Yeah," I agreed. Wait, what? "What do you mean, a relief?"

"I meant..." Brant paused, apparently stuck for words. He looked down at his feet and then back at his car, no doubt wishing he could make it there before the situation got any more awkward. When he finally looked back at me, he had a contented look on his face. "I just wouldn't have wanted it to go down like that. If it was going to, anyway."

"Oh." I waited a moment for him to say more, but he didn't. "So, was that a yes or no on the lemonade?" He checked his watch. Apparently, he had somewhere to be.

"Unless you have to get home to…someone," I suggested in case I had misinterpreted his single status.

"The only one at home is my cat, Linus, but he doesn't really care if I'm there or not. I think he prefers if I'm not, to be honest."

Again, I waited for him to answer my question, but he didn't. "If you would rather go, you can just say no." I tried to sound indifferent, but I was still coming off a little sour.

"It's not that. I actually hate lemonade, and I'm not sure I'm in the mood to pretend I like it."

I shrugged. "I have chocolate milk."

"Lactose intolerant."

I frowned. "Seriously?" I rolled my eyes. "How about a beer?"

"I have to drive, better not."

I scoffed and did a small circle on the porch to gather my composure. I nearly walked back inside and slammed the door on him, but instead opted for a more mature approach. "You do realize the beverage is just a ruse, right? I was trying to invite you to stay longer."

"Yes, I know that." Shame crept into his voice, and he lowered his gaze to the porch. "But if I walk back in, you will still give me something to drink, and as I said, I'm not in the mood to pretend."

"Okay," I conceded with disappointment. "But if we don't at least have a drink, then we'll just be standing inside having this awkward conversation instead of outside."

Brant perked his brow. "You see my dilemma now?" Brant perked his brow.

The silence stretched out for a moment, and I could see him turning his feet in anticipation of his exit. Rather than delay it any longer, I cued his exit line. "Well, you'd better get going. If you stick around any longer, I'll have to feed you dinner." I clapped my hands together and moved to the door.

"What are you making?" he asked.

I turned back around and let out a few thoughtful groans and puffed some air out of my lips. "I was gonna make spaghetti."

"Okay." Brant climbed back up the steps to the porch.

"What? You're serious. You want to stay for dinner?"

Brant nodded. "Like I said, Linus doesn't mind if I'm late."

I furrowed my brow. "So, a contrived beverage is too awkward, but an entire dinner is okay?"

Brant shrugged. "Yeah." He shifted past me, but stopped inside the doorway to look back at me. "Who knows, maybe you'll change my mind about that lemonade."

"We'd better be talking about a beverage still," I grumbled and followed him in.

The Dinner

"Tell me about yourself," Brant said as he sipped on his beer with his feet up on the adjacent chair. He had decided my spaghetti dinner would be heavy enough to soak up the alcohol. Somewhere between our pre-dinner conversation about my house renovations and the second beer, he had gotten quite relaxed.

"What can I tell you that you don't already know?" I asked over a mouthful of garlic bread. I was on the other end of the table, making the distance between us a little odd, but since this wasn't officially a date, I wasn't sure sitting next to him made sense either.

"How about what the hell you've been doing for the last fourteen years? Besides growing up. Good job on that, by the way."

I nearly choked on my beer as I washed down my last bite. I wiped my mouth and nodded. "Thanks, I was thinking of stopping here, but I'm told once you start..." I trailed off, letting the joke land where it may.

Brant gave me a small smile for my effort. "Why don't I tell you what I know, and then you can share something I don't know?"

"Okay." I sat back trying to emulate his relaxed demeanor.

He took another long swig of his beer before proceeding. "I know about the fire and all that jazz. I know you spent a few turns around the foster system before you were placed with your parents." Brant paused as if he weren't sure whether he should go on. "I heard they were killed in a car accident a little less than a year ago—which sucks. I'm sorry about that." I gave him a solemn nod, acknowledging his sympathy. "I also know you went to school for drafting, but dropped out just shy of your degree requirements to get your inheritance. I even heard you left behind a very coveted internship to come here."

I huffed out a breath and shook my head. "Geez, do people have nothing better to do than gossip about my life?"

"In Harold? No." Brant smiled, but I couldn't find the humor in being under a microscope. I had been so obscure in college I had gotten used to it.

"It's just that everyone in town is talking about me. I see them whispering to each other as I walk by. People I don't even know have started to introduce themselves like I should remember them."

"You don't, I take it."

"No."

"Well, you were only eight years old when you left. You're bound to have some gaps."

I wanted to tell him the gaps were all I had. My entire memory had turned to ash in that fire, but somehow I thought it might make me sound like a victim, and I didn't want that. It was true my life had taken terrible turns, but I was still doing okay. I just understood the hard truths of life better than the average person.

"You know it's not about you, right?"

I frowned. "Of course it's about me."

Brant shifted his feet off the chair and picked up his beer. He moved down the table and sat in the chair catty-cornered from me. His change in proximity made my heart thump a little, despite it being a perfectly reasonable distance for conversation. He leaned over the edge of the table and looked at me from beneath his brow. "It's not about you. It's about your parents." He leaned back again. "Your mother and father were part of this community. They had friendships with the people of this town. They had colleagues and co-workers. Your mother was on the PTA. Your father played golf at the club. The people of Harold aren't talking about Tori Blake. They are talking about Mark and Cassandra's daughter."

I bowed my head, chagrined not only that I was forgetting about my parents' personal connections to these people—who may well have been hurt by their loss—but also that Brant knew more about my parents' personal lives than I did. "That's true, I guess. I didn't really think of it like that."

"So," Brant said after a moment. "Now tell me something I don't know."

"You still want more information? There's hardly anything left."

"Tell me something you've never told anyone—not even your friends."

"Why would I tell you something I've never told my closest friends?"

"Because you said at the store you don't get personal with your friends."

"But you want me to get personal with you. A man I've known approximately..." I checked my watch. To my surprise, between dinner prep and eating we had passed nearly two hours. "Two hours."

"Yes," Brant said matter-of-factly, as if his request should be taken as a military order instead of a petition for conversational intimacy. "Are you afraid I'll judge you?"

"Of course you'll judge me."

"I can judge the statement, but not you. I have no comparison to past behavior and no expectations. You could say, 'I murdered a man,' and I would judge your act of violence, but I wouldn't be able to define it as out of character for you because I don't know you."

"You know, I'm *so* glad you brought that up because there was this one time..." I smiled, playing off the joke.

Brant's mouth turned up in a lop-sided smirk. "I'm sure they deserved it. Come on, tell me something important."

"This isn't fair. I don't know anything about you."

"You know more than you think." I tilted my head, curious about why he thought that. Granted, I had already met his brother, but that didn't compare to sharing untold secrets. "I want something juicy too."

"Why?"

"So I can use it to blackmail you later." He reached under the table and pinched my thigh just above the knee, making me jump and squeal like a schoolgirl. I couldn't help but laugh at his playfulness. I liked this side of him, and it had been a long time since anyone had flirted with me. In fact, judging by the number of butterflies in my stomach, I wasn't sure I had ever been properly flirted with. "Seriously, though, whatever you tell me stays between us. I promise." Instead of motioning a cross over his heart, he motioned double crosses over his eyes—miming the 'hope to die' portion of the traditional playground promise contract. I wasn't certain I had ever seen anyone use the gesture before, but it stirred something up in my memory banks. Nothing tangible, as usual, just an echo.

I shook my head. "I can't decide if you are teasing me or tormenting me."

He smiled widely. "Is there a difference?" He tapped his finger on the table, taunting me with his impatience.

I puffed my lips in thought. "I have no idea what I'm doing."

"Oh, come on, just one thing."

"No, that's the one thing I never tell people. I have money, an education—give or take the bachelor's degree—and now a house, and I have no freaking clue what the hell I am doing."

Brant leaned forward, resting his arms on the table. "I bet you thought if you came back to this house—your childhood home—that the pieces of your life would start to make sense."

"Yeah." I perked my brow, impressed he had gleaned that much from me already. "Actually, I came back to Harold to solve the mystery of who killed my parents."

Brant frowned and slipped his arms back off the table. "That's not going to be an easy mystery to solve."

"Tell me about it."

"Not to sound heartless, but why does it matter? I mean, what are you hoping to get out of it?"

"I don't know. That's the part that doesn't make sense, even to me. I have this big chunk of my childhood filled with question marks. I should be getting a job, buying a proper house, husband, kids, picket fence, whatever, but..." I debated how much to tell Brant. He had probably meant to draw out some kind of girly gossip about my sex life—or lack thereof. Instead, he was getting the down-and-dirty truth about my obsessions. "I couldn't let it go. I had to come back here. I had to know who started that fire—like, *OCD* had to know. Sometimes I feel like I'll never be whole until I understand what happened that day."

"What do you remember?"

"Nothing."

"No, I mean before the accident—the days and weeks leading up to it. Did your parents seem agitated?" I leaned over the table, holding my face in my hands. "You don't have to talk about it if you don't want to," Brant said, offering me a polite out for the conversation.

I looked up at him, prepared, for some reason, to tell him the truth. "Brant, I don't remember anything before the fire." That was perhaps a half-truth since I did have one very lucid memory, but that was as much a nightmare now as a memory.

"What do you mean? Like amnesia?"

"Sort of. It's like how you remember things that happened to you before kindergarten. You kind of remember a few things, but not very clearly, and you're not even sure you're remembering that correctly. Well, that's my whole childhood up to age eight."

"Wait, that means you don't have any memories of your parents." Just the one. "That's awful."

"Yeah." I took a sip of my beer, and Brant drank down the last of his. We sat there a long time, each of us looking at the table, searching our thoughts for the right words. "Sorry, I didn't mean to spoil the mood."

"You didn't. I'm just starting to realize why you're having such a hard time with the town knowing your history. It's like everyone got a copy of the Cliffs Notes to your life except you."

"Exactly." I nodded. "Now you know why I'm such a bitch."

"You're not a bitch," he scolded me.

"I'm pretty sure you thought I was a bitch when we first met."

"No." Brant leaned forward on his elbows and looked deep into my eyes. "The first thing I thought when we met was how beautiful you were." My mouth went dry, and it flopped open like a fish. "*Then* I thought you were a bitch," he admitted cheekily. I glowered at him as he got up. He retrieved his dirty plate and then came back for mine. He stopped beside my chair and looked down at me. I raised my eyebrow and waited for the needling to continue. He reached over and twisted a lock of my hair around his finger. He gave it a gentle tug before releasing it. "I don't think that anymore." He walked away with the dirty dishes, and a moment later I heard water running in the sink and the clanking of dishware.

Be still my heart, a man that does dishes.

The Confession

I watched Brant wash the plates and forks with fascination. He didn't seem to have any qualms about treating my home like it was his, and I was nearly certain he wasn't just trying to impress me. He was used to cleaning up after himself. I would have to thank his mother if I ever had the chance to meet her.

"You know, I get coming back here to tie up a few loose ends, put some faces to the names, but why move here?" Brant switched off the water and dried his hands. He leaned against the stove and eyed me warily. "You could have visited. Checked the place out first. But instead, you dove headfirst into an unfamiliar town, with virtually no job prospects for you, and bought a house sight unseen. What motivated you to do that?"

I bit my lip and shrugged. "What can I say? I'm impetuous."

"No, you're not." I blinked at his presumption to know me. He reached over and grabbed my notebook off the counter. It was open to my list of to-dos for the house. "Impulsive people don't make detailed lists with..." He glanced at the pad. "Cost estimates, timelines to completion, and—Jesus, did you label every light switch in the house?"

I reached over to snag the notebook out of his hand, but he lifted it beyond my reach.

"Oh my God, the faucets too."

"It's easier to keep track. Give me that!" I jumped up and yanked the book away.

"Seriously, Tori, you're a drafter—by definition you are a planner. You don't do things on a whim."

"Okay, fine, you're right." I closed my notes and stuffed them in a drawer. "I had been planning to come back to Harold for a while."

"Yes, but why?"

"Why do you want to know?"

"Why don't you want to tell me?"

"Brant!" I propped my hands on my hips, frustrated by this version of his playful side. He was definitely over the line of flirting and well into the territory of teasing. I hated being teased.

His eyes flickered over mine, and his mouth slowly dropped. "Oooh," he breathed the word. "This is about a guy, isn't it?" My eyes widened, and I froze like an animal about to become roadkill. "It *is*." I shook my head fervently, and he smiled. "Who do you even know here?"

"No one." I busied myself by putting the leftover spaghetti into Tupperware. By the time I got the skillet into the sink to soak, Brant was already reaching into his back pocket for his wallet. He drew out the business card I had given him with my phone number on it. It was Ed's card.

Brant looked at me, questioning the conclusion he had reached. I was eyeing him back, pleading for mercy. He didn't have to say it out loud, and neither did I. The truth was written in the tear that dribbled down my cheek without my consent.

"You can't tell anyone."

Brant shrugged. "I won't." Despite his previous claims to remain unbiased in the conversation, I could see the disappointment bleeding onto his face. His whole body seemed to slouch down like a sullen child.

"I mean it. I can't handle even one more piece of gossip about me."

Brant sighed and tossed the business card onto the counter. "I don't gossip. What you want to do with Ed Ladner is between you and him." He brushed past me and headed down the hall. "And his wife," he added. I heard his keys rustling, and I realized he was leaving. It was around the time I heard the door open I realized why he was leaving.

"Brant, wait!" The door slammed. I ran at a dead sprint down the hall to the front door. I crashed into it and yanked it open. "Brant," I called after him, but his long strides had already carried him halfway to his car. "It's not what you think!" I heard the words and groaned. It was such a cliché defense for adulterers that it bordered on being a misnomer. My next line should have been "we're just friends," but I ran after him instead. "Let me explain!"

My futile attempts to defend myself didn't slow Brant's steps in the least. He climbed into his car and started the engine. I had almost reached him when the car started rolling backward. With a quick twist of the wheel, Brant turned the car 180 degrees and sped down the hill, leaving me in a plume of dust.

The Rumors

"What is this about you requesting an exhumation of your parents?" Ed scolded me over the phone the next day. "What were you thinking?"

"It was just an idea." I stopped outside the Harold museum which was a small house converted into a commercial property. Even over the phone, I could feel Ed's glare. I hadn't exactly told him about my plans to investigate my parents' death. Up until now he'd thought I was more or less satisfying curiosity. Which was true, except my curiosity had a hungry motivation and a thirst for justice.

"What idea was that? What purpose would that serve?"

"I can't believe there isn't more to their death than a big accidental fire."

"Tori, contrary to your opinion of the Harold Police Department, they were efficient in their investigation. If they'd suspected foul play, they would have done autopsies. And just because you have questions doesn't give you the right to disturb your parents' final resting place."

"I know," I mumbled and kicked my foot into the step leading up the museum's porch. He was making me feel bad. I kept forgetting that these had been his friends. I wasn't just dredging up my history with my inquiries—I was dredging up his too. "I'm sorry. I didn't mean to upset you."

Ed sighed on the other end. His anger was waning, as it always did when I got pouty. "Look, hun, I have to go, but sometime we should sit down and discuss your parents. I mean, *really* discuss them. It would do you some good to talk about their lives instead of their deaths for once. Okay?"

"Yeah, that sounds good."

"We'll talk later—how's the house going?" he asked as an afterthought.

"It's okay. I was just about to start knocking down the walls into—"

"Good, good, can't wait to see it when you're finished. Call me if you need anything." He hung up before I could respond. I reminded myself he was a busy man and he couldn't spend all day chatting with me—especially now that he was married.

My mind wandered to the way things had ended with Brant. I had tried calling the store to speak with him, but he was always too busy to talk. Since I didn't have his cell number, I was going to have to resort to speaking to him in person—a notion that terrified me. Not so much because I had to clarify my relationship with Ed, an altogether uncomfortable prospect, but because there was still a chance my crush on him—albeit innocently naïve—was still going to be an issue Brant couldn't get past.

"Are you Tori Blake?" a sweet, kindly voice asked behind me. I turned and saw an older woman in her sixties standing at the front door.

"Yes, I called about—"

"The fire, oh, yes. Come in." She ushered me inside and shut the door behind her. "Everyone is always very interested in the fire, but I don't put a lot of pictures out for it. I prefer to focus on the positive accomplishments of our town and its members. Would you like some tea or coffee before we sit down?"

"Tea would be delightful," I said.

While Mrs. Plinth rummaged around in the kitchen, I meandered through the rooms on the main floor, examining the photos and memorabilia she had accumulated over her many years as the town's self-designated historian. A hobby for everyone, I thought.

"Hopscotch tournaments," Mrs. Plinth said when she found me concentrating on one particular set of photos. She handed me a teacup and saucer. On the edge she had placed two cubes of sugar, which I placed into the hot liquid to melt. "Can you imagine? Grown adults competing for the title of Champion Scotcher?" She chuckled to herself. "Oh, no one plays anymore. And adults are the worst. We grow up and we think that responsibility and maturity mean throwing away the things we used to do as children. And why?" She paused, giving me a stern look. "Who's going to stop us?"

I chuckled at her enthusiasm. "You're exactly right."

"This town used to do all sorts of fun things." Mrs. Plinth wandered over to a small table in the next room and sat down. I joined her, noticing the photo album already sitting on the edge. "Nowadays, people want champagne and fancy dresses. Every occasion is the same. Booze, music, and food. There's no creativity. There's no mental stimulation. At my age, the only stimulation I want is mental."

I laughed at her rant.

"Now, you, you're young enough to understand that life is not just a series of socially acceptable booze parties. You know the importance of play, don't you?"

"I'd like to think so," I said, although I wondered when the last time I had actually *played*. Sports, board games, video games—I wasn't even sure I had splashed in a pool in the last year. Perhaps I *didn't* know the importance of playing.

I glanced at the photo album, trying to decide how to transition our conversation to the photos of the fire.

"Your mother knew how to play."

My attention snapped back to Mrs. Plinth. "She did?"

"Oh yes, she was vibrant and curious. She had a friend she always went out with. Genie—something or other. They were thick as thieves. When they got together, you would have thought that they were eight years old again."

"Really?" I asked, interested in hearing more. "What else do you remember about her?"

"Your mother was always making new clothes for herself and you. She hated buying clothing off the rack. She thought a good sewing machine was the best investment a woman could put into her wardrobe. I can't remember how many times you two would show up at events in matching dresses or jumpers. Oh, I'm sure kids these days would hate that, but I thought it was adorable.

"Cass was also the best baker. She had a way of making her brownies so dense and her cakes light as air. She was an absolute wizard with flour and sugar. I'm pretty sure several inches of my waistline were caused by her lemon sponge cake."

I chuckled again. "What about my father? Do you remember him?"

"Oh, I'm afraid most of the to-dos I was involved with were more women's activities: bake sales, church groups, and school events. Your father was a nice man, so far as I knew. Friendly and gentlemanly."

"Do you know anything about what happened to them? I know it was written off as an accident, but you don't think anyone would want to start their car on fire, do you?"

Mrs. Plinth's smile faded slightly but returned. "No, of course not."

"Are you certain?"

Mrs. Plinth pinched her lips together. "Well, now, I don't know about murder plots, but there were some women in town that didn't prefer your mother."

"Why?"

"Cass was a very beautiful woman, and she attracted the eyes of several men. Men who were already married. I think some of the ladies in town didn't appreciate their husbands' lingering looks, but that is the burden of being a beautiful woman, as I'm sure you know."

I blushed, surprised she would lump me into the same category as my mother. I had seen pictures of her, so I knew how high a compliment it was. "You mentioned on the phone you had photos of the fire."

"Oh, yes." Mrs. Plinth pulled the photo album over to me. "I never go anywhere without a camera. On the day of the fire, I noticed smoke coming from the hill. I started photographing it right away. When I realized how severe it was, I drove up to take pictures of the aftermath before the police arrived to shoo me away. That's why I don't keep the photos out—too gruesome for a casual museum like mine." She patted my hand. "You take your time, sweetheart. There's a lot that can be learned from the past."

After Mrs. Plinth left the room, I flipped through the big book of black pages. Each page had one black-and-white photo displaying a different stage of the fire. The first ones only showed smoke and then the blaze. I was shocked to see the inferno was as high as the house. To my knowledge, though, the fire never touched the structure. The smoke from the car's tires eventually clouded the view of the fire.

That must have been when Mrs. Plinth drove up for a closer look because the next pictures were of firemen rushing around the house carrying hoses and extinguishers. I wasn't sure what Captain Bradford looked like, but I imagined the firefighter with the dumbstruck look on his face in one of the photos was him. He was obviously awestruck by the tremendous blaze.

I recognized the next photos—or at least one of them. It was a picture of me being pulled from the car and carried away—safe and sound. Mrs. Plinth had an excellent picture of the back seat. The fire chief hadn't exaggerated that my spot was the only one left untouched, as if my very aura had blocked thousands of degrees of heat and licking flames. Impossible, to be sure. I understood why the word *miracle* was freely bandied about on this occasion.

"Mrs. Plinth, who is this woman?"

Mrs. Plinth returned and looked at the photo of the burned car with a woman in the background. She was bent over with her face buried in her hands, presumably crying. "Oh, that's the friend I was telling you about. She took Cassandra's death very hard. In fact, she was never the same. She's a delightful woman to be sure, but she's marked by sadness, as we all are when tragedy befalls us." Mrs. Plinth gave me a sorrowful expression. I wasn't sure the description applied to me, but once again people weren't familiar with my memory loss.

"And who is this?" I pointed to the adjacent picture. It was a slightly different view of the smoking wreckage. From this angle, I could see the upstairs window of my childhood bedroom. A man was standing there looking down at the car.

Mrs. Plinth frowned. "You know, I don't believe I ever noticed him. Hmm, I guess it would have been one of the firemen."

"He looks too slender for that—they always look bulky in their gear."

"Oh, that's true. Maybe a policeman then."

I nodded in agreement, though I couldn't see a policeman just standing upstairs after that much chaos. Whoever this man was, he seemed to be content to watch the bedlam.

The Kitchen

Dust flew as I cut through the plaster wall with my reciprocating saw. It would occasionally snag on a nail, but otherwise the wall between the pantry and the kitchen was coming down fast.

I took a break to let my hand rest before I took on the next stud. I set down the saw and noticed an odd-looking nail head in the two-by-four. I touched it, and it dropped to the floor. I picked through the debris and found it again. After a moment of inspection, I realized it was a bullet—smooshed into a mushroom cap, but it was definitely some kind of ammunition. I set it down next to the sink and made a mental note to ask Ed about it.

I stepped out the back door, which I had kept open for ventilation. Once I was clear of the potential lung cancer cloud, I removed my mask and goggles so I could enjoy the fresh air and view.

My house was advantageously situated on the tallest hill in the county, so I had the best view of the sunset. The sharp descent on the backside of my property was a little precarious, but I knew better than to walk too close.

The breeze picked up as I sat on the ledge of the small back porch. It was a basic set of steps, but unlike the front, it was concrete and provided a sturdy seat. The air whipped around my hair, tangling it more than it already was. I closed my eyes and breathed in the spring air.

I was reveling in the idea of an ice-cold lavender tea when I heard the familiar *"kssshtt"* of a soda can being opened behind me, and I froze. A chill ran up my spine, but I refused to let my imagination get the better of me. I was mistaken.

It was just the wind.

It was just the pipes.

It was anything but what I thought it was.

Even as I tried to delude myself, I turned my ear toward the door to listen. There was a slight sound that might have been gulping. Then the exhale of a satisfied beverage drinker followed.

I twisted my body slowly, quietly. I didn't want to look. I didn't want to see who was inside my kitchen, but I had to.

I dreaded seeing the large man again. Man or ghost, I didn't want him in my house. But it wasn't him. It was something else.

With my survival instincts competing with my curiosity, I openly stared at the figure standing inside the kitchen in front of my fridge. It was the same man I had seen the other day standing on the other side of my screen door. Even now, only steps away from him, he was indistinct. Not ghostly, but as if he were standing in perpetual shadows. Which made no sense, because there was a stream of sunlight cutting right through the kitchen from the window. There were no shadows. Unless the shadows were coming from him.

My heart raced, and my eyes watered. This was not a hallucination. This was real, and yet not real. I opened my mouth, slowly formulating a question that would suffice to be spoken to a stranger, human or otherwise. "Who are you?" I whispered with barely enough volume to count as a voice.

The shadowy figure turned to me. The face was just as dark, but I knew it was looking at me. It took two long strides toward me, and I inhaled to scream. The back door slammed in my face as a shriek burst from my mouth.

I bolted off the porch and ran. It didn't matter where, as long as it was away from the house. Away from whomever, or whatever, was trespassing in my home.

The Police Station

I ran all the way to town, only stopping at the outskirts to catch my breath. When I reached the police station, I was wet with sweat and panting. I approached the desk sergeant, who looked at me with worry. "What's wrong?" he asked.

"There is a man in my house," I said, "an intruder."

The man picked up the phone and immediately asked for a patrol to be sent to my house. When I rattled off my address, he looked at me suspiciously. "What's your name?"

"Tori Blake," I answered.

"Weren't we just at your house the other night for the same reason?"

"Yes, but you never caught him. He was in my kitchen. He slammed the door in my face."

He looked me over again. "You still cleaning that place out?"

"I'm breaking down a wall in my house."

"Are you staying hydrated, getting enough air?" he asked.

I frowned. "What does that have to do with anything?" I frowned.

"I'm just making sure we really need to send somebody up there again."

"Are you refusing to help me?" I asked.

"No, of course not." The sergeant finished his call and asked me to sit. Twenty minutes later, he called me back. His eyes narrowed as I approached. "The patrolman said the house was empty. Same as last time."

"Well, he must have left."

"Yeah, must have." He crossed his arms. "This isn't going to be a running gag, is it? Because here in Harold we don't take kindly to mocking the police department."

"I'm not mocking you."

"It's just... that old house has fostered a lot of ghost stories. We do our best to keep that kind of thing under control. Tends to encourage vandalism and trespassing."

"I don't want that either."

"Good. Maybe next time you think you see someone in your house, you can double-check before you call in the police."

I stared at him, unable to fathom when I had become the nut-job in town. I nodded and left. Without my car, I was stuck walking home. But I didn't want to go home. Unfortunately, without my purse, I was at the mercy of kindness to find a trusting hotel for the night.

By the time I reached Ed's office, the sun was dropping low in the sky and I was trying to rationalize what I had seen. I had weeded through all the usual psychological illnesses when I spotted Ed stepping out the door with his secretary.

"Ed!" I waved and jogged over. I thought I saw him frown before he smiled, but I ignored it.

"Tori, what on earth are you doing? You're a mess," he said, looking over my state. I knew I was sweating like a cold glass in the sun, but I had forgotten about the dust and my goggles. I now looked like a mud puddle.

"I was doing some work on the house."

"Where are you parked?" He looked down the street.

"I..."

"Eddie, are you ready?" a woman's voice called from across the street. I looked over and saw a woman twice my age, but good-looking, sitting in the passenger seat of his SAAB. "We're going to be late," she said as she ducked down to get a better view of me through the rolled-down driver's side window.

I looked back at Ed, who was already giving her the one-minute finger and a genuine smile of apology. The smile instantly dropped when he looked at me, replaced by his politician's smirk. "Listen, kid, I hate to leave you, but we have tickets to the theater. It's not the type of thing you can be late for," he explained, assuming I had never been to a play.

"I..." I stammered, searching for the words "need" and "help." Unfortunately, the only words in my head were "love" and "you."

"Do you need a ride? "I can call a taxi," he added, as if he had not made his schedule clear.

"Ah, no. Actually, I'm sorry to ask, but I left my purse at home. Can I borrow some cash?"

"Of course." He dug in his pocket and pulled out his wallet.

"Eddie?" The woman impressed upon him her urgency, or perhaps she just didn't want him to give money to a shabby-looking woman on the street.

"Right there, hon," he hollered and handed me a couple of twenties. "That do it?" he asked.

I tried to remember if I had ever seen a motel for less than sixty dollars, but he was already putting his wallet back. I nodded and thanked him even as he was walking away. I waited on the sidewalk as he climbed into his car. There was some discussion of my identity with his wife, but the engine rumbled to life and they drove away before I could hear the rest of the exchange.

I stared down at my forty dollars and looked back up at my house, which was visible from here, as it was from nearly anywhere in town. I was being ridiculous. So maybe I had a poltergeist. That was no reason to sleep on the street like a vagrant. I had to go back—at least to grab my purse and get my car. Then I could leave again. Forever, if I wanted.

I continued to rationalize, but my feet didn't move.

"Tori?" Brant's voice called me out of my trance. I found him standing behind me with a bank envelope in his hands. "What happened to you?" His voice didn't sound sympathetic. He was just acting according to his compulsory gentlemanly behavior.

I looked down at my dirty, shabby clothes. I could only imagine what my hair looked like. "Renovations," I mumbled. I looked up the street and down the street, realizing I didn't even know where the hotel was.

"Do you need some help?" Again, he didn't sound sympathetic, but he at least seemed curious about my situation.

"Actually, yes," I said. I decided not to dance around the truth. "I need some money. I don't have enough for a hotel room." Brant stared blankly at me. "I'll pay you back. I just forgot my purse. This wasn't a planned excursion."

Brant looked at the storefront we were standing in front of, which was Ed's law office. He looked back at me and scoffed as he reached for his wallet. "This is new." He pulled out two hundred-dollar bills and handed them to me. I blinked at the amount he was offering, especially since he really did barely know me. "I've never paid for another man's tryst before."

"What? No, that's not what the room is for!" Brant didn't flinch at my explanation. He was obviously set on believing his own version of my story, and there was very little I could do about it. "Oh, forget it!" I threw the hundreds back in his face. "Screw you!" I crumpled the twenties and threw them at Ed's office door. "Screw Ed Ladner. And screw the police." I stormed off down the sidewalk. "I'd rather deal with a poltergeist than any of you!" I ranted as I went.

The Believer

I walked along the road, only marginally interested in the cars that were unhappy with my proximity to their lane. I still wasn't sure about going home. Whatever was happening in my house was not normal. If I were smart, I would get into my car and drive away forever. Forget the crazy haunted house. Forget my slightly obsessive crush on Ed. And forget that I was supposed to be making sense of my stolen youth.

Despite how frightened I was of these experiences, though, I couldn't help but wonder if something was pushing me away from the truth. I still couldn't wrap my head around the idea of a poltergeist, but perhaps my mind was creating these images to protect me. Not only had my mind made me forget the trauma of my parents burning to death right in front of me, but maybe it was also stopping me from retrieving the memories, too.

Had my brain turned against me?

A four-door sedan slowed to a crawl beside me and rolled down the passenger-side window. "I'm okay," I said and turned my head to smile appreciatively for the offer. My smile immediately shrank when I saw Brant staring back at me. "What do you want?"

"Why are you walking home?"

"Because I don't have my car." I continued to walk, and he inched along beside me, irritating the drivers on their commute home.

"Did your car break down?"

"Nope, it works fine. It's just at home."

"How did you get to town? Did Ed ditch you?"

"No! I ran to town."

"Why?"

"Because that's where the police station is, and I stupidly assumed they would help me."

"The police? What happened?"

I stopped and leaned down to look at him. "Why do you care? I thought you hated me now."

Brant shook his head and looked out at the road. "I don't hate you. I was just mad. I misunderstood what was happening the other night. I thought you were interested in me."

I leaned against his passenger door. "I *am* interested in you, ya moron."

"What about Ed?"

"What *about* Ed?"

Brant scoffed. "You're having an affair with him."

"No, I'm not!"

"You said you were."

"No, you surmised that all on your own. I have never slept with Ed. I have never even kissed Ed. We've hugged a few times—and one of those was at the hospital after my parents died. The only secret you uncovered the other night was that I have had a crush on him since I was fifteen. I didn't want you to tell anyone because it's humiliating. I moved to Harold to be closer to Ed, and a week after getting here I found out he's married. I was crushed, okay?"

Brant stared at me as if he still didn't believe me. His eyes sank to the passenger seat. He moved a pile of fabric swatches to the back seat and motioned to me. "Get in. I'll give you a lift." His audacity left me gawking at him. This back-and-forth, nice-guy-slash-jerk routine was making my head spin. I wasn't sure he was worth the whiplash. I pushed off his car and started walking again. "Hey! *I* gave *you* a second chance," he yelled out to me.

My feet stopped—cemented into place by the most powerful glue known to man: the guilt trip. He *had* given me a second chance. My attitude at the furniture store had not been my best moment. Frankly, none of my moments since I got to Harold could be classified as good, let alone best. At any rate, Brant was trying to make up for his stupidity, and my legs were willing to forgive him.

I dusted myself off as best I could and slipped into his passenger seat. He pulled back out into traffic, and I buckled myself in. For the first mile or so we were both silent—him watching the road, me staring out the window.

"So what happened?" he asked as he pulled onto the gravel road that would eventually lead to my long uphill driveway. I could feel my body tense with the prospect of walking back into that house. Two—possibly three—paranormal experiences were apparently my quota. "What happened?" he asked again. There was a sternness in his voice, as if he were containing his volume.

I shook my head. "I don't want to say."

"Why did you need the police?"

"There was another intruder."

Brant looked over at me and nearly slid into the ditch. He got control of the vehicle and kept his glances from the road to a minimum. "Are you kidding me? Someone was in your house?"

"I saw a man in my house last week. I called the police, but they didn't find him. Then today there was this guy standing in my kitchen, drinking a soda like he lived there. I asked him who he was, and he slammed the door in my face. So, I ran all the way to town. A patrolman checked the house again, but no one was there."

"Well, how did he get in? Do you need new locks? That basement has to have a dozen nooks and crannies someone could hide in."

I shook my head. "I wasn't sure the first time, but the second time I knew."

"Knew what?"

"I couldn't see his face, Brant. He was right there, but he wasn't. I don't think he *was* there."

"You mean like a ghost or something?"

"No." I sighed. "I mean, like schizophrenia or something. A brain tumor, maybe." I rubbed my face and leaned my head on the windowsill.

Brant stayed quiet for a while. I assumed he was considering—as I had just been—whether this relationship was worth the hassle. "I've seen a ghost."

I looked back at him, shocked he was admitting such a thing out loud. I was starting to tip heavily into the category of a believer, and I still didn't want to admit what I'd seen may have been real. "You've seen a ghost?"

"Yeah, my granny. I thought it was a dream. You know how those stories go: you wake up and the person is standing at the end of the bed."

"You don't have to make me feel better. I really don't believe in all that paranormal stuff, anyway." At least I hadn't a few weeks ago.

"That's funny, coming from you."

"What do you mean, coming from me?" I asked.

"I just mean I'm surprised the fire hasn't made you a little more open to miracles and magic, you know?"

"The only thing that fire did for me is make me paranoid about fire safety."

Brant chuckled at me, though I was serious. I had an inordinate number of fire extinguishers in my home. And two in my car—one in the backseat and one in the trunk.

"I can't speak for a doctor, but I suspect what you saw has nothing to do with your brain malfunctioning. That house has always been a little buggy." Brant nodded toward my house, which was coming into view ahead of us. "People have been seeing specters in there long before you came along. The police get sent up here on all sorts of wild-goose chases. This house has been empty for over a decade, but people still see lights on at night. A woman was jogging by one day and swore up and down she heard a baby crying inside. The kids used to come up here and try to break in..." Brant trailed off as if he were remembering something. Perhaps he had been one of those kids. "I don't know what kind of windows you have, but they don't break easily."

"That explains why the police won't help me."

"Yeah, the police know you saw what you saw. They just don't want to deal with it anymore. Truth is, I think it freaks the shit out of them."

"Great. I moved into a haunted house."

Brant pulled to a stop in front of the house and put the car into park. I surveyed the front windows, looking for movement inside. As I looked into the window of the upstairs bedroom, a chill ran through me. Not because I saw anything, but because it reminded me of the picture Mrs. Plinth had taken, with the dark silhouette of a man watching my parents burn to death.

"This really has you spooked." Brant turned to face me, resting his hand on my seat. "Shit, I shouldn't have told you all those ghost stories. They are just stories. No one has ever gotten attacked or anything."

"Except my parents."

"Don't," Brant said, the hard edge returning to his voice. "Your parents' death was a very unfortunate incident, but there are no ghosts or goblins responsible for it." There was a certainty about him that made me believe what he was saying to be true.

I nodded. "I know. I'm being foolish." I brought my hand to my mouth to bite my nails, and I realized how dirty they were. How dirty *I* was. I needed a shower, but the only thing worse than being in a house with a poltergeist was being *naked* in a house with a poltergeist. "Brant," I whispered. "Would you mind—I mean, if you have time...Would you come inside with me?" I expected him to dither or check his watch, but he smiled and shut off the engine.

The Shower

Covered in plaster, horsehair, and all manner of dust, I headed upstairs for an overdue shower while Brant waited downstairs. I turned on the faucet in the claw-foot tub and got the water up to temperature. I slipped off my dirty clothes and made the mistake of glancing in the oval mirror over the pedestal sink. My hair was gray with dust, and my face was streaked black where I had touched it. It was a wonder Brant had even recognized me on the road, let alone allowed my filth into his car.

I climbed into the shower and rinsed off what was left of my attempt to remodel. I eagerly accepted the sting of my tiny little cuts and scrapes as I removed the dirt from them.

After I was soapy and sudsy all over, I gave my legs a good shave. Just in case I...

Well, just in case.

Somewhere in my rinse cycle, I noticed a figure on the other side of the semi-transparent shower curtain. I gasped and cussed. "Brant, don't just walk in here. You scared me half to death." I waited for an apology, but it never came. "Brant?" I asked, now unsure whether the figure inside my bathroom was tall enough to be Brant.

The figure took a step forward, and I shut off the water. Once the dribble of the faucet stopped, I heard a rattling breath from the other side of the curtain—like the breath that precedes a coughing fit.

It took another step forward. An audible *thunk* on the floor as the step landed.

I was certain now this wasn't Brant, nor was it the large man, nor even the shadow man. The frame was too small for any of them, and I could sense the substance in the body before me.

It took another step forward. *Thunk.* It was limping.

The rasping breath pushed out intentional sounds. The figure was attempting to speak, but nothing was clear enough to understand.

It was only inches from the curtain. I could see the dark skin.

The smell of fire permeated the room. Gasoline, burned plastic, chicken feathers, and...meat.

One more limping step brought it into view. I could see blackened skin. It cracked and gaped—revealing the pink underbelly of adipose. The mouth opened. It took a rattling breath and pushed against the curtain. "Tori!"

Fear shot through me on every level I could imagine. Fear of death. Fear of pain. Fear of loss.

And fear of the truth.

The last one was the most surprising, since it was brought on by my suspicions that I already knew who this creature was.

My mother.

The Farmstead

I screamed and cowered down low in the tub. I continued to wail, huddled in a ball and rocking. When the curtain came crashing open, it wasn't the monster I had seen; it was Brant. He towered over me, looking around for an intruder but finding only me.

He was primed for battle, but as he looked at me tucked into a fetal position and bawling, his shoulders slumped. He grabbed a towel off the hook behind the door and threw it over me. "Come on," he insisted, urging me to stand. "Get dressed and pack a bag. You're coming home with me."

There was no discussion of whether or when. He helped me out of the tub and directed me to the bedroom next door. He didn't even wait for me to dress before pawing through two duffel bags at the end of my bed. "Are these all your clothes?" he asked.

I nodded. I hadn't really unpacked since I hadn't purchased a dresser yet. I didn't mention the second duffel bag was all dirty clothes. It didn't matter.

"Do you need any personal items? Something you can't buy later?"

I shook my head. It was sad, but everything I owned was expendable. I didn't even have any nice jewelry or fancy eye cream.

"I'll be right outside the door." Brant pulled out a pair of shorts and a t-shirt from the duffel bag and tossed them to me. I didn't care that they were technically PJs. Once he was out the door, I slipped them on. I dried my hair off as best I could and came out into the hallway.

Brant ushered me downstairs and handed me a pair of flip-flops. While I put them on, he stuffed a pair of tennis shoes into one of my duffel bags. In five minutes flat, we were walking out the door and getting into his car.

For twenty minutes I cried quietly, trying to figure out when my life had turned into the plot of a horror movie. Brant didn't console me or badger me with questions. I sensed him watching me, glancing over from time to time. I was grateful he didn't ask me what I'd seen, because I didn't want to describe it.

The sun was dipping low in the sky when we pulled in to an old farmstead. The ever-changing sunset cast painted stripes on the main house through the surrounding trees. The mammoth white structure was in desperate need of a coat of paint—not that I could judge on the matter of a home's disrepair. The red barn near the house appeared to be in excellent condition, but the surrounding sheds were barely being held up by the surrounding weeds.

Brant pulled up close to the house and shut off the engine. He climbed out and grabbed my bags from the back seat. He headed inside without a word. After a quick survey of the area, I followed him in.

I passed through a mud porch, which was piled high with old tools. They might have even been antiques, but sitting here, unused and unloved, they were just clutter.

I pushed through the decorative wooden door leading to the kitchen, and my mouth dropped. As first impressions went, Brant's home was a disheveled mess, but the inside was something else entirely.

The kitchen had stainless steel appliances—including an oven that could double as a bunker. The Corian marble countertops were beautifully matched with the slightly gray cabinets beneath them. The floor, albeit a little shabby, was beautifully refinished and somehow made the entire room seem warm and inviting.

Just as inviting was the smell of something meaty cooking in the oven. My stomach lurched with the hope that this overnight stay would include a meal.

Off to one side of the kitchen, was a modernized version of a mudroom. The open locker design had wrought-iron hooks for coats and rope baskets below for shoes. Naturally, all the hooks were empty, since that was the only way to keep it looking tidy.

"Brant?" I called out before leaving the kitchen. I hated to snoop, but I was dying to see more of his home.

As I left the kitchen, the disjointed floor plan gave me two options: proceed forward into the dining room or turn left to enter the living room. The dining room was smaller than I would have guessed, but nicely decorated with soft tones and fine art that I hadn't expected to see in a farmhouse. The only thing missing was a table. The card table was doing its job of holding fresh flowers, but even putting one more stem in the vase might have collapsed the table.

I veered over into the living room, which by design should have been the front of the house. I could see the front door was as fancy as the back door, but with the addition of a huge oval window. The fireplace on the wall nearest me had slate-style tile surrounding it with an oversized mantel that begged for stockings to be hung on it. On the opposite side of the room was an open staircase with a beautiful banister and thick spindles. The couch and chairs in the middle, I noted, were not unlike mine—classy, but comfortable.

Beyond the staircase, I could make out a bathroom and a bedroom. I assumed it was Brant's, so I didn't trespass any further. I peeked out the front door and saw a large front deck. It seemed to be a recent addition to the house. The fresh white wood hadn't suffered through winter yet.

"I think I'm in love," I shouted to wherever Brant was hiding out.

After a long pause, he responded. "I assume you mean the house," he called down from somewhere upstairs.

I chuckled. "Yes, but I think this place works in your favor too." There was no response. "I'm surprised you aren't married already. With a house like this, you're liable to get a girl to propose to you." There was no response to my effort at humor. "All you need is a nursery up there and you could put a girl's ovaries into high gear." I winced, realizing how stupid I sounded. "Probably a good reason not to bring girls here," I continued, although my mouth was doing me no favors so far.

Brant descended the stairs sans duffle bags. "I put your things in the second bedroom. There's a bathroom up there too."

"Thanks. I appreciate..." I trailed off, thinking about the long list of things I had to be grateful for. "You've really gone above and beyond for me today."

"Yeah, that's not usually my style." He crossed his arms, contemplating this.

"What *is* your usual style?" I asked.

He huffed out a laugh. "Well, let's just say despite my ovary-geared home, I am still single." He grimaced at me mockingly and pressed his hand into my back, guiding me toward the kitchen. "You hungry?"

"God, yes."

The Hungry

"Mmm, this is so good," I groaned over the roast melting in my mouth. I shouldn't have been wolfing down my food like a scavenger, but I couldn't help it. The day's events had left me seeking comfort, and food was number one on my list of consolations. "How do you keep it so moist?"

"If you care about calories, you may not want to know," Brant said as he helped himself to another bowl of his beef stew on the stove. He set his bowl by his chair and poured me a glass of milk. Aside from the calories, it was the healthiest meal I had had in a long while.

"Oh, good gravy, that's good gravy," I continued to lament.

He chuckled and sat on the stool next to me. "You act like you haven't eaten in a year."

"I've been living in dorm rooms and shared apartments for the last four years. So, no, I haven't eaten real food in quite some time."

"I used to be like that before I got this place. Then I grew up." I frowned at the suggestion that I wasn't grown up. He saw the expression and smiled. "There's a difference between being mature and grown-up."

"What's that?" I poked a potato and stuck it in my mouth before I realized how hot it was. I sucked down a quarter of my milk to cool my mouth enough to chew it.

"Mature means you're intelligent, honest, and respectful. Grown-up means you've taken all those skills and applied them to your own life."

"Cooking real food is what grownups do?"

"Yes, and creating a home for themselves."

"Oh, goody, I'm halfway there. How long did it take you to redo all this?"

"Oh, no, I didn't do this. My uncle and aunt did this. This was originally my great-grandmother's house. They sold it to me for a reasonable amount a couple of years ago, before they moved."

"Where did they go?"

"They're snowbirds. They wanted to spend more time in Arizona, so they decided to give this place up. They wanted family to have it and since my father already had a nice place in town, they gave it to me."

"How'd your brother feel about that?" I took another bite of beef.

"He didn't care. He's not into old houses. In truth, I don't think I would have taken it if they hadn't updated it already. I don't mind a little work, but...This wasn't just a little work."

"I'm starting to lean in that direction."

"Why did you take on that place, anyway?" Brant leaned his elbow back on the counter to get a better look at me. "It's not exactly a starter home."

I shrugged. "I think I thought it would help me remember them. Like a jump-start to my brain. That, and I wanted a project to keep me busy."

"Have you remembered anything about them?"

I waggled my hand, indicating a very conditional yes. "Bits and pieces. The things I do remember are so stupid. I can almost remember my mother's face." My thoughts turned to the charred skin of the woman outside my shower. It had been her face—just not as it should have been. "I mostly remember how her hair felt." I closed my eyes, trying to imagine her the way I wanted to remember her. "I think I would play with it while she was carrying me."

"What about your dad?"

I frowned and shook my head. "I remember him playing the piano. That's about it. Ed told me I was quite the daddy's girl, but those memories seem to be even more elusive." As if my trauma were directly linked to my father, I thought. I didn't mention to Brant that I had one other memory of my father—the memory of him yelling at my mother. But that was it. Two very lucid memories of my parents fighting and my parents dying. The rest was just a cluster of random crap that didn't add up to a childhood. "I can't even remember Christmas presents or birthday cakes, or—actually, I do remember going to a birthday party, but it wasn't mine." I thought back, piecing the memory together, from the taste of blue frosting to... "Oh, it was at the house of a little boy I hated," I said with the sound of revelation in my voice.

"Why did you hate him?" Brant asked.

"He was mean. He pulled my hair."

Brant chuckled. "That probably meant he liked you."

"Why do boys think picking on girls is the same as flirting with them?"

Brant grinned at me. "Why do kids do anything? To get attention. I'm sure that little boy, whoever he was, is sorry for what he did to you."

I scoffed. "Right."

"I hate to ask, but do you remember anything about that day?"

I bit my lip, debating—as I frequently did when people asked me this question—how much to tell him.

Brant narrowed his eyes. "You don't want to tell me, do you?" He grabbed my plate and took it to the sink to rinse. "It's okay. It's technically none of my business."

"It's just, I've heard so many stories from other people. I can't be sure if everything I see is from my own memory or someone else's."

Brant made a disgusted sound and put my bowl in the dishwasher. "There were a lot of rumors surrounding their deaths. I doubt much of what anyone told you was true."

"Oh, yeah?" I perked up, thinking this conversation may now be working to my advantage. "What sort of rumors?"

"Ridiculous rumors."

"Like what?"

Brant glanced back at me, a look of disappointment in his eyes. "I don't want to insult your parents' memory."

I shrugged. "Insult away. Frankly, it would be nice to hear something bad about them. Everyone builds them up to be saints. I'm starting to wonder if I even belong to them."

Brant hissed in a breath and leaned over the counter. "Okay, but it's pretty bad."

"I can take it," I said defiantly, even though I had no idea what he had in store for me.

"Okay, let's see. First there were the rumors of a murder-suicide."

I nodded, expecting as much.

"Next was your father killed your mother and accidentally killed himself in the process of disposing of her body. Then it was the one about your mother going insane and killing all of you in a fit of despair."

"Wow, people have a lot of time on their hands."

"Oh, I know, but it kept getting worse. There was talk of infidelity and money laundering, which led to a hitman theory. My personal favorite was when the rumors about a satanic cult started circulating."

"A satanic cult?" I glowered.

"Oh yes, and as painfully deluded as that one was, I was still hearing it a decade later. I even heard a few more to do with you, but I dismissed them."

"About me? I was just a kid. What rumors could I possibly stir?"

Brant chuckled and shook his head. "Not you specifically, just about your escape."

"My escape?"

"You know. How you got out unharmed?"

"Oh, you mean the miracle survival story? Please don't tell me I was sheltered under the wings of an angel."

Brant's smile diminished, and he tapped his fingers on the marble. "Oh, there were a few of those too, I'm sure."

"What exactly was the version you heard?"

Brant stared at me; his humor was lost altogether now. "The night it happened... As you well know, your house is visible from about anywhere in town. Some have a better view than others. A few of the townsfolk claimed the car was engulfed in flames as high as the house." I nodded.

Based on the pictures I saw, I knew that rumor to be true. "Almost everybody called it a miracle because you weren't burned at all, even though you were right in the middle of it."

"Almost?"

"There were a few people in town—the same people spreading the rumors about witchcraft, mind you—who started up some rumors about the fire being the work of the devil. Your mother was touted as a devil worshiper who apparently got in too deep with the man in red."

I started laughing and waited for him to join in, but he didn't. "Oh God, you buy into that theory, don't you?"

Brant shook his head. "Of course not. The dowdy housewives in those days were gossipy little bitches, and they can shove their theories up their asses." I noted the defensive tone in his voice, anger even. I wasn't sure it was really on my behalf, but I rather liked it, anyway. "A little girl walked away from a fire without having to get skin grafts. It doesn't matter why. Just be grateful."

"Yeah." I nodded in agreement as I slipped off my stool. I *was* grateful. I knew better than anyone that life doesn't always deal you a winning hand, so you might as well play the cards you have to work with. Brant and I may not have had the ideal *meet-cute* of a Hollywood movie, but he was handsome, fit, and a real live grownup.

I marched around to him, and he turned to me, questions lining up in his eyes. I pushed into his space, raised myself onto my tippy toes, and planted a hard kiss on his lips. I felt him tense and relax. I wrapped my arms around his neck, and he wrapped his around my back. When I pulled back from the kiss and looked at him, he had the same hunger in his eyes.

A moment later, we were lip-locked again, pushing against each other, hands roving. I wasn't wearing a bra—or underwear, for that matter—so there was very little to impede his enjoyment of my body.

He lifted me onto the island and pushed me down flat. He shoved my shirt up and kissed my stomach, then with just as much urgency pulled down the elastic band of my shorts and pressed his mouth between my legs. I lamented, rejoicing in gratitude for a generous lover.

As I writhed beneath him, pawing at the smooth surface beneath me, I couldn't help but think how much I loved Corian marble.

The Bacon

Brant had graciously offered to take our finale to the bedroom, or at the very least a softer surface, but in the heat of the moment I demanded he do me right there in the kitchen up against his still warm oven. It was a choice I felt a little embarrassed by now, in the clarity of the early morning. However, I didn't regret having sex with him. Not just because he was damn good at it, but because I finally felt like we had connected. We were at last on the same page.

The smell of bacon practically levitated me out of Brant's sheets. I slipped out of bed and plodded barefoot to the kitchen, obediently following my growling stomach. If Brant was as good at making breakfast as he was supper, it was going to be the best part of waking up.

"You keep feeding me like this, and you're going to get that marriage proposal with or without a nursery." I practically skipped into the kitchen and saw an elderly man cooking at the stove. He glanced back at me and smirked. "Oh, I'm sorry. I thought you were Brant."

"Mmm, I figured. I'm a little too old to be getting proposals from young women. Especially just for bacon and eggs." He glanced back at me again, taking in my pajamas. "Are you and Brant dating?"

"Oh... ah." I blushed thinking about my steamy night up against the appliance that was now sizzling bacon. "I think right now we're just getting to know each other." I gave the usual non-clingy response rather than proclaim Brant as mine, like a piece of property.

"Mmm, in my day, we called that dating."

"I suppose it's a subtle difference." I bet in his day they hadn't been aroused by contemporary kitchen designs. "Is Brant awake yet?"

"He's gone out for coffee. He'll be back soon. You take your eggs soft or hard?"

"Soft, please."

"Toast?"

"Yes, please." I looked around to examine my options for immediate escape, polite or otherwise. Then I realized my car was still at home. I would have to make conversation until Brant got back. "I'm sorry, I didn't catch your name."

"I didn't throw it." He handed me a plate of eggs and bacon. "Get it? Catch, throw?" I smiled and nodded. "I'm Dick, Brant's uncle." He tossed a couple of slices of toast onto my plate, fresh out of the toaster, and then extended his hand to me.

"I'm Tori." I took his proffered hand, and he gave me a quick but firm squeeze. I noticed a faded tattoo peeking out from beneath his short sleeve as he reached across to me. I didn't know much about him, but for some reason it made me think of the military—one of those tattoos that men get to show brotherhood with their army unit. Essentially, the manly version of friendship bracelets.

"Brant told me you and your wife did the renovations on this house," I said when he had returned to the stove. "I'm actually doing some work on my parents' old house. I would love to get some advice from you. This place turned out beautifully."

"It better have. We spent a fortune on it." Dick chuckled. "Practically caused a divorce, and then after it was finally done and we could enjoy it, the wife wanted to move south and get a condominium." He shook his head and shut off the stove. "But that's what you do, though."

"Move to a warmer climate, you mean?"

"No, I mean do crazy stuff that doesn't make sense cause your wife says so." He turned around and shrugged at me. "Because if you love someone, you do whatever it takes to make them happy."

"That's sweet."

He frowned. "Even when people do things that don't make sense, or contradict their usual behavior. It doesn't mean they stopped loving you. It just means the choices they were given weren't very good ones." His tone was serious, as if he were giving me advice in response to a previous conversation.

"Okay." I smiled uncomfortably and looked down at my plate. "I'll keep that in mind."

"Keep what in mind?" Brant surprised me as he moved in through the mud doors with a grocery bag hugged to his chest.

"We were just talking." I motioned toward the stove. Brant looked over to it and then back at me.

"Talking to whom?"

"Him." I pointed to his uncle, but he was gone. I looked around the kitchen, but I was alone. "Where did he go?" I got up and peeked into the living room. "He was literally just standing there."

"Who?"

"Dick."

"Dick?"

"Yeah, your uncle. He made me breakfast." I pointed back at my plate full of food, but there was nothing on the island. No eggs, no plate. Even the smell of bacon was gone.

"Tori, he couldn't have been here." Brant frowned at me and plopped his bag on the island. He unloaded coffee and orange juice.

"He was. We were talking face to face, like you and I are right now."

Brant sighed and leaned against the island. "You're confused."

"I'm not confused. He—"

"He's dead, Tori!" Brant snapped at me. "He died last year."

I stared back at him, begging him to be lying, but he wasn't. The look in his eyes was the same look I had. We were both very concerned about my state of well-being. "But..." I shook my head, realizing I had just had a full-on visual, auditory, *smellorama* hallucination. There was no denying it any longer. I was insane. I rubbed my face and left the kitchen.

A few minutes later, Brant caught up with me in the upstairs bedroom where my duffel bags had ended up. He tapped on the partially opened door to the guest bedroom before pushing it open further. He made no attempts to look away as I changed into a fresh set of clothes.

"Do you want some breakfast?" he asked.

I shook my head. "No. I think you should probably drive me home."

Brant looked around the room as if he were searching for a new conversation topic. "Look, Tori, I understand you are a little freaked out, but this kind of thing can happen. I mean, it's an old house."

"That's what you said about *my* house." I crossed my arms and dared him to keep trying to coddle me. "This wasn't a shadowy figure, Brant. I smelled the bacon frying. I touched his hand, for God's sake. We had a reciprocal conversation. There is something wrong with me. Something wrong in my head."

Brant rubbed his chin and propped his hands on his hips. "Have you ever had an incident like this before? I mean before you moved back."

"No, never."

"Don't you think if you had a brain defect your symptoms would be more gradual?"

"I don't know. All I know is that what is happening to me is not normal."

"You're right, it's not, but I don't think what you need is a doctor."

"What do I need?"

Brant grimaced. "I know it's a little soon for this, but I'd like to introduce you to my mother."

The Bully

"There's something I haven't told you," Brant said when we finally made it to the outskirts of town. He gave me a nervous glance before continuing. "I haven't been entirely honest with you."

"Oh, crap. If you're about to tell me you have a girlfriend, I will deck you."

"No, no, nothing like that. It's just...I know you. I mean, I already knew you."

I scoffed. "Yeah, you and everyone else in town."

"No, I mean you and I have met. We knew each other as kids."

"What?"

"I figured you didn't recognize me. It wasn't until our dinner that I realized you really had no idea who I was."

"And you didn't think to tell me we had met?"

"I should have said something."

"Of *course,* you should have said something. How well did we know each other?"

"Your mom and mine were best friends. You practically spent every day over at our house during the summer for a few years."

I stared at him, flabbergasted that he would intentionally hide this from me. I wasn't sure whether it was because he knew more about my past than I did, or whether it was because— "Christ, Brant, you slept with me."

"Yeah, I thought about delaying that, but...well..." He threw me a cocksure smirk that told me he didn't feel the least bit guilty about that.

"Why didn't you tell me?"

"Ahhhh, you and I weren't exactly friends."

"What does that mean?"

Brant cleared his throat. "Um, I may have been a little jealous of how much time my mom was spending with your mom. And I sort of took it out on you."

"What do you mean you took it out on me?"

"I bullied you pretty relentlessly." I shifted back in my seat and stared out the window. Brant kept glancing at me, waiting for my response, but I wasn't sure I had one. "I was a kid, Tori."

"The boy who pulled my hair? That was you?"

"Yes, and no. I was the one doing the hair-pulling, but at the time you thought it was my brother. That way he got blamed for it instead of me." Brant chuckled, amused by the memory of his little brother getting scolded.

"This isn't funny."

"Oh, come on, Tori, we were just kids."

"*You* come on. I have only a handful of memories, and none of them are good. You must have been a pretty big jerk if you rank as high as parental arguments and—" I shut my mouth before I revealed any more details about my shoddy memory bank. "I can't believe I just slept with my childhood bully."

"And you enjoyed every minute of it," he reproached me. He kept his eyes on me as long as his driving would allow, daring me to deny that I hadn't enjoyed last night. Which I couldn't. However, with the memory of a spoiled little brat overlapping with Brant's somewhat dictatorial manner, I wasn't sure a relationship was going to be possible with him, no matter how good the sex would be.

After a minute of silence, I turned back to him. "Can you take me to…Ed's office?" I had been about to say *home*, but aside from wanting to avoid my spooky house, I also didn't want to be in his car any longer than possible. Ed's office was closer.

Brant's jaw tensed, and he shook his head. "No." I took a breath, ready to defend my right to decide where I should be taken. "I really think you should speak with my mother before you do anything else," he interrupted my preemptive rant. "Please," he added.

When I didn't verbally concede, he reached over to touch my hand, which I pulled away from him. He put his hand back on the steering wheel, squeezing it tightly. "I know I screwed up, Tori. I know you're mad. But your meeting my mother has nothing to do with us. I actually think she can help you. I *hope* she can help you."

"Besides…" Brant pulled the car onto a steep cement driveway leading to a flat-roofed ranch-style house. There was an attached three-car garage that made the house look endlessly long. He parked his sedan in front of the third door and shifted into park. "If you want to know more about your parents, my mother is the best person to ask."

The Mother

I slipped out of the car and looked over the high brick fence bordering the street side of the property. Between that and an abundance of bushes, the house had a sort of courtyard instead of a driveway. Brant came around the car and moved toward me. I knew he intended to usher me forward with a gentle pressing hand to my back. It was one of those gentlemanly movements that made most women feel protected or claimed.

Regardless of what it was supposed to feel like, I was still pissed and dodged his grasp. He recovered after a pause and simply motioned me forward with his other hand. I headed to the front door, and Brant followed slightly behind me; his hands tucked behind his back.

"Why do you think your mother will be able to help me?" I asked as we reached the door. Brant tried the knob, but it was locked, so he rang the doorbell.

"My mother has a few uncommon hobbies."

"Like what?"

"Let's just say my mother has never been what you would call normal. My father calls her eccentric. My brother calls her weird."

"What would you call her?"

Brant's eyes glazed, and all humor drained from his face. "Dangerous," he murmured.

I frowned at him, trying to determine whether he was legitimately afraid of her, or whether he was simply concerned about the outcome of her behavior. "So, what does this have to do with me?"

Brant recovered from his trance and looked at me. "Tori, I'm not sure how to put this. My mom is a witch...and so was yours."

I didn't even have time to respond before the front door flew open and a woman with crazy red hair popped out to greet us with a screech. The redhead, presumably Brant's mother, wrapped her arms around me and gave me a big hug. "Oh, I knew it would happen someday. I told Rex, our boy won't be single forever."

"Mom. Mom!" Brant pulled her off me. "This isn't what you think. She's not—we're not—" Brant struggled to define our relationship. As if it hadn't been hard enough before the car ride over. "This is Tori Blake." His mother looked at him, baffled. "Tori, this is my mother, Genevieve Hart."

"Genie," I murmured, connecting the dots between my mother's friend and the woman in the pictures Mrs. Plinth had shown me.

I expected Genie to recognize the name and go into further theatrics, but her excited body movements stopped. For a moment, she remained frozen, staring at me. "Tori?" she whispered and took a step away from me. Her mouth dropped closer and closer to the ground. She pulled her glasses away from her face, letting them hang against her chest by the attached cord.

She pressed her hands against her face and took a few stuttered breaths before turning tail and running into the house.

I looked at Brant, and he closed his eyes and shook his head. "She just needs a moment. Come on." He raised his hand again to guide me forward, but brought it back again before he actually touched me.

I stepped into the house and was immediately boomeranged back into the 70s. I could see the living room slightly below us through the wooden spindles. The ornate posts topped a half-wall, which curved down away from the door in both directions, creating a horseshoe. It served as the back wall of the living room, while still giving the impression of open space. I wasn't fond of the decor, but I had a feeling Mrs. Hart was just the type to enjoy it.

"Do you want to fill me in on the joke here?" I asked when it was clear his mother was out of earshot. "What do you mean my mother was a witch?"

"I mean, your mother and my mother practiced witchcraft together as a hobby." Brant shut the door behind us.

"I'm sorry, I can't mesh the image of two women boiling frogs on one burner of the stove and making mac n' cheese for their kids on another."

"You're probably not as far off as you think. My mother was notorious for getting her herbs mixed up. I can't tell you how much I dislike lavender, especially in my spaghetti sauce." I snorted unexpectedly at his comment. I clasped my hand over my mouth to keep any other uproarious noises to a minimum. Brant smirked at me, which shouldn't have pleased me as much as it did.

"As amusing as that is," I said when I had allayed any chance of a giggle fit, "I don't see how moon rituals and scented candles are going to help me with my little brain malfunction."

"I don't expect you to take it on my word. I don't understand how this stuff works any more than you do, but I do have some experience with it. And if this were only about creaking floorboards and shadows in your closet, I wouldn't have brought you here." His hand drifted forward, brushing a strand of hair behind my ear. I didn't flinch away from the contact this time. "I don't think any of this is in your head. You described my uncle to a tee. I think you might actually be seeing ghosts." His fingers traced around my jaw, his thumb dragging across my cheek. His eyes were fixed on mine, only breaking to look down at my mouth. "I think if anyone can determine what is going on with you, it's my mother," he whispered, though neither one of us was listening to him. All I could think about was the night before and how good it had felt. And how much I wanted to do it again.

Brant moved his thumb to caress my lower lip. I opened my mouth slightly and sneaked my tongue out to lick it. His eyes widened slightly, tracking the movement like a predator. He shifted his hand down to my chin, and he took a deep breath like he was about to go underwater. Or perhaps he was just ready to dive into a deep, hot kiss.

The only thing that stopped him—the only thing that stopped another wild and heated sex act in an inappropriate place—was the sound of footsteps coming down the back hall toward the living room. Brant pulled away from me and took a short walk in the opposite direction around the horseshoe, as his mother came in.

The Witch

"I'm so sorry for that outburst." Genie came around to me and once again looked me over. I looked her over in return, searching for memories. Searching for a pointy nose and warts.

Genie's red bouffant waves were streaked with white. She had sparkling brown eyes beneath her reading glasses, which were perched back on the tip of her nose. She didn't look like a witch. She looked like a normal aging mother.

"You remember her, don't you, Mother?" Brant asked.

"Of course I remember her," she snapped at him. "I'm old, son, not senile."

"I thought you would be happier to see her."

"Happy?" Genie looked at her son, her eyes flitting over his features as if they hadn't seen each other in years either. She almost looked like she might cry, and then her mouth fell open. "Of course I'm happy to see her." She turned back to me and smiled, but there were tears in her eyes. "I cannot believe how big you've gotten. I mean grown-up, of course. I didn't mean to imply you've become large. What a stupid phrase." She glanced between Brant and me, looking almost nervous now.

"It's nice to meet you...Mrs. Hart," I said tentatively.

Genie's brow dipped. "Meet me?"

"Mom, just so you know, Tori doesn't remember you," Brant said. "She doesn't remember anything before the accident."

Genie looked me over as if she could verify it by looking at me.

"Bits and pieces of my childhood are still there, but I'm afraid it is mostly a blank slate," I clarified as if being mostly amnesiac was somehow better.

"I was your mother's best friend," Genie said. "You spent a lot of time at my house—in this house—when you were little." She motioned to the home as if simply being present should evoke memories. I knew it wouldn't. If being in my own childhood home didn't spur any memory dumps, I doubted her house would.

I had come to terms with the permanence of my condition. Time hadn't broken it. Hypno-therapy hadn't broken it. Coming back to town hadn't broken it. Whatever memories I had were just dribbles through the cracks. The rest were either erased or trapped forever.

"I cared for you and your mother a great deal." Genie frowned as if a thousand memories were returning to her. Since the pinnacle one was a tragic accident, it was no wonder a tear finally escaped her eye.

"Mom, can we sit down or are you going to stare at her until she's uncomfortable enough to leave?"

Genie blinked and looked at her son. She stepped away from me, offering me further entrance to the house. "I'm sorry, honey, I'm having a bit of a flashback. You do look a lot like her."

I descended into the living space and noted the gas fireplace built into the back of the half-wall that ensconced the room. There was no couch, only a bunch of chairs. The entire setup reminded me of a spaceship on Star Trek more than a living room.

Rather than take the helm, Mrs. Hart led us around the corner to a bright white kitchen with modern appliances. She motioned for me to sit at the breakfast bar while she dug in her fridge. I sat down at the counter, while Brant leaned against a pantry cabinet near me. I couldn't help looking him over as he stood there. Years of moving furniture had kept him toned. He wasn't bulky the way some men were. His loose-fitting clothes made assessing his physique difficult, but I knew he had a toned stomach and strong legs.

"So, if you don't remember me, what prompted this visit?" Genie asked. When Brant didn't answer, I dragged my eyes from his ass up to his face, but he was already looking at me. There was an amused smile there. I looked at Genie, and she had the same smile. I realized too late the question had been directed at me.

"What?" I asked, bouncing my gaze between them as my face reddened.

"I was asking you what prompted your visit." Genie pulled a bottle of orange juice from the fridge, followed by a bottle of champagne.

"It was Brant's idea."

"Oh?" She perked her brow at Brant to confirm this potentially scurrilous rumor. "And why was that?" Genie looked at me for the answer.

I looked at Brant for the answer, but he nodded back to Genie. He wanted me to explain my...situation.

I shifted in my chair as if I were about to give a speech. I wasn't sure I even wanted to tell her my problem. Witch or not, this was uncomfortable territory that could result in my name being further sullied by gossip and presumption.

"She's been seeing things," Brant finally answered on my behalf. I looked at him, a little annoyed that he was jumping into the water without me. He raised his brow back at me, insisting I tell her everything.

"What sort of things?" Genie asked as she mixed the orange juice and champagne in a larger pitcher.

I swallowed hard and spoke. "I think I've been seeing ghosts." Saying it out loud sounded even more ridiculous than in my head, but it was a relief to let it out into the world.

"Is that so?" Genie retrieved three glasses from her cupboard and slammed the door shut.

I shifted uncomfortably as her movements became swift and indelicate. "Brant thought you might have some insight into this situation," I explained, not understanding why she was getting perturbed. Perhaps her talent in the occult was not meant to be shared with strangers. But I wasn't really a stranger, from her perspective anyway.

"He did, did he?" Genie turned to look at Brant.

"Don't make a big deal out of this, Mother."

"I have never made a big deal out of it. It was you who made a big deal out of it. As I recall, you were the one who forbade me from participating in my craft in front of your friends."

"For Christ's sake, Mom, I was sixteen; it was embarrassing. I've apologized to you a hundred times."

"You apologized for yelling at me. You have never retracted your statements."

"Do we have to do this right now?"

Genie glanced at me. "If she is what her mother was, then yes, we do have to do this right now." I looked at Brant, concerned by the specification of *what* my mother might have been. We seemed to be well out of the territory of devout Wiccans and into something else. "I'm not going to pretend this isn't a smack in the back of the head, after a smack to the face."

"What do you want, Mom? What do I have to do to make you happy?"

"I want you to accept who I am and what I am."

"I do. I have always—"

"You still tell people I am a housewife."

"You *are* a housewife. You are currently a wife who spends her days caring for the household. There is nothing wrong with that statement, nor should you feel ashamed of it."

"I don't feel ashamed of it. I feel belittled. I am so much more than that. I control and wield the natural energies of the universe."

I mentally cringed. I had anticipated Genie might be eccentric, maybe even a little loopy, but did she just equivocally call herself a god?

"I know," Brant mumbled apologetically.

I turned my baffled gaze to him now. *He knows?* Surely Brant was only humoring her. He was an intelligent, grounded man. He had to know his mother was just playing with candles and meditating.

"I have changed the course of people's lives with my magic, and you know it."

Oh, good God, she really was delusional. I shifted my gaze to the floor, so I wouldn't reveal my discomfort or my complete and utter disbelief.

"Mom, I don't want to get into this right now. I am never going to introduce you in public as a healer or a psychic or a benevolent enchantress. If you would like me to mention your paganism in casual conversation, then I will, but in case you haven't been to one of our staff meetings lately, you should know Dad doesn't want your lifestyle to become an issue that would affect the store."

"I know exactly how your father and your brother feel about my *hobby*." She air-quoted the word. "It doesn't bother me that they refuse to acknowledge me because they have never witnessed what I can do. Never felt the strength of my will compel the elements." Genie frowned. "You have."

My head whipped back up, stunned by the accusation. Brant's gaze landed on mine but quickly drifted shamefully to the floor. Once again, I tried to decide how this seemingly normal man had managed to become part of his mother's obsession.

"Instead of it bringing us closer, it has driven us apart," Genie said mournfully. "Now, after all these years of that wedge being placed, you arrive with Tori Blake. As if I should instantly forgive your dismissal and perform the magic you are so ashamed of."

Brant struggled to maintain his relaxed position. "I'm not ashamed of your magic. I was never ashamed of it."

"Then what would you call it?"

"Fear, Mother." Brant leveled his eyes on his mother, pinning her with his disquieting honesty. Genie recoiled slightly, as if her proximity alone was the fuel for Brant's discomfort. "I didn't come here to argue with you, Mother," Brant said, shifting the conversation away from the immediate topic. "Tori is the one who needs your help.

She thinks she's going crazy. Hell, maybe she is, but before she commits herself, I thought maybe you might have a better solution. Something that skips the lobotomy. I may not like what you do, and I may not understand it, but yes, I know you are so much more than a housewife. Every fiber of my being knows how powerful you are. And if I have to beg you for forgiveness or acknowledge your craft to strangers, then I will do it. Just help her. Convince her she doesn't have a tumor in her brain."

Genie scoffed and looked at me. "She doesn't have a tumor. She's her mother's daughter. She's a necromancer."

The Necromancer

I sat there for several seconds staring at Genie, trying to find the definition of necromancy in my mind. My thoughts flitted from necrophilia to narcolepsy and back to necrosis. The only thing my weakened vocabulary was sure of was that my mother had done something with the dead. "She was a *what*?"

Genie poured three mimosas from her pitcher and placed the glasses on a decorative tray along with a single pink rose leaning in a tiny vase. She carried the tray past me to the patio door, where she motioned for Brant to open the sliding glass door. Brant cleared her path of slapping vertical blinds and slid the door open.

I could feel the slightly warm breeze coming into the kitchen, refreshing the otherwise stale air. Brant moved over to me, shoulders slumped and dejected. "I'm sorry about that. My mother and I have a strained relationship. I should have warned you before we got here. I was hoping she would play along for the sake of company."

"It's fine. I've had my fair share of arguments with my parents—my foster parents. What did she mean about me being a necromancer? What exactly is that?"

Brant frowned. "Um, well, you know that one movie? Where the kid sees dead people?"

"Yeah?"

"Well, it's like that. A necromancer communes with the dead."

I grimaced. "That doesn't sound like a good thing."

"I don't know about good or bad. My mother said magic isn't good or bad, just the people using it. She also said your mother was a very powerful necromancer."

"Powerful? How? Did she see more dead people than other necromancers?" I could hear myself saying the words, but I had no choice. I had to play along with this insanity until I could find a polite way to leave. I should have insisted on getting dropped off at Ed's office.

Brant shrugged. "I'm not really sure how it works; I just know she..."

"What?"

"I don't want to get into town rumors again. I think you should talk to my mother. She knew Cass better than anyone."

I followed Brant outside to the veranda. As beautiful, albeit dated, as the inside of the house was, the outside was even better. Decorative concrete blocks with floral-patterned holes provided the backyard with privacy from the neighbors. Trees, bushes, and countless strange plants populated the outskirts. Even the patio was packed full of ceramic pots containing flowers and herbs.

Genie was already lounging on one of her white patio chairs. Her tray of mimosas sat on the ornate metal table, minus one glass, which was clutched in her hand and half gone. She leaned her head back and shut her eyes, as if she were absorbing the early sun. "It's going to be hot this afternoon," she said as I pulled out a seat to join her. I noted that once again Brant stood off to the side as if he felt compelled to keep himself mobile during the interaction. "It will be hot in the afternoon for the rest of the summer," she said solemnly.

Genie lifted her head back up and looked at me. There was a sadness in her eyes I was certain she intended for my mother. "I used to love the heat. I would skip around in the backyard wearing a bikini top and short shorts. It used to drive the neighbors mad. The men never minded, but naturally the wives assumed I was trying to seduce their husbands." She scoffed. "Like I would be interested in those lazy clouts. My Rex has always taken care of me. He's a hard worker. Built that furniture store from the ground up."

I smiled. "It's a wonderful store, and your sons have excellent taste."

Genie looked at her son, the fervor of her previous irritation draining as she did. "My sons are good boys. I raised them to be respectful and truthful. My only mistake was not raising them to be mama's boys." She frowned. "That's the trade-off, you know. If you want responsible, independent men, then you have to teach them to survive without you."

Brant shied away from his mother's gaze. I was certain this was far more family drama than he wanted to introduce me to this soon in our relationship. "Mrs. Hart, would you mind telling me more about my mother? About her skills?"

Genie sighed and set a mimosa out in front of me. I thought it was a little early for alcohol, but I was certain she would classify it as breakfast since it had vitamin C in it. She set the other one out for Brant, and he finally took a seat next to me. He glanced at me and took a sip of the beverage before setting it back down. I did the same, but after one sip I realized I might actually enjoy it since we had skipped breakfast in lieu of getting information.

"How did you two meet?" Genie asked, looking between us. "I only heard about you coming to town a week ago."

"The store, Mom," Brant said, a little perturbed. "She bought furniture for the house."

"And now you're dating?"

"Mom, we aren't..." Brant looked at me and his sentence trailed off. I was already frowning in preparation for his clarification, which no doubt would have declared that we were not dating. We could have qualified as having had one date. We could have also qualified as a one-night stand. This relationship, whatever it was, had become heavy with baggage. As if my drama wasn't enough, Genie's was trickling over onto Brant's side. Despite an obvious physical attraction, I wasn't sure I would be seeing Brant after today.

Brant's eyes flickered over mine as if he were reading our impending breakup from my face. *It's not you, it's not me, it's our mothers.* "That's not a description that applies here," Brant answered diplomatically. Yet," he added with a stern look that told me I was going to be in trouble if I denied the possibility. He really was kind of a bully.

"We're still figuring each other out right now," I said.

Genie turned her inquisition on me. "Where are you living now?"

"In my parents' old house."

"The one on the hill?" Genie stared at me for a moment. "It's getting a bit worn down, isn't it?"

"Yes, I'm doing some renovations on it. Expanding the kitchen and redoing the bathrooms."

"My son has a renovated old house; you should go see it. You might get some ideas."

"Oh, I know, it's wonderful." Brant groaned beside me and shook his head. Genie beamed at me. I glanced between them, searching for the reason behind the frustration and amusement.

"Just getting to know each other?" Genie raised an eyebrow at her son.

I suddenly realized I had revealed that I had been to his house, a fact that instigated several presumptions in and of itself. I blushed and looked out at the yard. I noticed a slight change in the way the grass was lying. Not in a traditional horizontal pattern, but circular. Mr. Hart must have been getting creative with his mowing rotation.

"Mother, *if* we were in a relationship of that nature, you would be embarrassing both of us immensely by bringing it up. If we weren't, as I just said, then you would be trusting gossip over your own son, which I don't appreciate."

"Gossip?" My head snapped back to them. "Are we gossip already?"

"Oh, Brant, I'm just teasing you. I would be pleased as punch to have Tori as a daughter-in-law."

"Geez, Mom, we..." Brant looked at me, mortified that his mother had taken us from dating to in bed together to married in less than a minute.

Genie laughed and winked at me. "Oh, I think he does like you, honey. I haven't seen him this flustered since I caught him sneaking into the bathroom with a lingerie catalog."

"Mother!" Brant rasped. I bit my lip, trying not to laugh at his expense, but the look on his face was priceless. He shoved his chair away from the table and stood. "Excuse me. If I am going to continue to be the butt of your jokes, I am going to need something stronger than champagne." Brant stormed off to the kitchen in search of a more sedative drink.

"Oh, he definitely likes you," Genie assured me. "My eldest son is not usually a very excitable person. It's his best and worst trait. He usually tolerates my humor a little better, though. And by that I mean he ignores it."

I smiled at her and sipped my mimosa. For a moment, she just stared at me again. My discomfort at being compared to my mother was reaching its peak. Pretty soon I would be seeking out hard liquor as well.

"Your mother and I met when you and Lane were in kindergarten, I think...maybe preschool. The two of you were shoved together at tea parties and sandboxes for the next few years, while we hung out together drinking mimosas, laughing about our husbands, and dishing on the town gossip.

"Your mother and I were the last of the true stay-at-home moms. Most of the other moms were working in those days, and the ones that didn't, had their kids in so many activities they were never at home." She shook her head. "We would sit around this very table at least twice a week, sloughing off our household chores under the guise of a child's play date. It was the best time of my life, all too quickly followed by the worst." Genie drank down the last of her mimosa, and I took another sip of mine.

"Mrs. Hart, can you tell me what happened that day? The day they died? I was in the car while it was burning, but I didn't get hurt."

She stared at me, lips pursed for several seconds until her gaze floated to the table, staring into nothingness. "That fire was hotter than hell itself. Flames licking into the clouds. A puddle of molten rock."

"Then how did I survive?"

Genie leaned back in her chair and looked over her garden. "I assume your mother protected you."

"How? Magic?" I asked slightly sarcastically.

"You don't believe in magic, do you?"

I wasn't sure how to reply to that. I couldn't very well tell her I thought she was batshit crazy. "I believe in the power of the mind. I believe in miracles. I suppose if the mind could instigate a miracle, then I guess we could call that magic." I was pleased with my rationalization, especially since it allowed room for both of our truths.

"I suppose that's close enough for now." Genie leaned forward and took Brant's remaining mimosa. "When your mother first came into my life, I was a little guarded with my witchcraft. It had been a while since I had had a full-time friend, and I didn't want to scare her off.

"One day I admitted to using herbs in my garden to make spell charms for my sons. I tucked them under their pillows, so they would have good dreams. I expected her to laugh at me, or start searching for an excuse to leave. Instead, she asked me if I could make her one.

"She started telling me about her nightmares and the people that would visit her in them. I assumed, as she did, that it was all in her head. I made her a charm, but it didn't stop. I made her new charms, but that only made it worse.

Finally, I admitted to her that I had a certain amount of power with the ethereal forces and that I would like to bless her home." Genie frowned.

"You have to understand, I had never been to your mother's home. We always met here. She stopped over after her biweekly shopping trips. When I arrived at that house, I was stonewalled by a feeling I could only describe as oppressive. Being who I was, I immediately started to ask if her husband was being abusive to her. She denied this vehemently and insisted her husband was a good man. We actually had an argument because I believed so strongly that she was lying to me.

"After about a week, she came by, and we talked about various things, avoiding the topic of husbands. Then she got really quiet and said that sometimes in her nightmares, a man would come to her. He would hurt her. She told me with complete certainty that it was only a dream, but sometimes she would wake up with bruises she didn't remember getting."

"You think the oppressive feeling was from the man in her dreams?"

"Very much."

"How is that possible? I mean, you're talking about the aura of a nonexistent person, right?"

"Existence is subjective. For a necromancer, life and death are separated only by a thin veil. Your mother was not just communing with the dead; they were harassing her. It took us a while longer to figure this out, and I started to work with her. Opened her up to the experiences intentionally. We managed to train her to block out the aggressive spirits and allow the good ones to come through. Her confidence soared, and she was able to once again take control of her life.

"Our mimosas and gossip became as much fun as experimentation. With my skill and hers, we could run the town. My husband's business thrived. Her husband got a promotion. Our children stopped getting trifling colds. We were becoming so good at divination that we were able to start an underground business of fortune-telling."

"Really?"

"Oh, not like you're thinking. We would see people at parent-teacher meetings and get to talking about inane things. We would advise other mothers on how to handle certain situations. Banking, insurance, trips, and even style. It was amazing how often we could tell a woman what to wear to certain events and it would change the outcome of her day. Mrs. Teller down the street was a notoriously prudish woman when I first met her. Sweet as sugar and smooth as butter in a social setting, but despite all that, her husband was thinking of having an affair. He was struggling with it because he loved her, and yet there were so many fine young women passing right under his nose.

"Well, Cass and I wouldn't have it. She was far too nice to be cheated on, and I knew it would destroy her. So, one day we invited her over to the house and we had a face-to-face intervention. She was mortified at any suggestion that her husband would stray, but we assured her that if she dressed a little differently, her life would change for the better. I even donated three dresses to her since we were the same size in those days.

"So, three weeks later, at a bake sale, we see none other than Mrs. Teller walking in with one of my dresses on. I'm not sure if it was because I had never seen her dress up or if she was just upright with confidence, but I swear to God that woman was an inch taller, her breasts were a cup bigger, and everyone was looking at her.

"Now, I'm not saying I agree with the idea of getting your husband's attention by making him jealous, but damn if it didn't work. She was getting job offers for secretarial positions. She was getting phone calls from car salesmen, insurance salesmen. Every man in town wanted a shot with her. Mr. Teller was spending so much time fighting off her suitors he forgot all about his own prospects for adultery. He even went out of his way to sabotage their birth control, so he could get another baby in her ASAP." Genie laughed. "Now again, I don't condone the method, but as I understand it, Mrs. Teller went from a once-a-month, can-barely-get-off-the-couch husband, to a three-times-a-week, can-barely-get-him-off-her husband."

I chuckled. "Sounds like it was good advice."

"Yes, and because of it, my husband got an outstanding deal on his property purchase for the new store. A little bedroom finagling brought that negotiation into our favor in short order."

"The women behind the men."

"Damn straight. This town didn't run without us. Of course, that was years ago. Things have changed a great deal. Modern business practices demand monetary exchanges. Nobody wants a cup of sugar for advice; they want cash or credit."

"Isn't that the truth," I added since it sounded like the right thing to say. I hadn't been doing enough business in the world to really have a basis for comparison, but agreeing was always the best tactic when people ranted about the *old days.* "Brant said you considered my mother to be very powerful. What does that mean in terms of magic? Strength of power, or just the breadth of her skill?"

"Oh, your mother was...how shall I put this? She was a beacon to the dead. She drew in so many souls that we had to funnel the energies that could come through her or she would have gone insane."

"What about the man you were talking about? Did you get rid of him?"

Genie looked to her garden. "He was a constant difficulty for her. He wasn't easily dismissed. I'm afraid I have a few missing ingredients in that story. Your mother kept some of her trials to herself. I think she knew there was only so much I could do for her. And she didn't want me to worry. Her power was such that sometimes she just had to play the hand she had been dealt."

"What about me? Do you really believe I'm a necromancer too?"

"If you've been dreaming of dead people, then I should say so."

"Dreaming? Hell, I've been talking to them over breakfast." I chuckled, trying to make light of what earlier that morning had had me running for medical attention.

Genie tipped her head. "How do you mean? You see them while you're awake?"

"Yeah."

Her eyes narrowed at me. "And they speak to you?"

"Well, not usually, but this morning I had a conversation with a man who introduced himself as Brant's uncle."

Genie took a breath. "What do you mean by a conversation? Did you see an echo?"

"What's an echo?"

"It's when you see an apparition's past events. You're just walking through it as if you are the ghost."

"No, it was live-action. He was making breakfast for me. Sadly, the bacon was part of the hallucination too. He disappeared when Brant came in." Genie's frozen stare worried me. "What exactly is so concerning about that?"

"Sweetheart, your mother's convergence with the spirit world was limited to dreams and seances. She also never spoke to them, at least not in the way you're suggesting."

"What does that mean? Should I go ahead with the CT scan?"

"No. My concern is that you might be even more powerful than your mother." Genie stood and left the table, leaving me to divine my own presumptions about the dangers of being *more* powerful. "But there's only one way to find out," she called back to me.

The Graveyard

As I sat in the passenger seat of Brant's sedan on the way to our destination, I contemplated several excuses to get out of this field trip. However, I was also curious about what Genie wanted to show me. I still had my doubts about the so-called magic Genie and Cass had wielded. From the sounds of it, they were just a couple of nosy women who offered advice to downtrodden women. That wasn't really magic. It was women's intuition and good old common sense.

Brant hadn't spoken a word since we'd left the house. I assumed the day's craziness was blooming even beyond his tolerance. He obviously didn't get along with his mother for reasons of mystical indifference. Now that I was turning out to be something of an anomaly myself, he must have been questioning how he had gotten tangled up with yet another bizarre woman. Since this was all new to me, I had similar questions.

I turned to him, right as he turned to me. He reflected the same expression of worry back at me. "I'm sorry—" we both said in unison.

After a moment to acknowledge the coincidence, we chuckled. He returned his gaze to the road. "What are you apologizing for?"

"You having met me, I guess," I said sympathetically.

"What is that supposed to mean?"

"It means I've been nothing but trouble to you since you met me. I can't even pick out a couch, let alone deal with whatever this is."

"There's nothing wrong with needing a little help."

"Yes, but I get the feeling that being dragged back into a family ordeal was not what you had in mind when you accepted my dinner invitation."

Brant shook his head. "I'm a big boy. I can say no if I don't want to do something."

"This whole transition to Harold has been a shitstorm. First Ed turns out to be married. My inquiries about my parents' death have only brought me more questions. Then you turn out to be responsible for one of my bad childhood memories—which I'm still mad about, by the way."

"I told you—"

"And now here we are following your delusional mother to a graveyard."

Brant went still, dedicating his gaze to the road. "She's not delusional," he said quietly.

"I'm sorry, I don't mean to fling insults. I'm not sure how much longer I can listen to all this nonsense." Brant's gaze held on mine a moment—as much as his driving would allow. I could tell he was debating what to say to me. "Please tell me you agree. The stuff your mother is talking about is fantasy. Bad dreams do not translate to necro-whatever."

"Necromancy," Brant mumbled. "It's not a fantasy, Tori."

"Oh, Brant, come on. I know you were probably raised to believe in this stuff, but as an adult you had to realize it wasn't real."

"You don't have to believe in it, but you do have to accept that I believe in it." He turned a hard glare on me. Was this his relationship deal-breaker? "My father and brother don't even acknowledge what she does. They think of her as eccentric or a hippie, but that's because they haven't seen what she can do. I have."

"What have you seen?"

"That's not the point. The point is, you don't remember those days. You don't remember your mother. I do. I saw what she could do. I was the one peeking around the corner during naptime, watching them perform ritual seances. I saw what the two of them could do together."

"But you were a child. Don't you think—?"

"It was real," he snapped.

I nodded and let it go. I obviously wouldn't convince him that his mother's theatrics were all he'd seen—two half-drunk women chanting in the living room and lighting things on fire. The truth was, it sounded like they'd had a lot of fun together. Too bad it was at the expense of Brant's sensibility.

"What were *you* going to apologize for? Before I interrupted?" I asked, changing the subject.

"My mother takes great delight in embarrassing me, especially in front of women. She thinks she's funny. I'm sorry if anything she said about us made you uncomfortable."

"I'm sure it made you more uncomfortable than me. Speaking of uncomfortable, we should probably talk about last night."

"What about it?"

"I was thinking we should probably slow things down a bit. You know? I mean, given the turbulence, it probably would be best to...I don't know, maybe go on another date before we spend the night together."

"Yeah, whatever," Brant grumbled indifferently. I rolled my eyes and slumped against the door. "We're here."

I looked out the window as Brant slowed to turn onto a narrow driveway. We moved past black gates supported by stone pillars. As beautiful as it was, the remainder of the fence surrounding the property was chain-link—a cheap addition to the otherwise magnanimous entrance. "A cemetery?" I asked. "Isn't she taking this necromancy thing a little too literally?"

Brant shrugged. "I'm inclined to think so. But, since I don't actually know anything about the process, I can't really petition for a different experiment." He stopped the car and shifted it into park. He raised his arm to the back of my seat to look at me better. "Look, I don't know what's going on between us, and I know whatever was going on last night has probably changed because of this morning, but I'm not going to beg and plead for you to come back to my bed."

"I wasn't asking you to."

"The truth is, I had a bad feeling about you and me from the get-go, but I ignored it."

"What?"

"Maybe you and I weren't meant to be."

My chest ached a little from his rejection. "Why are you being such a jerk about this?"

"I'm just saying what you're thinking."

"I don't even know *what* I'm thinking! I just wanted to slow things down so I could figure out what it is I'm feeling before I'm in too deep."

"I'm pretty sure *too deep* started the minute I got between your legs."

"I meant too deep for my heart," I snapped.

Brant ripped off his seatbelt and opened his door. "So did I." He was out the door and slamming it before I could respond. I was about to run after him, but Genie arrived, smacking her knuckles against the glass right next to me.

"Hurry along, sweetheart," she sang. "The sun is getting much too high." She sauntered off grumbling about it already being too damn hot.

As much as I wanted to get answers from Brant, I really needed to let Genie perform her "magic." Although I did think she was two cards short of a full deck, she had a valuable insight into my mother. If I could get her off the topic of ghosts and goblins, maybe she could tell me more about her. Help me find her killer.

I got out of the car and looked around the hilly cemetery. Much like every other place of burial, there was a distinct difference between the upper and lower classes. Even in death, the richest among us had to distinguish themselves. I noted one such mammoth marble name stone that declared the ownership of the four smaller headstones below it.

"No, no, you don't want to talk to any of them." Genie came around the car and looped her arm through mine. She led me down the crudely blacktopped road through the center of the cemetery. "You'll have better luck with the fresh ones."

"Fresh?" I grimaced, but she was indifferent to my concerns. She tugged me off the path and through the grass past several rows of plots. I glanced back to see if Brant was joining us, but between the trees and the flamboyant name markers I had lost track of him. "Here we are."

I looked down at the grave we had stopped at. The shiny reddish-brown marble read "Tappert." The soil in front of it was barren and freshly packed. Mr. Eldon Tappert couldn't have been a resident for more than a day or two.

"Well, go on, dear," Genie prodded me. "Do your thing."

"What thing?" I asked. "I don't even know what I'm doing."

"Put your hands in the soil." I crossed my arms and took a step back, but she ushered me forward again. "It's just dirt, sweetheart."

"It's dirt when you're planting flowers. When you're planting bodies, it's hallowed ground."

"Oh, pish, it's dirt either way. Stick your hands in and call the spirit."

"I can't call a spirit."

"Of course you can. How do you think you're seeing them?"

I frowned and shook my head. "I don't call them. They just show up."

Genie threw her hands up. "Well then, stick your hands in the dirt and wait."

I sighed and kneeled down next to the plot. I looked around for an old crotchety groundskeeper to come out of hiding and shoo us away. The only notable objection to my hands digging in the new grave was a squirrel chattering from a tree branch above us. However, his objection might have simply been to our general proximity to his stash of nuts.

After entrenching my hands in the cool, moist dirt, I felt a little ridiculous. I was playacting the part of the witch, and no one had even given me any lines for it. My only concept of witches, up to that point, had been green faces at Halloween and ill-conceived horror movies about boiling cauldrons. So far, I was coming up short on both ends. I could try growing a wart on the end of my nose, and I could buy a big-ass pot, but I was quite certain I wasn't a witch.

"I guess Mr. Tappert doesn't feel like talking." Frustrated with my lack of progress, I leaned forward on my hands to get up, but I felt the dirt give out beneath my fingers as they hit a loose patch. I sank a little deeper, and then a lot deeper. My elbows. My shoulders!

I wanted to scream, but my head was already under the dirt. My entire body was sucked down into the grave, eaten alive by the earth itself. I called out, but the sound was only in my head. I tried to breathe, but I had no concept of it.

I waited to hit the concrete vault beneath, but instead of hitting it, I went through it. Down and down through the layers of wood, plastic, and satin. I stopped inside the vacancy of the casket. With no perception of my arms or legs, I couldn't even struggle to pull away from the face that was less than an inch away from me.

The man, not long dead, looked to be sleeping. Aside from his pale skin, sunken cheeks, and the abnormal smell of formaldehyde, I wouldn't have known any different. When his eyes opened, my heart thumped into a heavy rhythm for flight. Yet, without the use of my limbs, there was nothing I could do except stare right into those foggy, otherworldly eyes.

His mouth clicked open as if his jaw had rusted shut. He exhaled into my face. His breath reeked of putrid death.

"Go away," he rasped through atrophied vocal cords. "I'm trying to sleep."

I had no objection to the man sleeping, nor did I have any objection to going away, but of course that still wasn't up to me. I didn't seem to have any control over what was happening. "Can you hear me?" I asked as an afterthought, though I was quite certain the words hadn't actually come from my lips so much as my mind.

"Yes, and you are disturbing my sleep."

"Do you know you're dead?" I couldn't help but ask. It was probably rude in some way, shape, or form, but since I was clearly invading his resting place, I was already in for a penny.

"Not dead yet, only resting. It takes time. Just give it time. Now hush. Leave me be." He closed his eyes and shifted his popping jaw back into place. He was as before..."sleeping."

I felt an arm wrap around my body, pulling me up, or back, or somewhere. All I knew was the soil released me. My head flopped back against Brant's chest, and the sun once again breached my eyelids. I blinked it away, looking at Genie's nonplussed expression.

"What the hell was that?" I yelled. Tears sprang to my eyes as I added yet another level of trauma to my lifelong list. "I couldn't move!"

"Why the hell didn't you stop her?" Brant grumbled to his mother.

"I didn't even know she had gone under yet. Cass usually had to meditate for a few minutes first."

Genie kneeled down next to me. "Did you see him? Did he speak to you?"

"Yes," I admitted.

"How did it feel?"

Brant pushed his hand against his mother's shoulder. "That's enough, Mother!"

She looked at him, eyes filled with a delighted anger. "I thought you came to me because you wanted answers."

"I came to you because I wanted answers for her! Not for you. I thought you might try to help her. I should've known you would try to recruit her."

Genie rolled her head back and scoffed. "Oh, don't be so dramatic. Of course I'll help her, but I can hardly do that without understanding her." She raised her hand to her son's cheek and caressed it softly. "Just give me a little more time with her."

Brant's eyes glazed for a moment, but then he flinched away from her. "No!" The look on his face was not entirely anger. There was fear there. "This was a bad idea." Brant shifted behind me, and I felt myself rise from the ground. My head bobbled against his arm as he carried me away.

Genie crossed her arms as she watched him go. "This isn't going to go away, Brant. She's going to need my help. Just like her mother."

"Just hang in there, Tori. It will wear off soon, I promise," Brant assured me, but that didn't stop me from closing my eyes for a small nap.

The Awakening

I felt a sting on my face, and I opened my eyes. Lane Hart's wide eyes stared back at me, worried and relieved at the same time. I blinked away the remainder of my confusion, taking in the plethora of couches and chairs surrounding us. I was sitting on a suede Barcalounger with my feet propped up and a coffee in my hand. I looked down at it, trying to figure out when it got there.

"Sorry about that. Brant told me to keep you awake no matter what."

I touched my cheek where the sting was turning into a quiet burn. "Did you just slap me?"

Lane blinked and looked around at the random furniture. "Ah, here, keep drinking." Lane shoved the Styrofoam cup to my lips. The coffee was already half gone, but so far it was apparently not doing its job. "How long have I been out?"

"I don't know. You've been here for the last half hour. Brant said you got a pretty good smack to the head. What happened?"

I realized by the scuffs and dents on the surrounding items that I must be in the back of the Harts' furniture store. It seemed to be a storage area for clearance items.

Brant was nowhere to be seen. I was surprised he had taken me here instead of home. "Where is he?"

"He ran over to the coffee shop to get you a proper espresso. How are you feeling?"

I touched the soft suede beneath my fingers as I contemplated how I felt. Something was definitely wrong with me. It wasn't just the fatigue draining my energy and dragging my eyelids down. I felt as if something cold were wrapped around my heart. I felt as if death were singing me a lullaby.

"Hey, hey, hey!" Lane patted my cheek. "Don't close your eyes."

"I'm not," I said, though I couldn't actually see anything, so maybe they had closed again.

"All right." Lane's voice sounded mischievous as he took my coffee from me. "You're forcing me to do this." He reached beneath me, pushing his hand up my leg. For a moment I thought he was going to grope me or goose me in the ass. To my surprise, I didn't reach to intercept his hand. I was certain he could have unbuckled his pants and pissed on me and I wouldn't have opened my eyes.

I felt the pinch where my thigh reached my butt. It was the exact mix of probing and tickling that made one squirm like a worm on a hook. I shifted, trying to get away, but it only gave him the opening to get a better grip, as well as add a few dancing fingers to my soft underbelly. I screeched and curled into a ball. I fought his hands even as I laughed. He laughed with me and followed along with my contorted body. "

"Stop! Stop!" I begged. "I'm awake, I swear. Mercy!" I yelled as I fell into a giggle fit. Lane draped over my hip, laughing as well. When our eyes met, his smile broadened.

"Hey," he said simply. I smiled back at him, trying to remember him as a child. Was he the boy I had blamed my pulled hair on? Was it his birthday party with blue frosting? Was that why I hated frosting? Had Lane ruined it for me—or rather Brant? "You don't remember me, do you?" Lane shifted, and I rolled back over to face him. He kept his arm braced on the other side of me. I shook my head. "It's okay, I barely remember you. I'm told you were the first girl I dated."

"Dated?" I wrinkled my nose.

"Yeah, playdates." He winked at me.

"Oh." I smiled. "I don't think that counts."

"I'm counting it. In fact, by my estimate, you and I were going steady for about three years."

I chuckled and shook my head. "Wow, we're practically married then."

"Hey." Lane raised his hands. "I need to keep my options open. I mean, just because you were my first kiss doesn't mean you own me."

"I was your first kiss?"

"Um, unless you started earlier than kindergarten, I was your first kiss too."

I felt myself blush even though a childhood peck on the lips could hardly warrant any embarrassment. I was about to ask coquettishly if it had been a good kiss, but I noticed Brant standing next to an armoire across from us. The forbidding look on his face evaporated my joy. "Brant?"

"Hey, bro—" Lane turned to look at him. "What's wrong with you? You look like you just ate something rotten."

Brant's gaze sank to the ground, and he shook his head. "I was just...thinking."

Lane snorted and stood up. "God, you are so weird sometimes." He reached for the coffee in his hand. "You must get that from Mom."

Brant snapped back into reality and pulled the cup away from Lane. "I'll take it from here."

"Okay. She probably won't need the coffee anymore, anyway. I got her heart rate up all on my own." Lane aimed a finger gun at me, clicked his tongue, and winked before heading back out to the front of the store.

Brant approached me slowly and sat next to me. "How do you feel?"

"A little queasy, but I'm not tired anymore. What the hell happened back there?" I asked as I looked my body over for evidence of my trip down under. As near as I could tell, the only parts of me covered in dirt were my hands and forearms. "What was that?"

"If you're not ready to believe you're a necromancer, then there is no point in explaining."

I took a deep breath, letting the event replay in my mind. I didn't want to believe it. I really didn't want to. But that wasn't what my instincts were telling me. That wasn't what every fiber of my being had been screaming each time I had encountered my intruders. Even if my rational side was still trying to search for a medical cure, it was my primal side that knew there was no earthly explanation for what was happening to me. "Okay," I whispered. "I'm ready to listen."

Brant still seemed to be questioning my resolve, but I couldn't go cold turkey on my grip on reality. I would keep my finger on the abort button, just in case. Unfortunately, at this point I was very certain the button now involved heavy sedation and shock therapy.

"Sometimes your mother would go into deep trances when she was communicating with the dead. It was pretty scary stuff, especially when it happened right at the dinner table." Brant rubbed his face. "She even went into a coma once."

"A coma?"

"Yeah, but my mother didn't call it a coma. She said Cass had too much to drink and passed out. She made excuses to your father so she could spend the night. She didn't wake up until eighteen hours later. All because Cass tried to talk to a man who was less than one week dead."

"Why did your mother tell me to do it then?"

"To test you or prove to you it's real. I don't know. She should have pulled you out of the dirt the minute you zoned out." Brant took my hand, rubbing his thumb against my palm. "Do you remember anything?"

I nodded. "I remember being pulled down into the grave...literally. I couldn't move. I couldn't even breathe. And then there was this guy in his coffin. I spoke to him. He told me to go away because he was sleeping." Brant dropped my hand and stood up. He set the coffee down and paced between the two couches. "What does that mean?"

"It means you're a necromancer, like your mother."

"So, I'm a witch."

"No, you..." Brant looked around, but the room was empty. He pulled up an ottoman and sat next to me rather than take back his original spot. "My mother is a witch. She calls upon natural energies that exist all around us to cast spells. It's relatively harmless, as long as she remains a solitary practitioner."

"And a necromancer?"

"A necromancer draws power from the dead in order to use their gift. For some reason, drawing power from the freshly dead can hurt you. I don't really understand it, but there is a balance in energy, whether physical or metaphysical."

"How come I've never experienced this before now?"

"It's possible that, like your experience with my uncle, you just didn't know you were talking to a dead person. But my mother believes you are running into the same problem Cass had."

"And what is that?"

"There is something wrong with your house."

"You mean the house is putting my talent into overdrive?"

"Something like that. There have probably been several deaths in that house over the years. Maybe you are connecting with those spirits, and that in turn is feeding your skills."

"So, the more time I spend in the house, the more ghosts I will see."

Brant shrugged. "That seemed to be how things went for your mother."

"But Genie was able to help her, right? She helped her control the power."

Brant shook his head. "No, that's not why I took you to my mother. I didn't want her to train you. I wanted her to talk you out of living in that house. It's just bad news."

"Where am I supposed to live? I can't buy a house now. I've already sunk too much into this one. Ed will have a fit."

"Then don't buy a house. You can move in with me." I stared at Brant as if he had grown a second head. "You can sleep in my spare room." I continued to stare at him. "We'll figure it out. I don't want you to get wrapped up in my mother's version of reality. I know this all still sounds like potions and prayers to you, but I assure you it isn't. Combining a necromancer with a witch was a bad idea when Cass did it. It's an even worse idea for you."

Brant continued to lecture me about avoiding his mother, but my mind had already trailed off to another topic.

My parents were dead. If I really were a necromancer, I should be able to communicate with them. I could find out what happened that day. I could solve the mystery of their murder. Despite Brant's fervent warning, I had a feeling Genie was the woman to help me do just that.

The Competition

Talking with the freshly dead was obviously exhausting, and yet I felt great. It might have been the espresso, but I was enjoying an endorphin rush that could compete with a cardio workout. Not only was I not afraid of my skill anymore, I wanted to do it again.

There was some discussion about heading back to Brant's place, but I told him I had some errands to run in town and would be fine hanging out for the rest of the afternoon. I didn't tell him I was considering going back to my place to conjure my parents. That was a conversation best left for another time. Perhaps never.

Brant was walking me out when I heard my name being called across the street. I scanned the sidewalk for its source. "Tori!" Years of instinct overpowered my logic, and my heart skipped a beat. I smiled brightly at Ed Ladner as he jogged across the street to meet me. "There you are. I've been trying to reach you all morning."

"Oh, I'm sorry." I glanced at Brant. "I just had some other business," I stated carefully, not to make any insinuations about my relationship with Brant. Which, last I checked, was still on the rocks even though he'd asked me to move in with him. Complicated indeed.

Ed stopped at the curb, leaving us almost eye to eye with one another. He gave me what seemed to be a genuine smile. "You look good. Amazing what a shower will do," he teased and winked at me. He glanced at Brant, who was standing next to me—right next to me. "Hey, kid, how's your dad doing?"

"He's good, Mr. Ladner," Brant answered somewhat coldly.

"I keep thinking I need to call him up and have a beer with him."

"I'm sure he would enjoy that."

"Listen, Tori." Ed turned back to me. "The plumbing guys are ready to come in and move your pipes around, but they need to do it this afternoon or it's gonna be another three weeks. I thought they could at least get it started in the basement and then finish up when your demo is finished."

"Oh, right." I scratched my head, wondering whether fixing up the house was even on my agenda anymore. As attached as I had been to the idea of fixing up my parents' home, the thought of living there long-term no longer appealed to me. At this point, it was only going to be an investment, and a bad one at that.

"I see you missed a spot." Ed pulled my hand away from my forehead, noting the dirt on my hands left over from my morning digging in graves. "Here." He pulled a handkerchief out of his breast pocket and wiped my brow. "Don't tell me you've taken up gardening."

I could sense the shift from Brant as if he disapproved of the interaction, but I could hardly brush him away. As much as my connection to Ed had changed over the last few days, I still sought his approval and advice. "What do you say, then? Will you be around later this afternoon to let them in?"

"Um, well…" I glanced between him and Brant, not sure what answer to give. I was certain Brant would be willing to drive me home, but I didn't want to speak for him. Rather than jump in to offer his services, though, Brant seemed to be waiting for me to ask. "Yeah, I can be. How long will it take?"

"Oh, I don't know. Those guys are pretty fast. Why, you two have a hot date later?" Ed perked his eyebrows and made a clicking noise with his tongue.

"No," I answered far too eagerly.

"Yes," Brant answered at the same time. I gaped at him, unsure of how he expected me to tolerate more of his relationship whiplash. I must have been scowling at him, because he was giving me a black look.

Ed looked between us, seeing the tension there. He raised his hands in surrender. "None of my business, anyway."

I looked at Ed, being sure to brighten my face with a fake smile. "I was only asking so I could plan my day. I'm kind of without a car right now, so I am at the mercy of Brant and his work schedule."

"Your car isn't running? Is that what happened yesterday? Did you break down?" Ed grimaced at me. "Oh hell, and I just left you here to fend for yourself. I'm so sorry, Tori. I misunderstood the urgency."

"That's okay." I shrugged.

"No." Ed squeezed my arm. "It really isn't. I should have been there for you."

"It worked out okay." Brant reached over and rested his hand on my shoulder. "I was here for her." Brant moved his thumb, tickling the back of my neck. As good as it felt, his macho jealousy infuriated me. Ed may have been a failed pursuit, but that didn't mean he had to piss all over me in front of him. It's not as if Ed had any clue I was madly in love with him. Or had been.

Ed tracked the movement, staring at Brant's hand on my shoulder. "I appreciate that, sport, but it doesn't alleviate my guilt. Tori is *my* responsibility." If I had still been in a lovesick trance, I might have thought Ed was acting jealous. "I have to look out for her, you know? Keep her away from...trouble." I realized the critical eye Ed was aiming at Brant had very little to do with me. Whatever was happening here had started long before me.

"Let me make it up to you." Ed slid his hand down my arm until he was gripping my hand. "How about I take you off Brant's hands? That way he can get to work and we can spend some time together." Ed tugged me off the curb. I noted that it forced me to move out of Brant's grip. "I can take it from here, son."

"That's very nice of you," Brant said congenially, though I could see he was clenching his fists.

"Oh, no problem, buddy," Ed said with an unmistakable edge of condescension in his voice. "You let your dad know I inquired after him. He's one of my best clients. I want to make sure he's taken care of."

"Absolutely, Mr. Ladner. I know you are very dedicated to your clients." Brant looked at me when he said *clients*. "Oh, here, what am I thinking?" Brant said as he pulled out his wallet. "You'll need this." He pulled two twenties from his wallet and offered them to Ed.

Ed stared at the bills. "What's that?"

"The money you gave Tori the other night. She didn't end up using it. I wanted to get it back to you so you could adjust it off her account."

Although Ed was normally unflappable, his face went expressionless. His jaw rolled as he searched for the appropriate words to respond to Brant. I, meanwhile, wished I could crawl into the gutter and hide until they were done. The tension between them was palpable, and I was afraid I might get caught in the crossfire of a fistfight if they didn't stop soon.

Instead of blowing up, Ed laughed. He sighed after he had made his point. "Mr. Hart, I think you're confused about how this works." Ed motioned between us. "It's not about money. It's about a promise I made to her parents, and I take that promise very seriously." Ed's normally easy smile rose, defying the hard lines in his clenched jaw and narrowed eyes. "So you can keep that money. Consider it gas money." Ed stared him down, unflinching.

With no room left to defy the order, Brant slowly drew back the money and returned it to his wallet. "I'll see you later, Tori." Brant barely looked at me before heading inside.

Ed's shoulders slumped the moment Brant was gone. "That kid has always been a hothead." Ed turned to face me. "I don't know how you can stand him after what he did to you as a child."

I grimaced. "Was he really that bad?" I asked.

"You don't remember the…?" Ed looked at me piteously. I was, after all, a walking, talking headcase. "It doesn't matter, I guess—as long as he's nice to you now." I shrugged, trying to find the definition of nice somewhere in my description of Brant Hart. There were certainly far more bullheaded personality traits than I would have preferred, but I supposed in his own way he was looking out for me. That in and of itself was nice. Wasn't it?

"I just don't like seeing you get into a relationship this soon."

"Soon?" I furrowed my brow. It had been nearly two years since I'd had a steady boyfriend.

"So soon after getting into town. You've had a lot of changes lately. I'm not sure dating is the best choice for you right now."

I smiled at Ed, more than appreciating his fatherly advice. "Was that true, what you said about the promise to my parents?"

"Yes. I swore to your mother I would look after you."

"Until I inherited the money?"

Ed frowned and shook his head. "Tori." He rested his hands on my shoulders and leaned down to make sure we were eye to eye. "The money has nothing to do with the promise. It never has, and it never will. You will never be out from under my wing." Ed smirked at me. "You are stuck with me."

The teenager inside me rejoiced at the thought of having Ed's attention now and forever. I also felt my attachment to him, albeit naively romanticized, had been vindicated. "I love you." The words slipped out, a natural expression of emotion—honest, beautiful, and extremely inappropriate.

Ed's eyes widened, and his mouth dropped. After a moment, his smile returned, and he gently squeezed my shoulders. He pulled me close and wrapped his arms around me for a hug that lasted a good deal longer than our last. "I love you too, Tori."

The words fell over me like a warm blanket in an endless frigid winter. I wasn't sure why we had never said it before, or why I had been falling out of love with him before I could say it, but I meant it. And I knew he meant it, and that was all that mattered.

The Lunch

I scooted into the booth across from Ed, feeling a little giddy about having him all to myself. I was also feeling guilty for abandoning Brant. As soon as my life got back to normal, if it ever would, he and I really needed to figure out what the hell we wanted from each other.

"So, how did you come to be hanging out with Brant Hart?"

"We met at the furniture store when I ordered the couch and chair for the living room."

"Ah," Ed said, glancing over his menu. "*Are* you dating him?" He didn't look up, but I could tell by the slight rise in his tone that he wasn't indifferent to my answer.

"I don't know. We've only hung out a couple of times." I didn't specify that the last hang-out involved a sleepover followed by meeting his mother.

Ed stared at his menu a moment longer before slapping it down. "Okay, I am just going to ask. Are you...? Have you...?" Ed wrestled with the right wording. "Did you and he...?"

"No," I lied before he could find the right words. Aside from not adding to town gossip, I didn't think it was any of Ed's business who I slept with.

Ed wrung his hands and nodded. He looked around the diner before leaning in. "If you should decide to get serious with him, or someone else, we should discuss prenups."

I chuckled. Ed was always in lawyer mode, even off the clock. "You'll be the first to know if a diamond ring comes my way." He returned to his menu. After a quick perusal of my menu, I put it down. "Ed." He perked a brow, letting me know he was listening. "There's something I've been meaning to talk to you about."

"What's that?" He put down his menu and folded his fingers on the table.

"I know we've never talked about this before, but I assumed it was because I never asked."

"What's that?"

"What happened on the day my parents died?"

Ed's face blanched, and for the second time today, I saw his indestructible political mask shatter. "Oh, Tori. The truth is, we never talked about it because I didn't have any answers for you."

"So you don't know anything more than anyone else? Even though you were my father's lawyer and his closest friend?"

Ed frowned and squeezed his hands together. "Tori, your father shared a great many things with me, but he didn't share them with me as a lawyer. He shared them as a friend. I'm not entirely sure how much you want to know, but I can assure you none of it is going to help you understand why they are gone."

"The only thing I remember, aside from a few stray images of toys and play dates, is an argument. An argument between my parents right before the fire. The problem is, I don't even remember what the argument was about. I either didn't understand it or I just don't remember it. All I'm asking is whether you would know any reason why they would be so angry with each other."

The waitress came around, and Ed gave her a broad plastered smile. "You know, I think a hamburger and fries for me. No cheese, no mayo. Easy on the salt for the fries. And a Diet Coke too. Tori, any thoughts?"

I glanced down at the menu but didn't bother to pick it up. I got the feeling I only had Ed for the lunch break, so I had better hurry. "Same for me, but make my Coke regular."

The waitress wrote the order down and headed off to clip it on the rotary stand for the cook. I looked over the other patrons in the 50s-style diner. Most everyone was sitting at the bar, eating alone, trying to jam a meal into their lunch break. When I looked back, Ed was looking right at me.

"You look so much like her sometimes." Ed shook away the nostalgia and pulled out a pile of napkins from the dispenser. He laid them neatly in a pile beneath his silverware. "I suppose there's no point in keeping secrets for the dead. I mean, it's not as if it matters," he said somberly. "I just don't want you to have a bad image of your parents. Then again, personal opinions aside, we are all adults, and adults make mistakes, right?"

"Right," I agreed.

Ed tapped his fingers on the table nervously. "The thing is, this is a relatively small town. I mean, don't get me wrong, we do okay. Good commercial industry, lots of jobs, good schools, low crime." I smiled as Ed gave me the rundown on Harold as if he was trying to sell me on the idea of living here. "But of course, there's a lot of gossip. Everybody seems to know everybody's business, eventually. And even if it's not fact, the fiction usually isn't too far from it."

"And what sort of gossip did you hear about my parents?" I asked, already anticipating the bewitching tales of my mother through the eyes of the public.

"Tori, I want you to know I considered both of your parents my friends. I knew your father for a great number of years. He was like a brother to me. And your mother, well, as you might imagine, I was as loyal to her as your father."

"I can imagine."

"The thing is, sometimes life throws you a curveball, and you don't quite know what to do with it. There were a lot of rumors going around about your mother. Rumors I didn't approve of. I did my best to dispel them. I told people they were being ridiculous. And to my knowledge, they *were* ridiculous...at the time, anyway."

I frowned, thinking about what the locals would have to say about my mother's special skills. I was certain Genie had no qualms about broadcasting her witchcraft, but such things tended to get manipulated through the grapevine. That was probably how the Satanism rumors got started. "What do you mean?"

"Mark came to me one night. He had been drinking. There was a party at the house that night. I wasn't able to attend. He drove out to see me around midnight. He was knocking on my door so hard I thought he was gonna break it down. Honestly, I thought..." Ed shook his head and shifted his pile of napkins again. "All I knew was that he was upset and angry. I let him in, and he began to rant about Cass. I knew he had ignored the gossip, but being face to face with the truth was too much to deny. He was heartbroken."

"Heartbroken? What were the rumors about?"

Ed reached over the table and pressed his hand over mine. "There were multiple rumors about your mother having affairs," he whispered.

I shook my head. "She was cheating on my father?"

"Yes, I'm afraid so."

"There must be some kind of mistake. Everything you ever told me about them—she loved him."

"She did." He squeezed my hand. "Very much so. There's no denying that, but sometimes people make mistakes."

"You're not talking about one mistake. You're talking about several. They must be mistaken. Maybe she had something else going on in her life that people misinterpreted as...something it wasn't."

"Tori, I know you want to continue to have an unadulterated memory of your mother, and if you want to stop talking about this, we can, but I need you to know those rumors were true."

"You don't know that."

"Yes, I'm afraid I do. All too well."

I tilted my head, trying to understand what he was saying. His eyes drifted from mine, focusing on the table in shame. "You?" I whispered. "You...and my mother?"

He looked back up at me and nodded. "I wish I could explain it. The words 'it just happened' seem so clichéd to me, and yet...it did." I pulled my hand from beneath his. He looked down at my rejection, once again staring at the table. "There's no point in my trying to salvage your impression of me. The truth is, I never told your father about the affair. Even when I knew for certain she was cheating on him, I couldn't bring the others to his attention without revealing myself. So, I became a co-conspirator in her deception. Shame I can't even begin to alleviate, since it now seems to make me almost responsible for their deaths."

The waitress arrived, setting the food down in front of us in record time. She asked us whether we wanted anything else. Ed gave her another broad, equally fake smile and said, "No, thank you." When he turned back to me, he frowned. He couldn't even begin to understand how far he had dropped in my opinion. Setting aside the fact that my parents' magical marriage had been reduced to an atypical celebrity gossip column, my fantasy of Ed had been soured by the thought of him being an adulterer with my mother. "I suppose I'm going to have to live with that now. That frown. Oh, Tori, why did you have to grow up? Why did you have to become this smart, beautiful, inquisitive woman?"

"Is that why you got divorced from your first wife?"

Ed smiled. "No, I'm afraid I may have had another indiscretion involving a secretary who no longer works for me."

I scoffed and picked up my burger. I took a bite of it, along with several fries I could fit alongside it. I was barely able to swallow it since my throat was trying to choke on the emotions inside of me.

"Please don't cry," Ed whispered and reached out to me. He brushed his hand across my forearm before drawing it back again. I picked up my napkin and dabbed my eyes as well as my mouth.

"Is that why you do all this for me? As penance?" I asked.

"I do all of this because I loved them. I don't expect you to understand or forgive me, but don't think for one second my heart turned to stone after I cheated with your mother. Just because you screw somebody over doesn't mean you stop caring about them. It just means you're an idiot."

I sipped my soda for a little while. Ed ate, so he wouldn't lose the opportunity before his lunch break was over. "Is that why they were fighting that night? Because of her indiscretions?"

Ed finished chewing his food and swallowed before answering. "I think it's very likely. The fire occurred a few days after the party."

I shifted my glass on the table, letting it glide on its own condensation. "Do you think my father killed her?"

Ed glanced around at the potential ear-gawkers around us. "There is one thing I'm sure of: there is no way, not in this life or the next, that Mark would've done anything to harm your mother. And even if I am so naïve as to misinterpret his intentions, there is still nothing inside of him that could ever be angry enough to hurt you. Nothing."

He reached across the table, but this time I met him in the middle. We held hands for a moment, allowing the subtle tenderness I desperately needed. If nothing more, it assured me that Ed was not an entirely horrible person. Mistakes happen, and though it may have caused turmoil in my family, it certainly had not been the only factor.

Ed shifted his thumb along the back of my hand, and I gave him a small smile. As the moment continued to go longer, I felt a certain discomfort in the contact. It had somehow gone past the stage of tender and become more intimate. Since I wasn't quite ready to delve back into a teenage fantasy—that was now quite tainted—I pulled my hand away and continued to eat.

The Plumbing

By the time Ed dropped me off, I was relieved to see the plumbers were already in the driveway waiting to be let in and frantically calling my phone. I apologized profusely for the disruption to their day, trying desperately to hold back the hug I wanted to offer a large bearded man for arriving so promptly so I didn't have to be alone in my house.

While he and his assistant headed downstairs to shut off the main water and start shifting my pipes in preparation for my new layout, I headed into the kitchen. I wanted to see for myself that it was empty. There was no mysterious shadow man lurking in my kitchen drinking soda.

I supposed it wouldn't matter how many times I saw a ghost. Part of me was always going to think it was a brain tumor, or schizophrenia, or some other rationalization to explain the nature of my connection. I found some amusement in that, since everything in humanity's past consisting of religious impossibilities that those involved were supposed to take on faith. Over three-quarters of the American population believed in angels, but less than half believed in ghosts. That meant that most of the population believed in invisible beings with wings. And *I* was the crazy one because I was seeing an echo of human consciousness.

"Ma'am," the plumber interrupted my thoughts from the doorway. I looked back at his oversized frame smooching into the slender opening. "I'm gonna start removing the connections to the sink, if that's all right."

"That's fine. I have no plans for cooking in the near future, anyway." I motioned to my mostly broken-down wall leading into the dining room. I was a little disappointed with my progress. After standing in the house again, I remembered how much I wanted to bring it back to life. To bring some order to an otherwise chaotic past. As much as I disliked the idea of dealing with supernatural phenomena, I still felt connected to my childhood home in a way that no other place had made me feel.

As the plumber got down on all fours to inspect the sink, I noted he was wearing purple underwear. Which was a relief from the traditional plumber's butt crack people were usually privy to, but either way, I took it as a signal to get out of his way. I opened the back door and pushed through the creaking screen door. I carefully made my way down the back steps and strolled through my yard.

For the most part, the grass was a series of weeds long overdue for mowing. I wasn't sure what Ed had set up for lawn service, but I would have to look into it before my backyard turned into a prairie.

The area was extensive, but the triangular shape of the lot and the sloped ground made it seem less so. There was a long line of trees on the right side of the property, marking the end of my land and the beginning of a treacherous drop-off. Other than that, the only greenery on the property was a cluster of lilac bushes beside the garage.

The structure, I thought, was set a little too far back from the house. I was never sure why it had been built so far away. I pushed back the branches of overgrown shrubs and peeked through a dusty window in the garage. Through the cracked window I could see a rough concrete floor, covered in patches of oil. The back wall held a few shelves littered with jars of nails and screws, as well as a few greasy items I was sure I would never be able to identify. Against the far wall I saw something vaguely familiar: a silver and red tricycle with residual tufts of tinsel hanging from the handles.

I smiled at the memory of a hand pushing on my back, urging me to pedal faster. It felt safe, loving, and so despairing in its dissociation from my actual life. Despite my joy at having another little piece of my memory back, I wished it was gone again. So much of my life since the accident had seemed supplementary.

Returning to my parents' house had been meant to bridge the gap between my two very different lives and fill in the missing pieces. The memories should've been a welcome change, but I didn't know how to embrace my childhood without causing myself pain for the loss of it. Moreover, I didn't want to find more dreadful truths that would ultimately sour my image of my family. I'd come home to uncover more about my life, but it seemed I wasn't ready for the discoveries that were waiting for me.

I kicked the dirt at my feet and left the garage behind. I headed down to the lookout marking the farthest corner of the property. At one time, there had been a well-laid brick path leading to the concrete section, but most of it had been covered over with dirt and grass.

Just before the cliff edge, there was a slight drop-off. I descended the three steps leading to the small patio. Two small concrete garden benches gave me a spot to sit and enjoy the view. Over the years, the untended trees had grown haphazardly, leaving the once grandiose view filtered by so many leaves it was impossible to see how far down the drop was.

I moved to the edge of the patio, where an old rusty railing provided a safe haven for the patio observers. It was easy enough to drop off the edge when you were paying attention, let alone when you were admiring the sunset. I took a breath of the unadulterated exhalations of the local plant life and braced myself on the railing.

"Don't touch that!" a little girl's voice yelled behind me.

Even as I turned to see who it was, the railing gave way beneath me. It dropped onto the slanted grass and slid over the edge. I heard it *thunk* its way down, hitting who knows how many tree trunks and rocks before it reached the bottom.

My loss of balance caught me off guard, but since I was already turning, my headlong tumble turned into a sideways stumble. I was able to brace myself and prevent a deadly plummet. "Oh, my God!" I clamped my chest where my heart was thumping like a rabbit on speed. "Thank you so much for warning me."

I turned to see who my savior was, and I found a little girl not much older than ten. She was wearing a rather nice dress, albeit a bit too much of a tablecloth pattern for my taste. Her brownish blond hair was cut short and wrapped around her ears, making her look like an adorable little tomboy. She tipped her head at me and stared, as children do when they don't know it's rude.

"I'm Tori. What's your name?"

"Anna Bella Richards. And that's Anna Bella, not Annabelle," she clarified.

"That's cute. Your parents either have a sense of humor or a sense of irony."

"What's irony?"

"In this case, I think it means they like to do the opposite of what people expect."

"I've never seen you here before," Anna said in an almost accusatory tone.

"I just moved into this house." Anna glanced up the hill, then back at me. The critical expression on her face seemed to reveal her spoiled nature. "Where do you live?" I asked.

"You shouldn't talk to the new ones," she said with absolutely no foundation for a change in conversation topic.

"I'm sorry, I don't understand." Anna rolled her eyes and moved over to one of the cement benches. She jumped on top of it and twirled her arms around in circles as she balanced on the less-than-adequate surface. "Oh, honey, please don't do that. I don't want you to fall."

She snorted and stopped twirling. "You're not very smart, are you?"

"Excuse me? I think it takes a few brain cells to figure out those benches are meant for butts and not feet," I scolded her.

"That's so funny. My mother said the same thing."

"Speaking of your mother, don't you think she's probably wondering where you are right now?"

Anna shrugged. "She knows where I am. She would always watch me out the kitchen window while I played." She looked up toward the house.

I looked back at it, noting the convenient position of the kitchen window looking out onto the lawn. I suddenly wondered if maybe there was now a good reason for the particular placement of the garage. If it had been placed any closer to the house, it might've obstructed the view of the gully as well as the lawn. "You mean that kitchen?" I asked as I looked back at Anna with different eyes. "When was this?"

"Pbblst! I don't know. A long time ago. It doesn't matter."

I moved over and sat on the bench across from her, trying to decide how old-fashioned her dress looked. The house was well over a century old. The garage wasn't much younger, minus the updated door. "Did you fall?" I asked.

"Yup." Anna twirled once more. "Mama was watching, but she was too far away. She said not to twirl, but I did it anyway. I spun so hard and so fast I didn't even know where I was. I jumped off the bench and started walking. Mama screamed so loud. I could hear her all the way from the house, but I didn't know why." Anna pointed to the edge of the cliff. "I went the wrong way." A shiver ran down my body as I contemplated the horrifying image of a mother watching her daughter walk off a cliff and being too far away to prevent it. "That's why you shouldn't talk to the new ones."

"I'm sorry, I still don't understand what you mean by that."

Anna rolled her eyes again and threw her arms out with melodramatic exasperation at trying to communicate with me. "Don't you see? Only bad deaths keep you locked in place." She pressed her hands together. "Just because people die doesn't mean they want to hang around. You start talking to any random dead person, and they'll drag you in." She made a sucking sound and interlaced her fingers, apparently indicating an unbreakable connection.

"You're saying if I talk to somebody who's recently died, I could die myself?"

"The dead just want to sleep. If you wake them up, they stop dreaming. Nobody wants to stop dreaming, not if it's a good dream. They'll go back in, and they'll take you with them into their dream. Then you'll be stuck. Don't talk to the fresh ones."

"Thank you for the advice. You seem to know a lot about this subject." Anna shrugged. "What about the old ones? Can I talk to them?"

"The old ones won't talk. They are too far gone." She waved her hand upward, signifying how far she meant. I glanced up and couldn't help smiling. I wasn't sure the girl had meant to reaffirm my beliefs, but it was nice to know there was indeed an *up* for the dead.

"So, if I can't talk to the old ones, and I shouldn't talk to the new ones, who does that leave?"

Anna jumped down and plopped her butt on the concrete bench. "You have to talk to the ones like me. The ones who get stuck."

"The ones with traumatic deaths?"

"Yeah, I guess. I just like it here better. It's like a dream, but more real, so sometimes it's better."

"Doesn't your family miss you when you come here?"

She shrugged. "No, it's not really like that. It doesn't matter. The time away, I mean. It doesn't count."

I nodded, somehow reassured by that thought. Time was apparently a concept for the living. "Since you're being so helpful already, can I ask you something else?" I leaned forward as if conspiring with her.

"Sure."

"Do I need to help the people I talk to? Am I supposed to make them feel better about how they died?"

Anna's face scrunched up tight. "Why would you do that?"

"I don't know. I guess I thought maybe there was a reason I was seeing them. A purpose for it all. Like destiny or something."

"A fish is a fish. A bird is a bird."

It was my turn to scrunch up my face. "What does that mean?"

"It means you don't go fishing for a bird, and you don't go hunting for a fish, but if you snag a bird with your hook, and you hit a fish with your bullet, you can eat them just the same."

I laughed. "That's cute, but what does it mean to me?"

"It means things are the way they are for a reason, but sometimes you get lucky, and that's okay too."

"I see, I think. So, I'm just lucky that you happened to come by and save my life today?"

Anna shrugged and walked away, disappearing into thin air as she did. If there had been any purpose or destiny for her visit, she probably didn't know about it or care about it. She certainly didn't have to be part of the population who believed in guardian angels. Whether she was one or not.

The Calling

There were bad ideas, and then there were really bad ideas. Allowing myself to believe the dead were talking to me was a bad idea. Encouraging the dead to talk to me was a *really* bad idea. And yet there I was on my living room floor surrounded by candles and summoning the spirits of the great beyond.

In truth, it was a couple of scented candles, and I wasn't so much summoning as talking to myself. I had started the one-woman seance with a fancy speech about bringing forth the source of my life. Now, at the end of my attention span for nonsense, I was shouting for my parents.

"Mooooom," I droned as I stared up at the ceiling. "Daaaaaaaaad."

The only good thing coming from my efforts to contact the dead was I had found a few more cobwebs I had missed in my initial cleaning spree. Or were they new webs? I would need to pick up some bug bombs.

I got up off the floor with a groan and mentally chastised my stupidity for thinking I could simply will myself to contact the dead. I walked over to the piano and sat down before the ivory keys. I pressed a few of them to hear the tone of the instrument. "Oh, Daddy, help me," I murmured to myself.

"I'm right here, sweetheart," a voice said behind me. A hand reached around me and pressed a chord on the piano.

I jumped from the bench, pressing myself against the frame separating the front room from the living room. I could see my father bending over to play the piano behind a young girl. The image was not shadowy or transparent, but rather bright and blurred.

"See there? These three, then move to the left," my father instructed *me*.

I stared at my younger self with growing confusion. Why was I seeing myself? I wasn't dead. "Daddy?" My voice wavered. I crept forward and tried to touch him, but my hand went through him as if I were the ghost.

My eyes slid over the glossy wood floors to the old couch in the living room I had recently gotten rid of. It wasn't mouse-infested. It looked brand new. None of the furniture I had was there. I was seeing the house as it had been when my parents were alive. This was not in the necromancy brochure, as far as I knew.

"Mark," my mother called as she descended the stairs. She rounded the banister and stopped in the foyer. "Wrap it up, you two. We have to get to the school."

"School? At night?" my younger self asked.

"Not you, honey. You're going to see Mrs. Hart while Daddy and I talk to your teacher. Now run upstairs and get your shoes on."

I did as bid and trampled upstairs like a solo herd of cattle. Mark looked at Cass after I was gone and shook his head. "Don't tell me Miss O'Dell is still hounding you about those bruises."

Cass shrugged. "I've explained it several times, but she is still threatening to call the police. I think if she has a chance to meet you, maybe she'll see there's nothing to worry about."

"This is humiliating."

"I know, but at least she's concerned about Tori. Any other teacher would ignore the signs of..."

"Signs of what?" Mark asked. "Were you about to say signs of abuse?"

"That's not how I meant it. From an outsider—"

"Kids get hurt, Cass. We can't dress her in pillows."

"Hey." Cass moved to Mark and embraced his face. "I'm on your side, remember? We'll get through this. We have to show Miss O'Dell what a loving husband and father you are. Then this will all be over."

The vision disintegrated as Cass leaned in to kiss Mark. I stood in my living room, no longer concerned about an explanation for what I had just witnessed. I was more interested in the content of their conversation.

Apparently, I needed to pay my old schoolteacher a visit.

The Teacher

It only took two phone calls to track down Mrs. Margaret Clark, formerly Miss O'Dell. She was still working at the local elementary school, but instead of teaching, she was the principal.

As I walked down the halls of my old school, I once again searched my memories for familiarity. The smell drew on nostalgia, but there was nothing concrete until I hit the short stairwell that brought the next section up half a story. Something about the displacement in the architecture was odd enough to spur the seed of a memory. Books, homework, and endless spiral notebooks were all I could get from it, though.

Despite my lacking memory, I found the principal's office right where I expected it to be. I slipped past the receptionist counter as instructed and rapped on the fogged glass door behind it.

"Come in," Mrs. Clark called from the other side. I opened the door to find a younger woman than I expected sitting at the desk. I quickly calculated her presumed age and realized she must have only been in her twenties when she taught me. "Tori Blake, I presume?" She stood and came around her desk.

"Yes, Miss O'Dell—err—Mrs. Clark."

"Please call me Maggie," she said and shook my hand. "Have a seat."

I sat down in one of the two chairs in front of her desk. Rather than sit behind the desk again, she sat next to me. "Thank you for seeing me."

"Of course. I heard you were back in town. I'm thrilled you thought to come visit me."

"Oh, well, I—um..."

"I heard you took over your parents' old house. That must be an undertaking."

"It is."

"So, tell me about your life. What have you been doing since you left?"

Under normal circumstances, I would have despised telling anyone my life story, but I appreciated the way she referred to my "leaving town" rather than bringing up the fire as my exit reason. In fact, as she listened to me discuss my educational pursuits and failures, she just listened. She didn't pepper me with questions or mention my birth parents at all. Was Mrs. Clark perhaps the only politely enlightened person in Harold?

"That all sounds so wonderful," she said when I was done. "I hope you go back to finish your degree. No one should ever turn down extra income when they can get it."

"I will." For the first time since I dropped out, I realized how stupid I was being by not finishing. No surprise that it took an educator to convince me of that. "Maggie, can I confess something?"

"Go right ahead."

"I'm sort of investigating my parents' death."

Maggie sat back in her chair. "Oh." She had the look I'd expected, concerned and disappointed, but it faded and she smiled warmly. "I understand. You were so young. You must have so many unanswered questions."

"I do, and my memories are so...jumbled. I was wondering if you could help clear up something for me."

"Ask away. I've never lied a day in my life—except about my weight." Maggie chuckled and patted her belly, which was thick but by no means bulbous.

"I remember my parents coming to see you for an impromptu teacher's conference one night. It had something to do with the bruises you had seen on me." Maggie's face went white and her mouth draped open. "I thought you might be able to explain what that was about."

"Hmm, I can try. Do you remember the bruises?"

"No." I shook my head.

Maggie took a breath and stood up. She moved to her water cooler and drank down a cup of water. She brought one back for me, and I took a sip. "Well, Tori, I was very certain your father was abusing you. Your mother insisted he wasn't, but I could see she had bruises too. It was very hard for me to believe there wasn't some kind of abuse happening in your home."

"You never went to the police?"

"I wanted to give your mother a chance to do it instead. I wanted her to stand up for herself and defend you at the same time." Maggie shook her head. "I was naïve to think she could or would."

"How long was this going on? I mean, when did you discover my bruises?"

"Your bruises started about six months before the fire, but I stopped investigating them three months later."

"Why?" I asked, a little disappointed my savior would just throw in the towel so easily.

Maggie's eyes watered as she spoke. "On the night I was introduced to your father, your mother convinced me not to continue pursuing charges."

"What did she say to convince you?"

A tear fell from Maggie's eye. "I'd rather not say."

I reached over and touched her leg. "I really am sorry to pry, but it might be important to understanding what happened."

Maggie patted my hand and brushed it off her leg. "It was after I had spoken with your father. He turned out to be a lovely man, so I was fairly convinced the abuse was incidental, as your mother had suggested. He headed out to warm up the car while Cass and I finished talking. It was the usual chit-chat for about a minute, and then..."

Maggie's eyes glazed, and she swallowed hard. "Her face went so dark—I mean physically dark. I can't explain it, and I won't try, but that's what it looked like to me. She stood up and came around my desk. She pinned my hands down on the arms of the chair and got up close to my face. She said I had better start minding my own business or she would tell everyone in town I was a...cunt-licking dyke." Tears dribbled down Maggie's face. She sniffed and wiped a few away, but more followed. "I was young. I hadn't revealed my preference for women. I was mortified she even knew. *No one* knew."

I frowned. "My mother, the one everyone describes as happy and kind, said that to you—in those words?"

"Yes, I'm afraid so. I was in shock. Even if she hadn't threatened to uncloset me, I think the look on her face and the tone of her voice would have scared me into silence.

The strangest thing was how easily she went back to being herself. It was as if she were temporarily possessed. Mark returned, and she thanked me for my time. She never said an unkind word to me after that. It makes me wonder now whether she had a split personality or some kind of mania." Maggie gave me a sorrowful look. "It makes me wonder if she might have caused the fire in a fit of anger."

I knew the town had brought into question my mother's mental state. And given the fact that she was being inundated by ghosts at the time, it was easy to see how her sanity could have slipped. Was that the answer? Had my mother been under the influence of ghosts? Had she started the car on fire?

But how was the fire being fed? Did the power of necromancy come with jet fuel?

"I'm sorry you had to go through that, but thank you for telling me."

"I'm sorry I didn't fight harder for you, Tori. I hope what I've said doesn't change how you think about your mother. I'm sure she loved you. So did your father."

"Thank you." I shook Maggie's hand and headed back out of her office.

My thoughts were on my mother and her waning sanity when I hit the steps leading to the lower level. A sudden memory of falling down a set of stairs nearly toppled me. I grabbed the railing to steady myself. To my surprise, the memory didn't stop with my descent. I recalled looking up at someone high above me. A boy looked down at me. The image was hazy, but I could tell he had a pudgy tummy and that he was laughing at me.

I wasn't sure how I knew, but I was certain it was Brant. My childhood bully. He had taken delight in pulling my hair and apparently tripping me down stairs.

I cursed quietly to myself and trudged down the stairs. Of all the memories to uncover, why that one? As much as I rationalized that Brant was an adult now, I knew every bad memory I uncovered would sour my attraction to him, making it impossible for us to have a relationship.

Now who was being the whiplasher?

The Stairs

Somewhere between shoving my hands in the dirt, Ms. Anna Bella Richards, and Mrs. Maggie Clark, I had not only accepted my new reality of magic and spells; I was developing backbone with regard to my special ability. I wasn't sure I liked the idea of being a necromancer, though. There was no romanticism in conversing with the dead. It somehow seemed wicked or even dirty.

Being a witch like Mrs. Hart held more allure for me—casting spells and conjuring the details of future events. She may have presented a hokey image to me at first, but if her power was as real as mine appeared to be, she would likely be a valuable asset to me as I waded through the populace of the netherworld to find my parents.

There was something flattering about being able to converse with the dead, though. Initially, it had been frightening, but now that I understood what was happening, it was really no different from conversing with the living—albeit with a few caveats Anna had been nice enough to point out.

The only dead person I had not had a reasonably pleasant experience with had been the dark shadowy figure that was haunting my house. I didn't know who this mysterious man was or why I couldn't see his face, but I didn't like him. I sensed something from him that raised the hair on the back of my neck. Something...evil.

Perhaps his death had been more malicious than the others. Maybe he was defensive toward newcomers in the house. It reminded me of my discussion with Genie. She had mentioned my mother had dealt with a troubling spirit. But he had been only in her dreams. My troublesome spirit was slamming doors in my face.

Regardless of this ghost's afflictions or his resentments toward my presence in the house, I wouldn't walk away. If this house was accelerating my ability to speak to the dead, then I needed to spend *more* time here, not less. I had always felt like the answer to my parents' demise would be found within these walls, and I had been right. Granted, the path I was taking to get to them had changed rather drastically.

Renewed and emboldened, I spent the remainder of the afternoon breaking down the last of the wall between the dining room and the kitchen. I shoveled every last bit of plaster and lathe, leaving only the two-by-fours for the engineer to inspect before I cut them out.

When I was done, I took a careful inventory of the shadows in the room. I was almost certain my dark ghost would return to haunt me. I had decided he was connected to the house, most likely. I'd assumed my destruction of it would anger him, but perhaps he didn't care after all. Or maybe he just wasn't thirsty.

With my mind still set on contacting my parents, I headed upstairs for a shower. The idea of seeing my mother's charred body did not appeal to me in the least, but I had to try to contact her. Duplicating my horrific shower scene seemed like a logical step.

I rinsed and washed the dirt from my hair and body. All the while, I kept an eye on the blurry bathroom outside my curtain. No dark shadows appeared, male or female. Nobody uttered croaking words from the other side of the curtain. I was relieved, but also disappointed.

What was the point of necromancy if you couldn't contact who you wanted?

I wondered whether contacting my parents was somehow taboo. Were they meant to stay away from me? Was my gift limited only to those unrelated to me? And if so, who regulated this? Did I have a necromancy coordinator?

As I combed out my hair and got my pajamas on, I realized most of my clothing was still at Brant's. Virtually my entire wardrobe now consisted of the dirty clothes on my floor and the few items that had made it into my chest of drawers. I would need to start a load of laundry tonight if I wanted something clean to wear in the morning.

I gathered up my scattered clothes and bundled them up in my damp towel. I checked the bathroom and found some more dust-covered apparel before heading downstairs. When I reached the stairs, I felt a pressure hard and fast in the small of my back. With my hands belted around my mound of clothes, I didn't have the railing to help maintain my balance and I fell.

For a moment, the descent didn't seem real. I was merely floating above the stairs, elongated by the difference between the current level of my feet and the lower level that my face was about to smash into. With little time left to analyze directionality and speed of descent, I drew my head inward, tucking into my laundry, and did my best to curl into a ball. I pleaded with any ghost or divine entity to have pity on me.

The first collision was the worst: a tremendous impact to my upper back that knocked the air out of me. The second, third, and fourth impacts were just a series of rolls as I increased speed. Number five landed me on the hard floor not far from the door. My head was throbbing, and though I knew it was because of the wall behind me, I didn't actually remember hitting it.

On the verge of passing out, I looked up to the top of the stairs and saw a figure standing there. I couldn't identify who it was before my head swirled and I went out like a light.

The Blessing

I sat on the porch rubbing my neck and fiddling with a rosary my foster mother had given me. I had never adopted the idea of religion as she had wanted me to, and I was certain that only turning to God during times of stress was cheating, but I mostly wanted to hold on to it because she had given it to me. My world was turning upside down, and I needed something that felt normal—prosaic and fundamentally benign.

Just as the last of the light turned purple in the west, a car pulled up the drive. I stood up as Mrs. Hart stepped from her vehicle. "I'm sorry to call you so late," I said, apologizing for the frantic phone call I had made to her twenty minutes earlier. Thankfully, she and Rex were listed in the phone book.

"I'm so glad you called me, sweetheart," Genie said as she crushed me into a hug.

"Ouch!" I grunted as her arms gripped me a little too tightly.

Genie took liberties to raise my shirt and check my back. She frowned as she groped the budding bruises on my body. "You may need to get checked out tomorrow. There isn't much they can do for bruised ribs, but you could at least get some good pain pills." She winked and headed inside. "Now, as for—" Genie froze inside the foyer. Her shoulders slumped, and she looked disappointed.

"What is it?" I asked, searching her eyes for the answer.

"He's still here," she whispered. "He shouldn't be here." Her gaze rose to the upper level, transfixed by something. I followed her eye, but didn't see the dark shadow or the figure that had pushed me down the stairs. They could have been one and the same for all I knew.

"Who is still here?"

Genie snapped out of her trance and looked at me. "You remember that bothersome spirit I told you about? The one that haunted your mother's dreams?"

"Yes."

"That is the entity that has invaded this house. It isn't as strong as it once was, thank God, but it is nonetheless...awake." Genie's eyes glazed once again, now hypnotized by my hardwood floors.

"You can get rid of him though, right? Suppress him, like you did for my mother?"

"Oh, certainly. You leave it to me. I'll batten down the hatches and make sure he keeps to himself, though I can't guarantee it will last forever. As with your mother, the binding did wear off."

"I understand. I just need a little more time in the house. I think you're right that it's contributing to the frequency of my...communications," I said, trying to put a saner word to my otherwise ludicrous interactions. "I even had a vision—of the past."

"Of the past?" Genie frowned as she looked me over, as if the experience should have damaged me. "A memory?"

"No, I mean, sort of, but not mine. It was more of—oh, what did you call it? An echo? Only, it was a full hallucination—everything was as it was back then."

"That's wonderful," Genie said without any enthusiasm. "What did you see?"

"My parents were talking about a teacher who was concerned for my safety at home."

"Oh." Genie moved away as if she had lost all interest in the subject. "That would have been O'Dell. She was an overachiever. Nice, but nosy." Genie flopped open the big purse strapped to her shoulder and pulled a sage blunt from it. She pulled a lighter out next and lit the bundle of herbs. She began waving it around the piano first.

I meandered over to her, hoping to get caught up in some of the spirit-cleansing smoke. "Who is he?"

"Who?" Genie asked, distracted.

"The dark figure that was haunting my mother and now me. Who is he?"

Genie looked at me, eyes wide with worry. She licked her lips and finally opened her mouth to answer, albeit reluctantly. "He's—"

"What are you doing here?" Brant asked from the open door.

I turned and saw him standing in the foyer holding a plastic bag with a Chinese symbol on the front. He was giving his mother a wretched look of disapproval.

"I asked her to come."

Brant's eyes turned to me. His disapproving look was now aimed at me, but with the added ingredient of disappointment.

"I'll let you two sort this out while I cleanse the rest of the house." Genie slipped past Brant and went up the stairs. I noted that she kept a firm grip on the railing as she went up.

"What the hell are you doing?" Brant snapped at me. "I made it perfectly clear I didn't want my mother involved in this."

"I know, but it was an emergency." Brant rolled his eyes and stormed out. I scoffed and ran after him. "I was pushed down the stairs," I yelled at him.

Brant's feet stopped midway down the steps. He turned around, seemingly doubting my honesty, so I pulled the back of my shirt up to show him the bruises I could now feel with every movement. "Jesus!" He rushed back up to the porch and touched what must have been the biggest bruise on my back. The first impact, no doubt. "Tori, we have to get you out of here. This house is dangerous. Why didn't you call me?"

I pulled my shirt back down and moved to the far side of the porch where a bench swing was supposed to hang. I knew the swing was sitting in the garage waiting to be put back up, but I didn't want to listen to it creak in the wind, nor did I want to have to chain it up tight so it didn't break my picture window during storms.

I tested the railing before putting my full weight on it. I looked back at Brant's sweet concern for my welfare. I couldn't help but think about that nasty little boy who had pulled my hair and tripped me down the stairs. How cruel he had been. But could I really judge Brant for who he used to be? Was that fair? And yet, if I uncovered too many more bad memories about him, I wasn't sure I could sway my heart to be logical instead of emotional.

"Brant, I need to ask you a question," I said, steering the conversation away from the house for the moment. I couldn't very well tell Brant I wanted to stay in a dangerous house that was trying to kill me because I wanted to solve the mystery of my parents' death. He wouldn't understand the questions that were driving me. I was convinced no one could ever understand what it was like to have the memory of a heinous death without anything prior to justify it. "When we were young, did you ever hurt me?"

Guilt flooded Brant's eyes as he looked at me. He even slumped a little. "What do you mean?" he asked, even though he must have suspected what I was implying.

"I spoke to a former teacher today. She found bruises on me in the months leading up to my parents' death." Brant's face was muddled with confusion. "When I was leaving the school, I got another memory back. I remembered falling down some stairs. I remembered you standing on the top step laughing down at me. I think maybe you tripped me."

Brant shook his head and looked out over the property beyond the porch. The light was gone now. It was dark, and although I should have been thinking about settling in for the night, the smell of the Chinese food in Brant's sack was making my stomach grumble.

"I don't remember tripping you down any stairs. I never did anything to bruise you. It was mostly little things—break your crayons and pull the heads off your dolls."

I glanced back inside, where Genie was doing the rounds on the main level. She was back in the dining room behind the clear plastic barrier. She was waving her hands as if she were gesturing to someone. I didn't have a clear view of her face, but it looked like she was talking to someone. Perhaps this spiritual cleansing had turned into a spiritual ass-chewing. I shifted from the railing, getting close to the picture window. I wanted to see whether the movement I saw across from her behind the plastic was real or just my eyes playing tricks with me. Was she really conversing with the shadow man or was she being theatrical?

"Besides, I never did anything more than pull your hair after the second summer you were here, and that was only to get Lane in trouble."

I looked back at Brant. "Why did you stop after the second summer?"

Brant looked at me. There was more guilt in his eyes. He even looked a little sick. "Mom put a stop to it," he said, sounding almost childlike. I could only imagine what kind of punishment he could receive from Genie if she really put her mind to it. Not that anyone wants to get disciplined by their mother, but when your mother is a witch...

A fist pounded on the picture window next to me. I jumped and looked over at Genie, who was inches away from me on the other side of the glass. "Okay, you two lovebirds, I'm all done in here," she shouted through the glass. "Is that King Fu's?" Genie said, zeroing in on the bag in Brant's hand.

The Fear

"Did you get rid of him?" I asked after I had fetched a beer for each of my guests and myself. I sat down on the couch next to Genie, who was already stuffing her face with the Chinese food Brant had intended for me and him. I grabbed a box for myself while it was still hot. Brant was standing in the entryway between the dining room and living room. He sipped his beer all the while glaring at his mother. I couldn't imagine how disappointed he was to have his night upended by his mother. He had probably intended to be my savior with a hot meal since my kitchen was out of service.

He turned his attention to me. He closed his eyes and fluttered his lids as if so much eye rolling was going on behind them. I smiled at him and lifted a fork full of noodles up for him to take a bite of since his mother had confiscated his portion. Rather than politely decline, he moved over and leaned on the arm of the couch to take the bite from me.

"Oh, aren't you two cute," Genie said over the mouthful of food she was still working on.

Much to my disappointment, the cuteness of the moment ended. Brant shifted away from me rather than continue to flaunt any intimacy between us for his mother.

"Well, what's the verdict, Mother?" he asked, repeating my question. "Is the house clean?"

"There is no such thing as clean with this house, just less dirty."

"He's still here?" I asked.

"Oh, that bastard is still here, all right. Not as strong as he was, but it's only a matter of time."

"Why do you always refer to it as if it's a real person?" Brant asked.

"Oh, he is definitely real."

"But he's dead, right?" I asked. "He's just a nuisance ghost, isn't he?"

Genie looked from me to Brant and then smiled at us both. "Of course."

"Mother?" Brant leveled his eyes on her. "We aren't children anymore. You don't have to protect us from the boogeyman. Tori and I are unfortunately very aware of the existence of boogeymen."

Genie looked at him somewhat endearingly. "Yes, I suppose that's true. But this is only day one of Tori's introduction to magic. Don't you think we should take it easy on her? I mean, at this point, *you're* a more experienced practitioner than she is."

Brant glanced at me as if his mother had just revealed that he wore pink bunny slippers at night. "All the more reason to be completely honest with her."

Genie frowned and looked at me. "Are you sure you're ready for this? You weren't very open to the ways of the occult when you woke up this morning."

I nodded and took a long breath. "Yes, but it's been a very long day. I'm ready to hear what you have to say."

"Okay." She gave me a small smile before turning her attention to her son. "What do you remember about Tori's mother?"

Brant looked surprised by the question and even glanced at me as if asking permission to speak. He was still under the impression that the subject was difficult for me. He was probably more sensitive to the topic than I was. I nodded my permission, and he looked back to his mother, who was insistent he answer.

He shrugged. "I remember her laughter and her smile. I remember thinking she was the most beautiful woman I had ever met."

"Boyhood crush, huh?" Genie smirked at her son.

Brant tensed but maintained eye contact with his mother. A game of defamatory chicken was being played. "I guess," he said and took a swig of his beer.

"Half the town was in love with your mother," she said to me as if rationalizing Brant's admission. I knew she meant it in a flattering way, but knowing her history with affairs made it seem far less romantic and far more pornographic.

"What else do you remember about her? How would you describe her manner?"

"Why are you asking me? You knew her better than I did."

"Humor me, son."

Brant sighed and thought about her question. "She was cheerful...affectionate." A warm smile bloomed on his face as if he were remembering a specific encounter with her.

"And what about when she thought no one was watching her?" Brant lifted his gaze back to his mother. He stared at her almost accusingly. "Go on, Brant. When

Cass was alone, or when no one was looking at her. What did you sense from her?"

Brant glanced at me. He pinched his lips shut as if refusing to speak. He took a long breath, then answered. "I felt fear."

Despite being a clearly awful admission in terms of my mother's situation, Genie smiled. Brant seemed embarrassed by the entire conversation, but she was proud of him.

I looked at Brant hoping to get some clarification on this, but he wouldn't look at me.

The Excitement

"I know you don't want to talk about this stuff," Genie whispered on the porch. Brant had slipped out for some fresh air, and when he didn't come back, his mother joined him. Something about the turn in the conversation had made Brant uncomfortable, even more so than his usual irritation with his mother's antics. "But it needs to be talked about."

"No, it doesn't," Brant insisted in a hushed tone. "I have nothing to do with this." I felt guilty that their private conversation was as clear to me as if they were in the room with me, but I could hardly blame myself. It was the single-pane windows that were leaking sound as easily as a winter wind.

"Nothing to do with this? You have as much to do with this as Tori does."

"Not anymore. I am a grown man, Mother. I am not going to play this ridiculous game with you anymore."

"What game? It was never a game."

"To you it was. To you, it was fun. You and Cass both. Running around town manipulating people with spells and charms, disguising your fortune-telling as impromptu advice. It was all one big game. Until it wasn't."

"You blame me for what happened, don't you?"

"I blame you both." There was a long pause. "I know you were trying to help. I just wish you had…"

"Had what?" Genie asked, her temper rising.

"I don't mean that. I mean, you should have stopped while you were ahead."

"While we were ahead? And leave her to struggle on her own?" There was a pause. "Is that what you would have done? See someone in pain and leave them to suffer?" Another pause. "No, I don't think so, Brant. You and I may be very different people, but we are also very similar. I know that in my position, you would have done the exact same thing. And you *are* doing the exact same thing."

"What are you talking about?"

"Tori."

"This is different."

"It's not different. Tori is struggling with the presence of the dead. You are seeking out witchcraft to help her."

"I don't want your magic!" Brant's voice rose well beyond the whisper. "I never wanted you to bring her deeper into this."

"Then what do you want from me? Do you really think this will go away like a bad cold? It didn't for Cass, and it won't for her."

"Then she can move away. Get away from this house and Harold."

"That isn't our decision to make, and even if it were, the darkness would likely follow her. She's better off fighting it off now while it's still early."

There was a long pause. "I just want her to be okay. I don't want her to go through what Cass did."

"Neither do I," Genie insisted. "But this has already started. He is here. If I'm right, then he never really left. I know you can feel it."

"I don't feel anything."

"Don't lie to me. This house is a breeding ground for lost souls. He thrives in a place like this. It has to make your skin crawl just being near this place." After a long pause. "Please, Brant, don't turn away from the craft now. I know how frightened you are of it, and I know that is my fault. You were too young."

"Much too young," Brant snapped.

"Yes," Genie admitted sorrowfully. "I took advantage of you. It was wrong and cruel and...I can't imagine the pressure I was putting on you, but you have to know I only did it to protect you."

I heard a creak on the porch, and the front doorknob twisted. "It might have been about protecting me at first, but once you knew I had a skill for it, you just used me."

"That isn't true."

"It is true. I know because the more fear I felt from Cass, the more excitement I felt from you. I don't blame you for what happened, but I do blame you for not recognizing your limitations sooner." The front door swung open, and Brant stomped back inside. He headed upstairs, and I heard the bathroom door shut. Genie trailed in, and I flipped through the channels on the television, pretending I hadn't been listening to their every word.

Understanding it, however, was a whole other problem.

The Empath

B rant sat on the couch with me, watching the television even though I was certain his vacant stare didn't count as watching. I wanted to ask him about the conversation on the porch. I wanted to know what part his mother had played in my mother's death—or he, for that matter—but I didn't want them to know I had been eavesdropping. I also wasn't sure he would tell me. Whatever issues Brant had with his mother's witchcraft seemed to be gained out of first-hand knowledge, something I was sure he would be loath to admit.

Brant turned to look at me and narrowed his eyes at me. "What?"

"*What* what?"

"You are staring at me. Are you going to ask me a question?" I swallowed hard and bit my lip. "Spit it out, Tori."

"Why was my mother afraid?" I asked, not quite chickening out but sidestepping the obvious questions.

"Your mother had started communing with a particularly bad spirit. He was essentially a poltergeist, I guess, but she was the only one experiencing his disturbances. It was starting to interfere with her life. She wasn't sleeping. She was hardly eating. The only time she felt safe was when she was at our house." Brant looked away, staring at the television again. "My mother thought she could help her, and for a while it did help, but then something went wrong. Something neither of them could fix."

"What?"

Brant looked back at me and frowned. "I don't know if I can answer that. Mom wasn't much for censorship when I was growing up. I heard almost everything that went on in that kitchen. But the conversations started happening while I was at school, or outside playing. Suddenly, there were bigger secrets than witchcraft in my house."

"And this is the same spirit that's haunting my house?"

"Yeah."

"Do you know who he is? Or, I mean, who he was when he was alive?"

Brant's eyes glazed in thought, but he shook his head. "I don't know. They always referred to it as *he* or *the house*. At the time, I just thought Cass was having nightmares. I didn't understand until much later that her boogeyman was real, and by then it was too scary for me to want to understand. That was when I stopped thinking magic was cool. That was when I stopped seeing my mother as some dime-store psychic, like my brother did." Brant turned to me and twisted his finger around a lock of my hair and tugged it gently. It should have brought back memories of the bully who had pulled my hair, but instead it brought memories of him pressed against me. "My mother means well, Tori, but I think you should limit her involvement in this. Why did you invite her over? Why didn't you call me?"

"Things are very confusing between us. And as generous as your offer of moving in is, I can't take you up on that."

"Yeah." Brant disentangled his finger from my hair and got off the couch. "That's probably for the best."

"It is?" I asked, slightly annoyed that he was readily agreeing with my decree instead of fighting for me to come home with him like he had been earlier that day.

"Yeah, I've had a bad feeling about us since we met."

"A bad feeling?" I crossed my arms, thoroughly on the edge of a hissy fit. "Did you have a bad feeling about us when you were screwing me?"

"I wasn't exactly thinking straight at that moment."

"Oh, so when you are cock-deep in me we are a good couple, but any other time not so much."

"Tori, I don't mean it like that. I just have this feeling about us."

"A feeling?"

"Yes. Look, I can't explain—I don't *want* to explain. I just think you're right that we shouldn't occupy the same house, in case things don't work out between us."

I laughed. "Wow, I've never broken up with someone before I've officially dated them before. This is new."

Brant rubbed his face and closed his eyes. "That's not what's happening here. I don't want to get my hopes up for something that may not happen."

"Oh, that has commitment issues written all over it."

"It's not me. It's you!"

"Me!"

"Yes, you and Lane!"

"What?"

Brant shook his head and paced the floor. "I didn't think anything of it until I saw you two together, and then…"

"He tickled me to wake me up. It's not like we were—"

"Getting married!"

My mind went blank for a moment as I watched Brant pace across my living room. "Excuse me?" I finally uttered.

"I get these feelings sometimes. It's like a wave, but it's not coming from me. I can feel the emotions of others."

"You mean like an empath."

"I hate that word. It makes me sound like a character from Star Trek."

"Well, what do *you* call it?"

"I don't call it anything. My mother calls it clairvoyant."

"You're psychic?" I asked, feeling a little exposed.

"It's minimal. Very minimal. It's not like I can read your mind."

"But you can see my future?" I asked.

Brant stopped pacing and stared at me. "At first it was just a feeling. I couldn't see the entire picture yet. Then the other day, when I saw you and my brother together, I got the full vision."

"And what's that?"

"I saw you standing next to him at an altar. You were in a wedding dress; he was in a tux. And you...were looking at him endearingly." Brant bit his lip as if punishing it for speaking the words. "You and Lane were getting married."

I stared at Brant, eyes glazing as his words set into my heart like tiny little stabs. "So let me get this straight." I stood and faced off with him. "You think our relationship was doomed from the start because you had a vision I would marry your brother." I cocked my head to one side. "That is a load of—"

"They are never wrong," Brant snapped before I could finish. He seemed defensive now. Defensive of his gift. "My premonitions are never wrong. Not once in the twenty years that I've gotten them have they ever been wrong."

We both stood in the living room, mad and hurt and searching for a way back to where we had started, but we had come too far. His bullying, his mother, his premonition. My ghosts, my amnesia, my obsessions. It was all too much for a casual fling to surmount.

I wasn't sure how I felt about Lane Hart. He was cute and closer to my age. He was an incorrigible flirt and no doubt fun to hang around, but beyond that I barely knew him. However, I did know how I felt about Brant Hart. Much like my childhood, he was teasing and tormenting me, only this time he was doing it with my heart.

"Get out," I said without any exceptional rise in my volume.

Brant watched me, possibly searching his mind for the right words to rewind time or undo what he had just said. However, there was no spell to reverse time or stupidity. He settled for a very slow departure of gathering up his belongings and trudged to the door. He stopped at the entrance and looked back at me. I met his gaze with my stoic facade.

"The truth is," he whispered, "I don't deserve you, anyway." He ripped open the door and went out before I could agree or disagree with his statement, though I was certain I was in agreement at the moment.

The Bullet

"Tori!" Ed greeted me with open arms when I reached his office the next morning. "What brings you in so early?" I gave him a long hug, relieved to be speaking to another human being about something other than mystical happenings.

"Is everything okay?" he asked when I pulled away.

"Everything is fine. I just had a very long day yesterday."

"Troubles with the plumbing?"

"No, but we do need to discuss the house."

"I told you, these old houses become money pits."

"Actually, I was wondering if I could get a little more information about the house."

"Sure, what do you need?" Ed pulled out a chair in front of his desk and I sat down. Rather than sit in his usual spot on the other side, he sat next to me in the other chair. "Lot lines? Zoning laws?"

"No, I was hoping to get more information about the former residents."

"Former residents? You mean besides your parents?"

"Yes, the people who lived in the house prior to them. And, well, anyone else who has lived there."

"Why on earth would you want to know all that?"

"When I was breaking out the walls, I found this." I pulled the bullet I had found in my wall during the demo from my purse.

"Is that a bullet?" Ed pulled a pair of glasses from the inside pocket of his suit and examined the small metal object in as much detail as he could without a microscope. "Fascinating. It's in rather good shape for passing through a wall."

"That's what I thought. I was considering that maybe it had passed through something softer first to slow it down. Like a person."

Ed barked a laugh at me, which made me jump. "Look at you, Detective Tori." He gave my knee a squeeze and removed his glasses. "You're ready to walk into the police station and close up some cold cases, aren't you?"

"Not exactly." I took the bullet back and deposited it into my coin purse, which had long since become my depository for coupons and gift cards instead of coins. "It just reminded me that a house like mine probably has a very rich history. People may have even died there." I left out the part that I suspected the house was a pool of dead energy fueling my necromancy and manifesting an evil incarnation that wanted to kill me. Ed was a nice guy, but he would have had me committed if I had told him that.

"You do realize it could just as likely be a stray shot from two drunk hunters and nothing corrupt."

I shrugged. "Regardless, I want to know who lived in the house before me, and...how they died."

"Mmm, this is starting to sound less like a crime novel and more like a haunted house story." He winked at me.

"I'm serious. I tried to find something at the library, but I don't know where to start, and the microfiche machine wasn't working—or I don't know how to work it." Ed smirked at me. "I thought I'd check with you. See if there was a way of digging up old property records. Maybe some death certificates."

"It's possible, but why so morbid?" Ed leaned over his knees, frown lines marring his usually congenial face. "You're a young woman and a rather wealthy one at that. You should be out shopping and getting your hair done, not ripping apart houses and solving forty-year-old crimes."

"I've never been a shopping girl. I'm not like other girls."

Ed smiled warmly at me, his eyes glinting with pride. "No, you are most certainly not like other girls. You've always been direct, headstrong, and respectful. I've always appreciated that about you." His gaze lingered for a moment, then he sat up and took a breath. "I tell you what. I can't stand the idea of you fretting away at the library. Why don't I send my aide to the courthouse to do a little digging on your behalf? We'll get together at the end of the week to go over it. Sound good?" Ed put back on his glasses and dragged his overstuffed calendar book off his desk and into his lap. He clicked his tongue as he flipped through the pages. He paused on one and stabbed it with his finger. "How about this Saturday? The wife will be at a women's charity event, and I'll be desperate for someone to make me a proper meal." I blinked, wondering how I was going to make dinner while plaster dust was still settling into every crevice of my kitchen. "I'm kidding, sweetheart. I know what your kitchen must look like. I'll bring dinner. You like Italian, right?"

"Right," I said, surprised that he knew my favorite food, but then again, he did pay my bills. He had probably surmised that Carlito's—my most frequent expense during college—was not a salon.

"Great, it's a date." Ed cuffed me gently on the back and then pressed against it to usher me up in a not-so-subtle hint to get out because he had work to do. "Twice in one week. The town will be talking," he said as he guided me to the door of the office.

I tried to laugh at his joke, but I wondered if the town *would* be talking. The fact that his wife was out of town would make it seem more lurid. I hadn't exactly stopped by with the intention of getting more time alone with him. I'd only wanted his advice on how to look up the history of the house. Apparently, his aide would handle that. I wondered how she would feel about doing my dirty work for me.

As I left Ed's office, I considered going back home, but I wasn't ready to face renovations or poltergeists yet.

The Cold Case

"Hi," I said to Officer Higgs when he arrived at the front desk following my request.

"Hi." He smiled back at me in that perfect way men do when they are being genuinely friendly. It made me hate the ring on his left hand even more. "What can I do for you?"

"I was wondering if you could tell me who this bullet went through before it ended up in my wall." I raised the bullet to show him.

If I had asked any other policeman, they would have rolled their eyes and walked away. Higgs, however, let out a breathy chuckle and nodded for me to follow him back to his desk.

Twenty minutes later, Higgs slammed a file down in front of me. I looked up at him, and he nodded. "I'm pretty sure that's the murder victim you're looking for. Annette Pratt. Shot and killed by her husband in 1943."

I thumbed through the file, looking at the old black-and-white crime scene photos. I was surprised at how discomforting they looked, even without the telltale red of bloodshed. "Why did he kill her?"

"Who knows? It's always an affair though, isn't it? He killed himself right after, so there was no chance to even incarcerate the bastard."

I grimaced, thinking that death was its own punishment, but there were still people who believed in happily ever after for the dead. From what I had been exposed to so far, there was no guarantee heaven would be your destination. You might get stuck on Earth—talking to a necromancer like me. How much would that suck?

I turned a page in the file and saw the male suspect/victim lying dead on the floor of the kitchen with a gunshot wound to the head. Omer Pratt. I analyzed his features closely. Could this be him? Could this be the dark shadow that has infested my house? Hibernated for years only to arise the moment a necromancer was within reach to torment? Was this the evil Genie and Brant felt inside my house?

"He beat the crap out of her, shot her, and then put one in his head. I'm sure that bullet you have is the one that went through her." Higgs sat down in the chair next to his desk that was meant for his guest. "What are you getting yourself into, Tori?"

I huffed out a breath. "I'm trying to figure out who's haunting me," I said with a half-smile, even though I was fully serious. I wasn't sure why the identity of the shadow man was so important, but maybe if I knew his name, I could try to communicate with him. Talk him into leaving my house. I was certain it was a ridiculous plan, but I had to try something.

Higgs didn't quite smile back. He nodded and turned his attention to another officer passing by. "How are you doing up there?" he asked when he had the all clear.

"I'm not stir-crazy yet, if that's what you're asking." Higgs nodded, but he still looked a little concerned. "Hey, I don't suppose you know this, but were my parents ever brought up on charges of child abuse?"

Higgs furrowed his brow. "Not that I know of—nothing on paper, anyway. Why?"

"I heard some rumors about bruises and abuse. I don't really remember anything of that nature."

"Mmm." Higgs shifted uncomfortably and glanced around the room. "Listen, Tori, I didn't want to say anything the other day because I thought this was a passing phase for you, but there is something you should know."

"About what?"

"About your father." Higgs leaned forward, resting his elbows on the corner of the desk. "A few days before your parents died, they had a party. There were twenty or so people at the house. Everybody was pretty drunk. It was a boisterous kind of event. The thing is, after the fire, a man who'd attended that party came forward and reported that Mark and Cassandra had been arguing several nights earlier. He said Mark had threatened to kill her."

I swallowed hard, trying to reconcile that statement with the man everyone described to me. As if it wasn't bad enough thinking of my sweet, gentle mother as the whore of Harold, but now my loving, doting father was an abusive beast. It didn't make any sense to me, unless the picture being painted for me was gilded by Ed's guilt.

"It doesn't really matter, because the fire was always inexplicable. Whatever happened between your parents had nothing to do with that fire." Higgs rested his hand over mine. "I know that isn't the answer you were looking for."

It wasn't the answer I was looking for, but maybe it was the answer I needed. My mother had appeared to me once as a burned corpse. Perhaps my father had appeared to me as well, but I hadn't recognized him. Was the dark shadow man haunting me my father? Had his anger in life bound him to the house?

I closed the file and slipped my hand out from under his. "Thank you for your help, Officer Higgs."

"Danny, and you're welcome." He once again gave me a genuine smile. The warmth it offered made me want to curl up at his feet like a cat in front of a fireplace.

As I left the police station, I couldn't help but think about the many disappointing men in my life. My father had not been the man I'd pictured him to be. Ed was not the man I daydreamed him to be. Even Brant was stomping all over my expectations—premature as they were.

With each new bad memory being uncovered, it was hard to deny that Brant and I might not have been destined for a happily ever after. With so much bad history between us, it was even clouding my attraction to him.

Maybe Brant was right. Maybe Lane was the man for me.

Regardless of whether he was or wasn't, I felt compelled to give it a try—at least for Brant's sake. After all, his visions were never wrong.

The Revenge

By the time I reached the furniture store, I was not only looking forward to asking Lane out; the prospect of doing it right in front of Brant delighted me. Revenge was not my usual strategy for getting a man's attention, but I was too mad to be thinking rationally, let alone maturely. If Brant was going to trust his vision over his own heart, then he could see his self-fulfilling prophecy coming to life before his very eyes.

I entered the store and saw Brant just ahead of me. He was staring at me fearfully as I stomped down the center aisle of recliners. I headed right toward him, and he frantically made his excuses to the customer he was speaking with. He no doubt suspected I had arrived to make a scene, which I had, but not the one he expected from me. "Tori, what are you doing—?"

I brushed right past him, ignoring his question. He babbled something in my wake, but it was unintelligible anyway. I knew where I would find Lane without even asking—down at the far end of the building, standing by the coffee machine, eating donuts. There was nothing appealing about a man with no work ethic, even less when he had raspberry filling dribbled on the front of his shirt and powdered sugar on his mouth.

He was handsome in a boyish way, but I hadn't felt any particular attraction to him the first time we'd met. Even now, with a crooked smile on his face, laughing at his co-workers' jokes, I knew he wasn't for me, the way that I know I don't want sprinkles on my ice cream. It certainly isn't a distasteful addition to your ice cream and would make it look more appetizing, but some people just don't want sprinkles.

And Lane Hart was sprinkles.

"Lane!" My shout made him jolt to attention like he was in trouble for something. His eyes got big at first, then turned to tiny slits as he tried to figure out who I was. This was off to a great start.

"Tori?" he finally put two and two together as I reached him. "What are you doing—?"

I cut off his words in the same place as his brother's. However, this time it wasn't a dismissal that put him in a state of confusion. It was my lips.

It was childish, I supposed, to start a conversation with an open-mouthed, publicly inappropriate kiss, but I wanted to make it obvious to Brant that I was doing exactly what he wanted. Rather than mess around with awkward conversation and a coquettish dance, I decided to go for it and see what I really thought of Lane.

Naturally, I could hardly tell anything by a kiss with a near stranger. Initially, the taste of powdered sugar put me off, but then I could taste his minty toothpaste, which put him back in the plus column. I surprised him, and he even laughed into my mouth at first. His hands were tentatively holding my shoulders, waiting to rip me away at any moment, but of course, he hadn't. What man would?

Lane seemed to relax a little. His mouth got a little braver, accepting my kiss and even participating a little. I had to admit; it was a good kiss once he got into it. Nothing I would object to if it weren't for the wrong man being attached to the lips.

A low, rumbled harrumph sounded behind us, and Lane pushed me away. He licked his lips and looked behind me like a scolded child. "She kissed me, bro."

"Yes, I saw," Brant answered. I didn't want to turn around and look at him. I knew I had hurt him. I knew because I had hurt myself in the process. Even though he'd practically told me to do just this, I felt awful. I felt cheap and wrong and unloved.

I turned back to look at him and saw the despair in his eyes, even though he was glaring at me. He was clutching his clipboard hard against his chest, his knuckles turning white with the intensity of his grip. "Is there some reason you are making out with my brother in the store?" His voice was deceptively calm, almost indifferent, but I could see how anguished he was.

"I came here to ask him out on a date," I said.

"Is that so? Is this how you usually ask men out?"

"No, I'm usually more subtle, but that hasn't been working out for me lately, so I thought I would try a new approach."

"You want to go out with me?" Lane asked incredulously, obviously flattered.

"Well, you're the only other man I know in town."

"In your age bracket, anyway," Brant added. I knew he was referring to Ed and my empathy for his pain ebbed a little.

"I can't date you," Lane scoffed.

"Why not?" I whipped around, offended I was again being rejected again.

"That's like against the rules. It's like sloppy seconds."

"Watch it, Lane." Brant stepped forward, and his brother took a step back.

"Well, I thought you and she were... You said you two were hitting it off."

I looked at Brant, who wouldn't answer.

"We were," I said snidely. "Then we weren't. Oh well, guess it wasn't meant to be. Can't fight the future, right? Speeding train, blah, blah, blah."

Lane looked between us, trying to figure us out. "Look, I'm not going to date your ex, man."

"She's not my ex. We were never going out," Brant said. "You should go out on a date with her. She's beautiful, sexy, and intelligent. She's obviously a very good kisser. Why not get to know her better?"

"Are you seriously okay with this?" Lane asked.

Brant paused, trying to formulate the words since *yes* was probably not an accurate statement. "I think you and Tori would get along pretty well. If things work out, then so be it. If not, no harm done, right?"

Lane looked at me, frowning at me. "Do you really want to go out?"

I shrugged, having lost all my enthusiasm for hurting Brant. It wasn't really fair to Lane either, but I was certain he wouldn't be emotionally invested in me anytime soon. "We can catch up on old times."

"Okay, how 'bout Friday night?"

"See you then," I said curtly and walked away. I quickened my steps to the front entrance so I could get outside before the tears in my eyes overflowed.

The Date

U ntil Lane pulled up to his mother's house Friday night, I had not truly defined the word *awkward*. I looked out at the familiar drive and turned to question Lane. He was already hopping out of the car and bounding around to my door. He opened it and motioned for me to come out. "I thought we were going to dinner?" I asked.

"We are. This is my mom's house. You won't get a better meal in Harold than here."

"But this is a date."

"I know. I always bring my first dates here."

"Can I ask why?"

Lane sighed and raised his index finger. "One, my mom is a super cool lady, and if the girls don't like her, then..." Lane clicked his tongue and swiped his neck with his index finger. "Two." Lane continued to count off his reasons. "Girls like to know a guy is involved with his family. It shows commitment or something. Three, I am way more comfortable in this environment than in some stuffy restaurant. And four, my mom is a fantastic cook." Lane laced his fingers through mine and kicked the car door shut with his foot. He looked around and leaned in a little closer. "And just between you and me, my mother doesn't charge me for dinner, and her liquor cabinet is always full." He winked at me and gave me a broad, toothy smile.

I couldn't help but smile back at him, even though he was basically saying he was too cheap to take his dates out to a restaurant for the first date. I had to admit he did have a certain charm about him. Goofy, but endearing. That was something, at least.

Lane entered the house, announcing his presence with a loud "hello." I had almost forgotten about the definition of awkward until Genie came around the corner from the kitchen. Her open-mouthed smile dipped a little when her eyes hit me. "Tori?" She looked behind us, no doubt searching for Brant or Lane's actual date.

"Oh, good, you remember her. Tori, this is my mother, Genevieve Hart. You can call her Genie, though. My mom actually used to babysit you."

"Not exactly, dear." Genie glanced down at our linked hands. She frowned at me, worry deepening the wrinkles on her forehead. "We've been over all that already. She stopped by with Brant the other day."

"Oh, great, then we can skip all the boring getting-to-know-you conversation stuff." Lane headed into the living room, leaving me with his mother. "Where's my beer, old man?" Lane mockingly scolded his father, who barely acknowledged his request except to point toward the kitchen.

"Tori, dear, what's going on? Why are you on a date with Lane? What happened between you and Brant?"

I felt the sting of embarrassment grip me, and I felt like crying on the woman's shoulder and begging her to fix everything for me. *Make your son love me. Make him be normal.* "I think that's a question you should ask Brant."

"All right." She waved me in and as we emerged from behind the lattice divider, Mr. Hart jumped to his feet. "Rex, this is Tori Blake, Lane's date. You remember her mother, Cassandra. She was my friend back in the old days."

"Nice to meet you, Tori." Rex was a tall man, but he had a slight hunch in his back. His eyes were deeply wrinkled, revealing his age to be that of a fifty-something man, not quite as young as his wife, or at least not as disguised. His dark brown hair was thin and lay flat on his head. Much like his sons, he had handsome features and a warm smile.

"And you, Mr. Hart."

"Oh, heck, call me Rex." He shook my hand gently, his eyes catching on mine as he examined my face. He glanced back at his wife. She mouthed and motioned something behind my head, and Mr. Hart's eyes lit with acknowledgment. "Yes, now I remember you, dear. You...ah...your mother—used to come here and visit my Genie. Those two girls were thick as thieves and twice as ornery." Rex released my hand and shook a finger at his wife. "I came home on more than one occasion and found them both drunk on the patio, giggling like schoolgirls. Meanwhile, the oven was empty, and so was my stomach. I had a good mind to separate them, but it didn't take more than a minute between the two of them and they had me drinking a martini and ordering out for pizza." Rex smiled at Genie, and she smiled back.

"Your mother was a good addition to our family. She was missed dearly when she passed." Mr. Hart patted my back and, to my surprise, a little moisture bloomed in my eyes. I was sure it had nothing to do with my mother, and more to do with someone speaking so fondly of her. The rumors of her infidelity had put me off the path of trying to remember her, but it was nice to know some people had good memories of her as well.

"Thank you, Mr. Hart."

"Rex, I insist."

"Thank you, Rex."

"Hey, Tori, come check this out," Lane called me over, and I excused myself. "Have a seat." Lane thumped the spot beside him in the oversized recliner he was lounging in. I calculated the space it offered the two of us and determined there was no way to get in without squishing myself beside him. Adding to the weirdness of the evening, I had decided to wear a low-cut top.

He motioned for me to jump in again, so I just toppled myself over the arm and slumped up against him. He smiled over at me. "Starting to feel more like a date already." He lifted the control pad from his lap and handed it to me. "Okay, this is forward, this is your brakes..." Lane continued to explain the details of my controller and how to get the maximum speed for my car to win the race. After a few practice sessions, I started to feel like I was on a date.

With an eighth-grader.

The Video Game

"**N**o!" I screamed louder than necessary as my wheels spun out beneath me. "You jerk!" I elbowed Lane beside me, and he laughed. I no longer cared about the space on the chair. We were both hunched over on the edge of the seat anyway, each of us trying to outrun the other car on the screen.

"I told you to watch out for my missiles."

"Lane, you two finish up," Genie hollered over at us.

"Yeah, Mom!" he yelled back.

"Oh, yeah? Try this on for size." I shot a missile of my own and disrupted Lane's progress. I squealed as I passed him on the track. "Take that from the girl who only started playing twenty minutes ago."

"Oh, I can still beat you," Lane boasted. "I have super-speed." He pressed his button, and his side of the screen went into a blur as he rocketed past all the competing cars, including mine, and finished the race uncontested.

"What?" I screeched at the words appearing on my half of the screen. *Loser.* "No way! You cheated!" I gave Lane a playful shove.

"No, I didn't." He laughed at me again. "Just because you used up all your power plays in the first five minutes."

Lane poked my side, making me flinch. "Oh, that's right. I forgot you were ticklish."

"No, tickling is for emergencies only." I laughed and pushed his hand away. He poked me again, and I tried unsuccessfully not to flinch. "Let's play another one."

"No, I think I found a new game to play. *Torture Tori*." Lane's smirk widened, and he jumped out of the chair. He whipped back around and started tickling my stomach. I squealed and laughed, barely able to breathe. I felt ridiculously juvenile, but at the same time I couldn't remember laughing so hard or so much. Lane certainly wasn't boyfriend material, but he ranked pretty high in the annoying older brother category.

"Lane!" Genie scolded, and we both looked up to see what punishment we were about to receive. Genie was standing in the living room with a perturbed frown on her face. I couldn't blame her for being mad. Only a few steps away in the kitchen, she was slaving away to make a feast for both of us, and we hadn't even offered to set the table. Instead, we were acting like children and wrestling on her furniture. I should have been making polite conversation and complimenting her interior design style.

However, it wasn't until I glanced back to the foyer that I saw perhaps the real reason for her ire. Brant had arrived and had just come around the decorative divider. He was staring at Lane and me, examining our interaction with the critical eye of a jealous ex—or almost-ex.

I felt mortified, especially because my shirt had ridden up on my back as I'd tried to squirm out of the chair. Lane was still straddling me, hands on my bare stomach, both of us panting and only temporarily ceasing our frolicsome laughter to find out what his mother wanted.

"Dinner is ready. Why don't you two put away your toys and wash up?"

Genie's words hit me like a brick. I was certain she had meant it sardonically, but it was no doubt something she had told us in the past, perhaps during one of our playdates. The memories of toys, candy, and Lane's annoying airplane noises flashed into my mind. Genie's younger self stood over me and repeated the same words, but this time with a cheerful smile.

In the memory, I looked behind her to my mother and asked permission to play a few more minutes. My mother dipped her brow at me and shook her head. *"What did I say about Mrs. Hart's house?"* she asked.

"Mrs. Hart's house, Mrs. Hart's rules," I repeated the strict no-lip policy my mother had enforced during our visits.

Genie dipped her brow at me, and I cleared my throat. I hadn't meant to say it aloud, nor had I meant to make it sound like a sarcastic response to her request. "Sorry, Mrs. Hart, we were just playing." I adjusted my shirt and scooted myself back into the chair out from under Lane.

"Well, as thrilled as I am that you two have finally learned to play together, I would prefer to eat dinner while it is hot." Genie headed back into the kitchen.

Lane offered me a hand up, and I took it. However, when we were upright, he didn't let go of my hand. "What are you doing here, Brant?"

"Mother invited me to dinner. She said, we needed to talk."

"Hmm, she didn't mention it to us," Lane said.

"She called a bit ago. I hadn't left town yet, so I took her up on the offer. I didn't realize you were bringing Tori here. I thought you were going out on a date."

"This *is* the date, bro."

"Video games and tickle monsters?" Brant raised his eyebrows, unimpressed by Lane's romantic efforts.

"Tori's having fun, aren't you, Tori?" He looked at me for the answer, and I smiled. "You don't have to lie for him. He dumped your ass."

I cleared my throat and nodded. "Yes, I'm having fun."

Brant looked at me, his eyes revealing how hurtful my words were. "Apparently I was right about you two."

"Look, bro, I don't get this. First you wanted her, then you didn't, but now you're critiquing my choice of date. I don't know if you've noticed, but she was laughing and smiling before you got here, and now she's not. So, either be nice or back off, but get your sour grapes out of my face." Lane walked away, tugging me along with him. I didn't bother to look at Brant's reaction. I was on a date with his brother. Brant was no longer my concern.

The Ouija Board

G enie had elected to have dinner alfresco. The patio table was situated under a pergola just off the house, in view of the yard. Large brown striped cushions equipped the chairs, and they were even more comfortable than the recliner inside, although it helped that I had the whole chair to myself.

Lane sat beside me, while Brant sat across from me, next to his mother. I had hoped he would sit across from his brother, but there was plenty of room for glares between them no matter where he sat.

The first few minutes of the meal passed without incident. The food was passed around with pleases and thank yous interspersed properly. When my plate was full, I tasted each component in turn. I was relieved that Lane had not oversold his mother's talent. Genie could have opened a restaurant with her green beans alone.

"Mrs. Hart, this is delicious," I said after a boisterous groan of approval. "I can see where Brant got his talent for cooking."

Lane looked up at Brant. "You don't cook."

"Sure I do."

"What, grilled cheese?"

"Believe it or not, *bro*, I do manage to feed myself seven days a week. We can't all run home to mommy when we are hungry," Brant mumbled before taking a sip of his wine.

"Well, you can sign me up for a standing invitation, Mrs. Hart," I said, eager to change the subject. "I don't get a lot of home-cooked meals."

"Oh, Mom loves cooking. Don't you, Ma?" Lane poked his fork toward his mother, who nodded and smiled as she finished chewing her bite. "I used to bring my friends over all the time because they said my mom was the best cook in town. My friends' moms always made stuff from a box or used the microwave. Not my mom. She likes home cooking. Right, Ma?"

Genie winked at Lane as she sucked a piece of food from her teeth. I noted that she wasn't technically agreeing with him.

"I say used to because they stopped coming over when I was about nine." I glanced at Lane to see whether or not this was a touchy subject. He was staring at Brant. "Gosh, what was it that stopped them from coming over?"

Brant slowed his movements, staring down at the center of the table. Genie set down her fork and glanced between the men. Mr. Hart seemed oblivious to it all, his appetite unaffected by the tension.

"Oh, that's right. My big bro had a hissy fit in front of them."

Brant grabbed his wine and took a long drag, finishing the glass in one swig. "Excuse me, Mother." He stood up. "Whatever you wanted to speak to me about will have to wait for another night."

"Come on, bro, I was just getting to the good part." Brant paused as if he knew leaving wouldn't stop his brother from telling the story. "So, Mom comes out all dressed in her wicky—wacky—what is it, Ma?"

"Wiccan, darling."

"Yeah, Wiccan robe. You see, Mom's into all that natural shit. Earth power, love goddess, mother nature. She likes to play with aromatherapy and do yoga." I glanced at Genie to see what she thought of this interpretation of her craft. She smiled congenially at her son. Mr. Hart had no opinion on it other than to ask Brant to pour him more wine since he was up.

"It was getting close to Halloween. She thought, hey, why not give these boys a night to remember? So, she gets all dolled up and calls us all outside for a seance." Lane chuckled and leaned back from the table. Brant watched him carefully, ignoring the wine that was overflowing from his father's glass.

"Hey, easy, son. I want to drink it, not swim in it." Brant adjusted the bottle with barely a glance at his father.

"It's going super good," Lane continued. "We're all a bunch of tough guys, so none of us would say we were scared or anything. Moms got the Ouija board, the crystals, a lock of witches' hair, and some goat's liver she got from the butcher. She starts chanting, and we all join in."

I glanced at Genie, not liking the sound of this story. Had she really been using children to perform an actual seance? Judging by the tension sheeting off Brant's body, he didn't like the story either. Especially since he had lived it.

"I don't know what set Mr. Attitude off, but all of a sudden he comes home and sees us in the backyard playing the Ouija board and he flips out. He kicks the board. He rips our hands apart. Then he lays into Mom." Lane chuckles. "Now, mind you, I had seen Brant and Mom go at it before, but this was the first time I actually thought the cops were gonna get called. Of course, my friends are uncomfortable, so they all leave and never come back. Forget about sleepovers. Forget about girlfriends for the next six years too. Yeah, thanks for that, man." Lane raised his glass to toast his brother.

Brant stood stock-still, staring at his brother for a long moment. The fact that he wasn't jumping over the table to strangle him was impressive since he looked like murder was on his mind.

Brant shifted, making Genie shift her chair back. However, Brant didn't attack. He leaned over the table and spoke quietly to Lane. "What did the Ouija board say, Lane?"

Lane paused, then shook his head. "Hell if I know, I was on the far end."

"What did your friends say it said?" Brant asked.

"Brant, that's enough." Genie stood.

"It was enough five minutes ago, Mother, but you didn't stand up then, so sit back down."

"Brant," Rex scolded his son, but no one paid him any mind.

"If you are going to tell the story, Lane, then tell the whole story. What did the planchette spell out?"

Lane snorted derisively. "We were just messing around. She was giving us a good scare, that's all."

"Of *course,* that was all she was doing. Mom would never use innocent children to activate a spell she couldn't perform on her own."

"Christ, Brant, you always took this shit so seriously." Lane turned to me. "He really thought Mom was a witch, and that she was gonna accidentally unleash hell on us with her spells."

"Obviously, he was wrong," I said to Lane. "Your mom is certainly a kitchen witch, but that's all. Right, Mrs. Hart?" I looked at Genie. She smiled and shrugged, once again neither admitting nor denying anything. I glanced at Brant before looking back at Lane. "But I am curious. What did the board spell out? Was it a name or something?"

Lane shook his head. "No, nothing like that." Lane glanced at his mom, then back to me. He shrugged. "The guys closest to it said it spelled out, 'I will kill the children.'" I was certain my eyes were as wide as saucers, but I contained the gasp that should have followed that revelation. "Scary stuff, huh? Mom was the best at Halloween pranks. Right, Ma?"

"That's right, sweetheart," Genie said.

I looked at Brant, and he looked at me. I couldn't imagine a world where a son had to prevent his mother from performing dangerous spells. Spells that might summon something that could ultimately kill children. I wasn't sure what had happened that night so many years ago, but I was certain Brant had done the right thing by stopping it.

"How about some dessert, Genie?" Mr. Hart clapped his hands together, disrupting the moment and returning us to the all-important topic of food.

The Doubt

I sat on the patio with Lane, sipping coffee and watching the sun go down. Genie and Brant were inside the patio doors arguing about something. I wasn't sure what specifically, but since they kept looking out at me, I imagined it might have something to do with me. Perhaps Genie wasn't happy about my sudden changeover to her other son. Neither was I.

It wasn't the best date I had ever been on, but then again, it wasn't the worst. Lane, on the other hand, seemed oblivious to our lack of connection. "So, do you want to go back to my place?" he asked, tracing his finger along my arm.

I laughed and shook my head. "Do you have more video games there?"

"No, but I do have a bed."

I pinched my lips together, containing my smile. "Lane, I had fun tonight, but I don't think we are a good fit."

"What? Why? You're hot, I'm hot, bam!" He smacked his hands together.

"Okay, think about it this way. We go to your place, we have sex—"

"Okay!" He jumped up, ready to run for the door.

"Then what?" I added.

"What do you mean?"

"I mean, what do we talk about?"

"We've been talking all night."

"No, we've been playing video games and you've been picking on Brant all night."

"Is this about Brant?"

"No, but it is about the fact that you and I have nothing in common."

"Why did you go out with me then? Was it just to make Brant jealous?"

"No, actually, it was to make him happy. Or prove him wrong. I don't even know. I think he thought because we were childhood friends that he might be stepping on your toes if he dated me before you had a chance to get to know me as an adult."

"Oh." Lane frowned. "I don't know why he thought that. I hated you when we were kids."

I blinked in surprise. "You did?"

"Yeah, you would scream at me to stop pulling your hair and then hit me or pinch my arm."

"I did?" I smiled behind my hand.

"Yeah, like all the time. Mom would get so mad at me. The stupid thing was, I never even pulled your hair."

I laughed. "I'm so sorry. If it makes you feel any better, Brant was the one pulling my hair. He wanted to pester me, and he liked getting you in trouble too."

"What? That jackass!" Lane jumped over my extended feet and ran into the house. He ripped open the patio door and pointed an accusing finger at Brant. "You son of a bitch! I owe you for two years' worth of pinches!"

"What?" Brant questioned the statement, but he was already starting to smile. "Hey, you should know better than to pull a girl's hair. That's not nice."

Lane roared and charged at his brother. Brant caught him around the back and flipped him to the floor. Before long, they were wrestling on the kitchen floor, and it was all Genie could do to get out of the way without toppling over them.

I chuckled at their antics. Although they were still fighting, at least it was brotherly fighting, and it was only inadvertently because of me. As I looked over the garden in the dusking light, I noticed the pattern in the grass again. It was clearer in the soft, slanting light.

I stood and moved to the edge of the brick patio overlooking the lawn's mowing pattern. There was definitely a circle in the grass, but it didn't continue. Instead, the traditional pagan star sat at its center. I was certain Mr. Hart wouldn't have mowed the grass this way, but Genie might have put down fertilizer in those spots to make it invisible to the naked eye, but symbolic nonetheless.

I was curious why Mr. Hart said nothing about his wife's practices. Was he honestly oblivious, or did he just ignore them? I couldn't imagine practicing a type of faith without the consent or support of one's family. Brant seemed to be the only one who believed in his mother's power, or in magic in general. And even though he possessed his own clairvoyance—trusting it beyond all common sense—he still rejected his mother's use of magic.

Genie had clearly taken her spellcasting too far that Halloween. And if she was willing to do that, what other magic had she performed with my mother to back her up? Cass had supposedly been a powerful necromancer. Add that to a powerful Wiccan, and what do you get?

Nothing good. I was certain of that.

When Lane finished wrestling with his brother, I asked him to take me home. He dropped me off at home, and I immediately went upstairs to change into my pajamas. When the doorbell rang, I assumed it was Lane, trying for one last effort at a goodnight kiss. I was certain he understood my motives for not wanting to pursue our relationship. I couldn't say I disliked him the way I had originally thought, but I definitely couldn't see a future with him. At best, we could be friends.

"No means no, Lane." I ran down the stairs and swung the door open wide. Brant stood on the porch staring back at me, his eyes panicked and worried. "Brant? What are you doing here?" He glanced around the house before returning his gaze to me. Before I could ask him again, he dove forward, cupped my face in his hands and brought his lips down on mine.

The shock of his attack left me backpedaling, but his grip on me kept me from falling backward. He slowed his kiss from a ravaging attack to a slow-progressing seduction. When his lips finally fell away and we were both breathless, he looked at me in earnest. "Choose me, Tori."

I opened my mouth to tell him I already had once, but he pulled away and walked out. I stepped onto the porch and watched him jog to his car. He paused to look at me one last time and got into the vehicle. If I had had any sense in my head, I would have run after him and tackled him so he couldn't leave, but I didn't.

The File

Ed Ladner had dressed down for his evening in with me. Although dressed down for him meant a sweater vest with a pair of slacks. I smiled as he brought in his briefcase in one hand and a large basket full of food hanging from his other arm.

"What on earth did you bring?" I asked, taking the heavy basket from him. "This feels like a meal for six."

"Ah, I wasn't sure what you had for flatware, so I brought plates and glasses and...well, everything."

"Always prepared, aren't you, Ed?" I set down the basket in the living room to take a peek inside.

"Of course."

I frowned. When he said he brought plates and glasses, he meant good china and wine glasses. "Oh, Ed, you shouldn't have done all this. I put my dining room table in storage."

"That's why it's in a picnic basket."

"You really want to sit on my living room floor and drink wine?"

"Of course." Ed bit his lip. "Or we could sit on that lovely sofa and use the basket as a table."

"Sounds perfect."

Ed situated himself on the sofa and brought out the first course, served on his glass plates. I knew the glass would be easier to eat on, but I felt bad that he had to take the dishes home to wash them since my kitchen plumbing was offline. After he served me, he brought out a candle and lit it with a lighter he had stowed in his pocket.

"Seriously? You even brought a candle?"

"Of course," we both said in unison and laughed.

"As eager as I am to dig into this salad, I'm wondering whether you remembered the reason for this meeting." Ed narrowed his eyes at me and tipped his head at me. "Of course you did. What did your aide find?"

"I'll tell you between courses. I'm famished." Ed and I polished off our salads and started nibbling on the mushroom cap appetizers. Once his initial appetite was satiated, he looked around the room and pointed to the crown molding. "They don't make houses like this anymore. I know everyone says that, but it's so true. The detail that goes into these places, and most of the time they sell for half the price of a new house. It's a shame. I'm so glad you decided to keep it."

"I think you thought I was crazy when I first mentioned it, but I'm glad you approve now," I said, taking a sip of wine.

He looked back at me. "My approval means a lot to you, doesn't it?" I looked up at him like a deer in the headlights. "It's okay, I don't mind being your sounding board. Actually, I like it. I think when you were younger, it was a bit trying."

"Mmm, I did call you quite a bit in the early days, didn't I?"

"It was understandable. You had just lost your parents. I was really the only familiar face in your life. Had it not been for the will, I might have been able to help you more."

"What?"

"Oh, I don't know." Ed shook his head. "You know when something tragic like that happens, you have a tendency to want to reach out and help. Even if you can't or shouldn't."

"Sure."

"Well, among my other duties, I entertained the idea of adopting you."

"Really?"

"Only for a millisecond. I was in no position to be a father. If I had been, I would have had kids already. Truthfully, there were a lot of petitions for custody after the fire. Brant's mother, Genie, wanted to adopt you. Even some people who barely knew you offered to foster you. It was humbling, really. You never know how a community can rally until something truly tragic happens."

"But they were denied because of the will?"

"Yes." Ed gave me a somber smile. "It was well written. No loopholes. It was designed to protect you from persons seeking monetary gain from your custody."

"Is that why my foster parents never adopted me?"

"Yes, but they petitioned many times. They loved you a great deal, you know."

"Yeah, I know." I nodded introspectively. I hadn't been the easiest child to raise. I had been extremely fearful of my new environment, and it had taken my foster parents months to get me to trust them. I'd never understood why, since they had been perfectly civil people. They had never been abusive, and I could count on my hand the number of times they'd raised their voices at me. With so many lacking memories, I should have been a blank slate for them. But something about what happened to me in that fire had made me reject everyone around me. I never wanted to get too close...to anyone.

"Now, about this house." Ed reached down for his briefcase and brought it onto his lap. He clicked open the clasps and lifted the lid on his stash of documents. He pulled out a small file folder marked with my name and address. "I don't know if this particular ghost story will keep you up at night, but it certainly will me. But you were right about that bullet."

"Oh?" I feigned ignorance rather than spoil that I had already solved the mystery of the bullet in the wall.

"A couple of people were shot and killed in this house back in the forties."

I glanced at his notes. "Who else lived here?"

"Ah, after that, the house was sold to a young couple. They had a child, but she died on the property at age nine. Some kind of accident involving the bluff back there."

My mind immediately went to Anna Bella. Though I no longer doubted she was a ghost, it was somehow vindicating to know she had been a real person. I wasn't imagining it all.

"They sold the house shortly after her death. It went to a man by the name of Charles Victor. He was unmarried with no children. He lived in the house for the remainder of his years. Oh yeah, I remember this story from when I was young. Charles died in this house, but since he didn't have any family, his body wasn't discovered until two years later."

"Eww." I grimaced. "How does that happen?"

"As I recall, Charles was a pretty unlikable guy. Most people didn't mind not seeing him around town. In those days, the mail got dropped through the door slot. His bills were drafted until the account went dry. It didn't take much investigation to figure out he wasn't cashing his Social Security checks."

"How did he die?"

"Rest assured, the coroner ruled it a natural death. No foul play. Charles was an obese man, so they suspected a heart attack finally did him in."

My mind wandered back to the first vision I'd had of the large man tromping and wheezing through my house. Was that Charles Victor? Could he be my dark shadow as well? His body didn't fit, but perhaps it didn't have to. Was that darkness the manifestation of his anger? If I had been left to rot in my home for two years, I might be inclined to haunt the future inhabitants.

Ed handed me the file, and I skimmed through the pages that included printouts from local newspapers. "Your aide was very thorough," I said.

"Always," Ed said proudly.

I found a wedding photo of Mr. and Mrs. Pratt. It had obviously been taken long before presumed infidelity had driven a wedge between them.

I paused at the next newspaper article, which discussed the tragic death of Anna Bella Richards. Under the graceless headline of "Child Falls to Death," was a photo showing a young couple with their daughter. According to the cake in the picture, Anna was just turning nine. I cringed as I considered how traumatic it would be to lose a child at such a young age. It was hard enough losing parents, and I wasn't even reasonably sure my situation counted as grief since my memories of them had been erased before I could properly mourn them.

I didn't think someone could photograph orneriness, but I could see sinister little thoughts brewing in Anna's head behind her smile. She was determined to disobey her mother and twirl to her heart's content anywhere she pleased. It almost made me laugh. Though her demise was not funny, there was a certain irony in that stubborn little girl standing watch over the ridge like a mother hen, clucking at anyone stupid enough to get too close.

"Can I keep this to look through the rest later?" I asked.

"Of course, it's all yours."

I closed the file and set it aside. "Thank you for doing that and thank your aide for her hard work."

"You're welcome, and I will. To tell you the truth, though, I thought you'd be more excited about your murder mystery being solved."

"I am. They just weren't the answers I was looking for. I was kind of thinking: House Built on Old Indian Burial Ground." I waved my hand in the air, mocking the headline news I had hoped to find.

"Is this about the intruder the police didn't believe was here?"

"Sort of. I thought there might be a pattern of deaths in the house. It wouldn't explain everything, but at least I could blame it on some supernatural curse."

"Oh, Tori, I wish I could make sense of all this for you. The fire was so abnormal, I know. It was bound to stir concerns about curses and bad juju, but the reality is, the car caught fire. Your parents died. You survived. And that is all that matters." Ed reached across the couch and squeezed my hand.

"Cars don't just catch fire, Ed. And even if it did, you're telling me all four doors locked and wouldn't open? All four windows were rolled up and wouldn't roll down?"

Ed grimaced. "Tori, I beg you. Don't go down this road."

"What road?"

"The road where you ask so many questions that eventually you get the answers you need, but don't want. In the end, they will still be gone."

"This isn't about them anymore. There is a huge chunk of my life missing. You have no idea what that feels like."

Ed shifted and narrowed his eyes at me. "I have no idea what you're going through? Of course I do. I have been on this path with you every step of the way since it happened. Or did you once again forget the midnight phone calls? The night terrors?" I looked away, embarrassed by my pathetic history. "How many times did I fly out in those early days to explain the bruises that were being blamed on your foster parents?"

Bruises? My mind flashed back to the early days of foster care when I would wake up after a fitful sleep with scratches and bruises all over my body. I had forgotten all about it. Apparently, my so-called abuse had continued after my parents were out of the picture. Even after Brant. Did that mean I had been doing it to myself all along? My night terrors must have started before the fire. However, my night terrors were always a playback of my parents' death. If the terrors had started before the fire—what had been spurring me into irrational, violent fear then?

"Christ, Tori, who did you call when you...?" Ed shook his head and looked away. "I'm sorry. You're right. I have no idea what you've been through. If I had, I would have been able to do more than be a sounding board for you."

"No, you're right. You helped me a lot. I didn't mean you don't understand my situation, just that...fourteen years later, I still have questions, and no one seems to have answers, even though nearly the entire town witnessed the incident."

"Tori, I hate to remind you of this, but the only person who knows what happened that day is you. If your memories haven't come back by now, I doubt they ever will."

"I know, but I have to try."

"And if you don't like what you find?"

"I want the truth. No matter what the truth is."

"All right." Ed sighed, resigned to being outvoted.

"Ed," I whispered. "Can I ask you some personal questions?"

Ed grimaced and put down his briefcase. "Uh-oh, that sounds serious."

"I'm concerned my mother may have had an affliction that caused her philandering."

"What do you mean by an affliction?"

"I know this sounds strange, and I have virtually no proof to back up this statement, but what if my mother was...?" I debated telling him she might have been possessed. Even if he was open to the idea, it painted a rather morbid picture of his encounter with her. "What if she had a split personality?"

Ed shook his head. "I think you're reaching."

"No, I'm serious; just think about it. When you two had the affair—" Ed cleared his throat and shifted his gaze to the floor. "—was she acting like herself? Did she instigate the intimacy or did you?"

Ed shifted again. "Um...it was a long time ago, and I've spent every day since trying to forget about it."

"I understand, and I promise I'm not asking so I can lay blame or pass judgment. I only want to know whether this was a flirtation that turned into something more, or if it was a sudden change in character."

Ed scratched his head and relaxed into the couch. "It was sudden. I had been fighting with my wife on and off for a while. We were on the verge of divorce, but neither of us wanted to pull the trigger. No one wanted to be the asshole. I came by to talk to Mark. He wasn't home, but Cass could see I was upset, so she invited me in. We sat and talked about my problems for a bit, then she told me she had just the thing to make my sorrows go away." Ed barked out a laugh. "I thought she meant bourbon." Ed paused as he recalled the event. "She went into the kitchen for a little while and when she came back..." Ed glanced at me. "Are you sure you want to hear this?"

"*Want* is a strong word, but I do need to hear this."

"When she came back, her dress was sopping wet. I laughed at first and made a joke about her taking a shower in the kitchen sink. Then I noticed the fabric clinging to her body. She wasn't wearing any undergarments, and I could see...I could see through the wet fabric. I asked her what she was doing, and she said, 'I'm making you feel like a man again.'

"I told her I couldn't do that to Mark. I told her she was my friend and nothing more. I even got up to leave." Ed paused again as he thought about that. "She pushed me back down like I was a rag-doll. She climbed on top of me and... I'm sure you can imagine the rest. I'd like to say she forced me, but obviously there was participation on my end."

"What about after?" I asked almost clinically. Ed seemed even more disturbed by this question. "Please."

"When we were done, she got off me and started looking around like she was looking for something. She finally looked at me and burst into tears. I knew exactly how she felt. I had wanted to stop, but couldn't. I wanted to erase it, but I couldn't. It was the worst mistake of my life. Hers too, I think."

"Maybe she was a sex addict and couldn't control herself," I suggested.

"That's all well and good, but what was *my* excuse? The strange thing is, I had never cheated on my wife before that day, but after...I couldn't *stop* cheating. Took me years to get back on track with monogamy."

I considered that statement. If my mother had been possessed, as Mrs. Clark had suggested—presumably by the evil force lingering in my house—how did that affect the men my mother had slept with? Had my mother been spreading misery like an STD?

After dessert, Ed cleared our plates into the trash and piled them neatly back into his basket. I walked him to the door, and he gave me a chaste kiss on the cheek before leaving. It was nice to spend time with him outside of the office, to skip the superficial pleasantries and actually talk. He'd seemed more relaxed, even fun. I couldn't help but wonder what my life would have been like if he had raised me. What would life have been like if I had stayed in Harold instead of leaving? I was certain a lot of things would be different, including me.

The Will

My investigation of my parents' death had certainly taken a turn. As convinced as I was that a supernatural source had caused the fire, I still wanted to know who had been the guiding hand. Who was the dark figure residing in this house, influencing my mother—and possibly tormenting my dreams?

Charles Victor, the man left for dead for two years?

Omer Pratt, the angry wife-killer?

Whose soul had enough damage to transform a simple ghost into a poltergeist?

Or was this more than a house-haunting? Perhaps Mrs. Clark was right, and something had possessed my mother.

People had always described my mother as shy and soft-spoken. I couldn't imagine a change in her character that would have inspired her to behave so lewdly with Ed, or with any of the men she'd supposedly slept with.

From Ed's description, she had been strong enough to put him back on the couch. She'd forced herself into a position to negotiate with their bodies instead of their common sense. That was not the normal strength of a petite woman. Either Ed was exaggerating her strength, or something had been fueling her to an abnormal level.

Possibly the same something that had fueled a fire to 2800 degrees.

But if I was considering the notion of possession to describe my mother's behavior, then I doubted what had been controlling her had even been human.

Was it a demon? Some unholy creation born in darkness searching for someone to torment? If there were ghosts, then surely demons were not too far from the realm of believability. Could a necromancer speak to a demon the same as she did the dead?

Maybe not on her own. But maybe with the help of a witch.

I sat back into the cushions of my sofa thinking about the lengths Genie had gone to in order to summon the magic she wanted. She'd used Cass. She'd used her own son—and even other people's children. How far had Cass and Genie gone?

Who had they pissed off?

I noticed the file folder Ed had brought over the other night. I opened it back up and leafed through the latter portion I hadn't been through yet. Mortgage records, birth and death certificates, more articles and photos. Most everything was a photocopy, but there was an envelope marked with my name at the very back. I wondered why they separated it and sealed it. It almost looked like it didn't belong in the mix. If it hadn't had my name on it, I might have left it be and asked Ed about it later.

I pushed my finger through the paper fold, shredding the envelope open. I pulled out a thin stack of papers. They were photocopies as well, the original no doubt tucked in a file cabinet at Ed's office.

I stared down at the last will and testament of Cassandra and Mark Blake. I couldn't really believe what I was looking at. Was this a mistake? Clearly not, if my name was on it. Had Ed meant for me to see this, or was this his aide's doing? Had she slipped it in at the last second? But why?

I read through the odd language of legal jargon, trying to understand the specifics of my parents' wishes. There was a long list of details involving the estate and its belongings. Though my parents technically left me everything, there had been a lot of money to shuffle in order to care for me until I came of age. Ed was named my temporary guardian as well as my executor of my estate. Nothing new to me.

However, several crossed-out paragraphs in the will surprised me. Between the lines, I could see I had been meant to be adopted by Genie and Rex Hart and remain in the same school. A reasonable choice, since it would have kept me in a similar environment and with people I already knew. But why did they change it? If Genie and my mother were such good friends, why hadn't she become my foster mother?

I flipped through the pages, which explained what my parents wished regarding medical care should they be left in a vegetative state or rendered mentally incompetent due to an accident or disease. Besides being my temporary guardian, they also put Ed in charge of "pulling the plug" on their life support up until my twentieth birthday, after which I became their medical proxy. I thought it strange they didn't choose eighteen, since I would have been the legal next of kin and an adult. However, I also couldn't imagine being responsible for choosing the date of my parents' death at any age. Having gone through a set of surprise deaths twice in my life, I was certain having a chance to say goodbye sounded better than it actually was.

I flipped to the last page, which contained two hand-written paragraphs. The first was a fancy script describing the next hand-written statement to be a legal addendum to the will and testament. The next passage revised the exclusions in the document.

In the next paragraph, scribbled, slanted penmanship demanded my adoption be prohibited by any family, friend, or foster parent for ten years—effectively the duration of my childhood. I was not to live in the home of my birth, nor return to it for any visits. My foster parents were strictly prohibited from bringing me back here.

Ed had never mentioned that I was forbidden from returning to the house. Now that I was an adult, the restrictions had been lifted, but he must have considered it an odd amendment to the will. No doubt my mother had already known the nature of the house when she wrote this and wanted me as far away as possible.

The scribbled words got bigger and the ink lines became thicker as if the hand writing it was moving faster, exuding urgency in the poor penmanship. My brow crumpled as I reread the next statement three times.

Immediately following my evacuation from the home, the property was to be burned to the ground.

I looked at the four signatures at the bottom of the written page: my mother, my father, Ed, and a name I vaguely recognized as a member of Ed's staff. Although Genie had been the fourth witness on the original version of the document, she was not present for this amendment. I sat back and stared at the signatures. All were dated on the same day. The day before the fire.

I don't know how, but my mother had known she was going to die. Or at the very least, she'd felt as if she were in imminent danger. Her spells were no longer keeping the monsters at bay, and she wanted to keep me safe.

Despite her lacking signature, I was certain Genie would have known about this amendment. She knew more about my mother than anyone, but for some reason, she was only giving me pieces of their history.

The only question was whether she was hedging to protect me from the truth, or lying by omission to absolve herself.

The Echo

"I need answers, and I'm not leaving until I get them," I said when Genie answered the door. She stared at me blank-faced. The smile that had formed when she saw me fell flat. "I know you are trying to protect me from my mother's infidelity, but I need to know what happened to her. I need to know why she changed her will the day before she died."

Genie's expression changed to stern disappointment before she turned around and went back inside. "Come on in," she called back to me.

I followed her into the kitchen, where I found Brant sitting at her island, midway through a sandwich.

"Brant, what are you doing here?" I asked, surprised I hadn't noticed his car outside.

He swallowed his bite. "I'm on my lunch break. It's not an infrequent event."

"Oh," I said, feeling a little stupid.

"What are *you* doing here?" he asked me, but turned his attention to his mother. She waved her hands and shook her head, refusing to be accused of a secret meeting.

"She didn't know I was coming."

"I think Tori was hoping I would have more answers for her about her parents."

"You don't? You didn't tell me she had changed her will. You didn't tell me about the bruises my teacher found on me. I was starting to have nightmares like her, wasn't I?"

Genie shifted uncomfortably before nodding.

"That's why I was banned from that house. I was a necromancer too. He found a way to get to me, and she wanted me away from Harold to keep him from using me like he was using her. Even if that meant uprooting my entire life."

"Yes, I think that is the bulk of it."

"He isn't a ghost, is he?" Genie shook her head. "What is he?"

"I don't know. I'm not sure I want to know. That type of evil doesn't require a title."

"The devil?"

Genie perked her brow. "No, I think the devil prefers more pious prey. Your mother wasn't exactly in that category. I think *demon* is a good word for him, though. Something dark and angry that goes bump in the night. Something that feeds on fear. Something that shouldn't exist."

"Is there any way to...get rid of him? For good?"

Genie took a long breath and turned to look out her kitchen window. "Until I walked into that house again, I thought he *was* gone."

"You think my return to Harold rekindled him?"

Genie sighed and wrung her hands together. "Tori, I really don't know. I wish I had more answers for you, but the only one that can help you is long dead."

I nodded. "Well, then it's a good thing I'm a necromancer."

Genie looked at Brant and then me. "I don't think it works that way."

"It would if you helped me."

"No, I don't think so. The only thing I can do is help you have another vision. An echo, like you saw the other day."

"Okay, let's do that," I said eagerly.

"Mom." Brant stared at his mother. "No."

Genie looked between us. Two hopeful faces, pleading for opposite outcomes. She finally caved and turned to me. "I'll get my coffer."

When Genie returned, we situated ourselves in the living room on the floor. I got a distinct sense from Brant that what we were about to undertake was not only unwise, but possibly even dangerous. And yet, Genie seemed at ease with the idea, excited even. She rattled around in her trunk, pulling out candles, talismans, and a large pedestal bowl. She set the bowl down between us and smiled at it. She rubbed her finger along the rim, then suddenly snapped out of her reverie to grab a long purple scarf out of the trunk. "Almost forgot." She grimaced as if she had made a major Wiccan faux pas and handed me one end of the scarf. "Wrap this around your wrist—tightly. As if you might need it to pull yourself up from a deep trench."

I glanced at Brant, hoping he would tell me how truly stupid I was being, but he was staying out of this. Slumped over his knees in the corner chair, he only looked up to meet my gaze. The expression on his face was empty, but I sensed he was resigned to allowing this forced echo to transpire, if for no other reason than to appease my need to get information about my past. Some secrets were better left buried, but if the presence following my mother had somehow found its way to me, then no amount of dirt was going to help me. I needed to know as much as I could about the past and my mother's final days.

"Are you ready?" Genie asked, forcing me to look away from Brant. I checked the scarf; it was cutting off my circulation, so I assumed it was tight enough.

"Ready." Genie reached back into the trunk and pulled out a long, glinting dagger. "Not ready. What's that for?"

"I need a lock of your hair. I'm going to bind you temporarily to your mother so we can specify the echo we want to see."

"And then?"

"Then we do a little dance, shake a little, and go into the most tranquil hypnotic state you will ever experience. Trust me, you will feel amazing when we get back."

Once again, I looked at Brant. I felt like I should kiss him goodbye in case I didn't make it back. Genie reached over and sliced off a piece of my hair. I frowned at her random selection but didn't flinch lest she cut my skin in the process. She pulled a baggy from the trunk containing a small lock of hair twisted with a rubber band.

"Is that my mother's hair?"

"Yes."

"You kept it?" I couldn't quite grasp the logic of keeping a part of someone after they were dead. It felt clinical to me, or perhaps just weird.

"I haven't opened this trunk since..." Genie frowned and glanced at Brant. "Your mother and I didn't want to lose hair every time we performed a spell together, so we bagged up a couple of pieces and reused them over and over again."

I nodded in understanding, but I now had a new reason to feel uncomfortable. I was sitting around the very objects my mother had used to perform magic. We were about to embark on a flash from the past, but I was already in one. Everything around me was dripping with memories of the dead.

Genie tossed my and my mother's bound hair into the pedestal bowl. She dug around in her box and found one of her own locks and tossed it in. She poked her finger against the tip of her dagger and placed a drop of blood on the rim of the bowl. My eyes got big, anticipating my pain next, but she never requested my blood. I could only assume it was a requirement for the person performing the ceremony. Despite my skill set, I was just along for the ride.

We joined hands, and Genie walked me through verses of her spell. It wasn't English by any means, but I couldn't quite tell what language it was. Ultimately, it didn't matter. Words were words. Right?

My eyelids felt heavy, and I let them close. The room spun as dizziness settled into my head. For a moment, I was floating, and then I was falling, and then, for some reason, I was upside down.

"Oh, my goddess!" I heard Genie squeal beside me, and I opened my eyes. I was staring back at my own reflection, and it made me jump. "Look at me!" Genie stared at her own reflection, touching her youthful body. "I wondered if it would work, and it did."

"What?"

"That piece of hair was almost twenty years old—oh my goddess, this is what I looked like at twenty-eight—no. How old was Brant? Oh, hell, who cares? Look at me! I could spend the whole spell looking in this mirror."

I heard a knock on the door behind me and looked back. White plastic and mauve decorated the cramped little bathroom we were in. We were staring into a mirror trimmed with a thick plastic lacy design. The fans on the wall above the toilet were white plastic with mauve roses glued to them. Judging by the strings of hot glue collecting dust around them, it had been a DIY project for the homeowner. Even the tissue paper on the sink was covered by a monstrous white container decorated with the same plastic roses. This was decorating hell. This was the beginning of the 80s.

"I don't think you can spend all night staring into this mirror. At some point, someone will want to use the bathroom."

"Oh, it doesn't matter." Genie poked at her cheeks, giving them a natural rouge before turning to face me. "They can't see—holy crap!" Genie jolted back, cowering against the tall pantry closet door. "What? How? Oh, goddess."

"What is it?" I turned to the mirror and checked myself. There weren't any horns growing from my head, nor was I draped in roadkill. Short of that, I was certain her response was unjustified.

Genie relaxed and peeked back at my reflection. "Honey, I don't want you to get upset, but I might have made a teensy tiny mistake in binding your hair to your mother's."

"What sort of mistake?"

"I think...Instead of entering an echo state like I have, you may have astral-projected as well." Genie bit her lip.

"I don't know what that means!" I yelled at her.

"Cass, who are you talking to?" the woman outside the door asked.

I looked at the door and then back at Genie. "I'm inside my mother?" She nodded. "What the hell were you thinking?"

"Quiet! Shh, let's just go with it."

"Go with what? How can I observe my mother's behavior if I *am* my mother?"

"I'm not sure you have to do anything. This is still just an echo. I think."

"You think?"

"Shh!"

"Cass, are you okay in there?" the bathroom eavesdropper asked.

"Say you're fine," Genie instructed.

"I'm fine. I'm on the phone."

"What?" she asked.

"No, no, no!" Genie scolded me. "No cell phones."

"Shit!" I hissed. "I'm on the...drone. Just droning on to myself," I babbled." Genie frowned at my lame verbal recovery. I shrugged.

"Well, hurry up, honey, I gotta pee." Genie motioned for me to open the door. I did and found a short brunette on the other side. "Thank you." She ran in without regard to my presence, removed her pants and squatted on the toilet.

"That's Eleanor Reynolds. She was another lady we used to hang out with," Genie explained as we scooted out of the bathroom. "No magic, of course. She was a good little Catholic girl. Not that it stopped her from sleeping with two of her senior students."

"Eww." I moved away from the larger partygoers in the living room and instead sneaked into the galley kitchen off to our left.

"It was a different time."

"Why does everyone say that about their generation, but then turn around and question the morality of the next generation? In the 70s, it was pot and sex. In the 80s, it was cocaine and rock 'n' roll. In the 90s, it was ecstasy and chat rooms. There is always something the next generation does to piss off the last ones." I leaned over the yellow countertops in the kitchen and closed the extended bi-fold doors that closed the pass-through, giving us more privacy.

"Not everyone was sleeping around, or doing drugs, but to be fair, it was a sexual revolution. Birth control was becoming mainstream. And frankly, pot was just fun. Speaking of." Genie moved over to an ashtray by the microwave. She took a deep breath of the lingering wafting smoke. "Do you think I can get a contact high in an echo?"

"I wouldn't know. I'm not in an echo, remember?"

"Hmm. This is Brad Huey's house. His wife recently left him, so he had a denial party." Genie looked around and twisted her lips. "I think it's safe to say we have not actually traveled through time. This event has already happened, so you shouldn't be able to change the event."

"Then why was I able to talk to Eleanor in the bathroom? Why am I able to move and talk to you if I am in an existing memory?"

"I'm not sure."

"I thought you were the expert!"

"I'm sorry, honey, but you are way more powerful than she was. I think your added magic overshot the target."

"Hey, pretty lady." A tall, broad-shouldered man entered the kitchen and tapped his joint on the edge of the ashtray.

"That's Brad. He's the host."

"Where's your husband tonight?" Brad asked.

I chuckled and put my hand up to my face to disguise the movement of my lips. "What do I do?" I mouthed to Genie.

"I think you are overwriting the memory. I think you have to let go and allow the events to happen on their own."

I paused and waited for the words to come to me. Or for the man to assume I was an idiot and walk away. I felt the forceful expulsion of air from my lips and then I heard my mother's voice. As she spoke, my body fell backward within my own vision. I was now in the back seat.

"Oh, you know Mark—work, work, work. I thought I would come out with Genie and have a good time."

"I bet you did."

"What is that supposed to mean?"

"You know, you and I have the same problem." Brad moved closer and rested his hand on the counter beside me.

"What's that?" my mother asked.

"We have spouses who don't appreciate us. Or in my case, didn't. But that's no reason to get all worked up. In fact, I feel pretty fucking good, actually." Brad took a long drag of his joint and blew it out. When he looked back, his eyelids were dragging and his expression conniving. He leaned into my mother's ear and whispered. "Why don't I take you back to my bedroom and show you how much I appreciate you?"

To my relief, my mother pulled away from him and slapped him, the sting in her hand evidence of how insulted she was.

"Oh, come on, Cass, don't be a spoilsport."

"I am not cheating on my husband."

Brad's face frowned. "You're kidding, right?"

"No."

Brad scoffed and motioned to himself. "You mean you won't cheat with me."

"Anyone."

Contempt marred Brad's face as he looked me over. His gaze settled on my face and barked out a laugh. "Who do you think you're fooling? Your legs are spread wider than a turkey on Thanksgiving."

"You asshole!" Genie yelled into his face, but naturally he didn't see or hear her.

"You know, the only thing more pathetic than a slut is a picky slut." Brad marched away, flicking his joint into the sink on the way by.

"That prick!" Genie complained. "Oh, don't cry," she said to me, but I wasn't. I could feel the acidic burn of saltiness in my eyes and the tears pouring down my cheeks, but I wasn't the one crying.

It was my mother.

The Rumors

I ran, or rather, my mother ran. She dodged people left and right. A few took notice of her emotional state, but no one bothered to follow her. I could hear Genie behind me—unsure of who was in control, she was still trying to ease my grief. I, on the other hand, was observing the faces at the party. Trying to distinguish one drunken lout from another. I was hoping there was at least one recognizable face. I couldn't have made it to age eight without meeting a neighbor, a teacher, or at the very least an overly friendly baker that might have pinched my cheeks and insisted I stuff my mouth with processed sugar. It wasn't possible for me to have no recollection of the people in my life prior to the fire.

The crowds finally parted, and I caught a glimpse of Genie in front of me, except it wasn't my Genie. She was young, the same as the one following me, but her hair and her dress were different. Her natural waves were frizzy, and she had glued her bangs into a bouffant blob. Her dress was still reminiscent of the 70s, a bohemian style with a chevron pattern. It looked like a dressing gown instead of a party dress, but somehow she was pulling it off. The huge bug-eyed pink-tinted sunglasses, however, were a bit too much.

Genie, the real Genie, saw the expression on my face and tore herself away from her group. I veered right, and she veered left. We met at the patio doors and pushed through to the veranda. We shut the doors behind us, and she turned to me.

"What happened?"

"Brad propositioned me," my mother answered and wheeled around to pace over the bricks.

"He's an asshole," Genie stated simply. "His wife left him. That's proof right there."

"Why does everyone keep thinking I am open for business?"

"They just misinterpret nice for *nice*."

"No, it's more than that, Genie. He thinks I have slept with all the men in town. He really believes it."

"But you haven't, right?"

"Are you asking me?" Cass snapped.

"No, I'm asserting it. Because if you were sleeping around, you would have told me about it."

"You've been hearing the rumors too, haven't you?" Cass asked somberly. She sounded defeated, as if the whole world was against her.

Genie sighed and nodded her head. "Sure, I hear lots of rumors in this town."

"They can't be true."

"Yes, I know. You keep saying that, but..."

"What?"

"Why do you keep phrasing it like that? Just say they aren't true. Say it is a lie. Tell me that under no circumstances have you ever been in bed with another man."

"I don't remember sleeping with any man other than my husband."

Genie frowned and shook her head. "Oh, Cass, not remembering is not the same as never having done it. You know that, right?"

"I love my husband."

"Of course you do. I have never questioned that. But you have to be honest with me. Once and for all. Can you think of any reason these men are spreading this rumor? You said you don't remember sleeping with anyone, but do you have missing time?"

I turned away from her, staring out into the backyard of a neighboring house. She moved around to face me. "You have to tell me. I can't help you if you don't tell me."

"It's him," she whispered. "I don't know how, but it's him."

Genie frowned and looked down at the ground. Her face shifted to anger, and then her eyes welled with tears. "We will get through this. We will find a way to get rid of him."

"How?" I shook my head, more tears falling onto my cheeks. "He's so strong, Genie. I don't know how much longer I can fight him. If something happens to me..."

"What? No, don't be ridiculous. Nothing is going to happen to you."

"If something does happen to me, I want you to promise me you will take care of Tori."

Genie shook her head slightly, then nodded. "Of course I would. Like she were my very own. But nothing will happen to you because we are going to get that fiendish prick out of your life. For good this time." Genie gave me a hug, and I squeezed her back, breathing in the scent of incense and pot lingering on her clothes.

The Trespasser

I sat across from Genie, my Genie, staring hard at her. "You remember this conversation, don't you?"

"I do now." She nodded. "I also remember those glasses. Oy, what was I thinking?"

"You knew she was having affairs."

"No, I didn't. She denied it up until that night—this night. She didn't truly acknowledge the problem until the next time I saw her."

"Why didn't she remember having sex with the other men? Did she block it out?"

Genie shrugged. "I don't know. She just always said she couldn't be cheating. Not that she wasn't, or that she didn't. Just that she couldn't. It was definitive enough for me. She wasn't a liar, and I wasn't about to doubt her honesty again. Once I knew it had something to do with him and his influence, I understood it wasn't her fault. She was being played with like a puppet." Genie leaned over her knees. "Unfortunately, it was too late by the time she admitted it to me. He was in so deep. No amount of charms or spiritual cleanses would get him out of her."

I felt a shift in my vision, and I sank backward. "She's taking control again," I warned Genie, before I felt the reins slip away.

I stood up and turned to go inside the patio doors. As I reached for the knob, I turned my head to Genie. "Get back, witch!" The raspy words poured from my mouth, leaving an oily flavor on my tongue. They weren't my words, nor were they my mother's.

Genie's eyes widened. "It's you. How can you see me? This is just an echo." She gasped and shook my mother's body. "Tori, get out of there! He's in there with you!" Her words pierced my mind, but they faded right along with her image. She disappeared entirely, leaving only a slight blur where she had been standing.

I opened the patio door, marched between the partygoers, past the kitchen and bathroom. At the end of the long hall, I pushed open the hollow door. On the other side was a bedroom, bland and brown. Brad was sitting on the bed, looking at a framed picture from his wedding day and crying. He looked up and glared at me. "What do you want?"

I closed the door behind me and moved in front of him. I took the picture from him and stared at it. After a moment, I spat on it. "She was a bitch, anyway." My mother's voice sounded unfamiliar. It was a slightly lower register, but enough that it didn't sound quite like her.

"That's my wife you're talking about," Brad snapped.

"Oh please, she barely qualified as a wife when she was here."

"How dare you?" Brad got up, but I pushed him back down. I wasn't sure how strong my mother was in this state, but he seemed genuinely surprised by her force.

"How dare *she*?" I moved onto the bed, straddling his supine body. He started to sit up, but when my pelvis settled against his, he froze. "Wasted a perfectly good man by being a frigid bitch."

"I thought you didn't want me."

"I want what I want when I want it."

"And what do you want?" he asked, interest piquing in his eyes as well as in his pants.

"I want you..." I slammed my fist into the frame, breaking the glass and cutting my knuckles. Surprisingly, it didn't hurt. I pulled the picture out of the frame and tossed the frame away. "...to look at this picture of your wedding day..." I pierced the photo with my necklace, allowing it to hang off it like an added charm. "...while you fuck me."

Brad wasted no time in negotiating the specifics of his order. As soon as I released him to get my panties off, he removed his pants and was ready for my return.

The scene was too much. Never mind that I didn't want to engage in echo pornography. I was in my mother's body. It was all just too weird. Somehow I shrank away from it all. I was hoping I would awaken back in the living room with Genie and Brant, but a few moments later, I emerged back in the bedroom.

I was on the bed, my dress shoved up over my chest, one breast popping out over the fabric of my bra. The wedding photo had since fallen by the wayside.

Brad was off the bed, turned away from me, zipping his pants. He stood there as I rushed to cover myself and search for my panties. When he finally turned back to me, he gave me a weak smile. "That was great." He moved to the door but turned back. "I won't say anything to anyone about this. I don't want to add to the gossip. I know my marriage was shit, but I don't want to break up yours." He left, shutting the door behind him.

I jumped out of bed, all at once noticing the pain in my hand. I looked at the bleeding knuckles and the glass on the floor. I noticed Brad's wedding picture on the edge of the bed crumpled and covered with smudges of blood. I picked it up and stared at it. I could only imagine my mother's thoughts. Her own marriage was in danger of the same fate as Brad's. How long until my father recognized the rumors as fact?

My mother turned to the mirror over the dresser and leaped backward with a shriek. I could only see my reflection, but there was a darkness in my features, like something was on the other side of my face, stacked between my mother and me.

"Leave me alone!" my mother screamed at the dark figure invading her, much in the same way I was. "Leave me alone!" Her anger turned to grief, and she fell onto the bed, weeping into her hands. "Please, just leave me alone." Her voice faded.

I debated my options. I needed to leave, but I wanted to try something first. I pushed forward, allowing myself to take over the body. It wasn't a memory. It was an echo. I wasn't trespassing in the past. I couldn't change the events. At least in theory. Unless, of course, this *is* what happened in the past.

I pushed forward, placing myself back in the driver's seat. I took a breath and sat up. I looked into the mirror, at what should have been my reflection, but now the darkness had moved forward, superimposing itself even over me.

It was the same darkness I had seen trespassing in my house. The features were clearer at this distance. The face looked male, but it also seemed to morph as if multiple people were contained within, each taking a turn to come forward.

"Can you hear me?" I asked.

Laughter came from my throat. Not my own.

"Who are you?" I asked.

"I've been waiting for you," the raspy voice spoke through me. "They tried to keep you away, but I knew you would return. It's only a matter of time until the debt is paid."

"What debt?"

The laughter continued, but I shrank away. I rejected the body, the echo, and the sensations that came with it. I was struggling mentally and physically. I didn't realize I was back until I heard Brant soothing me.

"It's okay, Tori. I've got you." Brant shushed me and pushed my hair back.

As soon as I knew I was safe, I passed out.

The Exile

"How was that possible?" I asked Genie.

"I don't know." Genie paced the kitchen, drinking her wine straight from the bottle while I sipped on the water Brant insisted I drink.

"He saw you inside an echo. He spoke to us. He even seemed to know I had been gone, but was now back. Which is impossible, because he possessed her fifteen years ago."

"I don't think demons operate by the same standards of time as humans."

"If that's true, then it doesn't matter if I was gone for fifteen minutes or fifty years. He would have always been in that house, squatting and waiting for me."

"Did you discover anything more about your mother?" Brant asked.

"No, just further proof that she was the whore of Harold."

"Don't you dare sully your mother's name! She was a good, kind woman."

"Mrs. Hart, ten minutes ago I was playing out her seduction of Brad Huey. I'm pretty sure we are past the point of slanderous gossip. I know she wasn't the one in control, but we have to stop pretending it didn't happen.

Help me piece this together. I understand the end result was their burning to death. I understand this demon is responsible. What I don't understand is the catalyst for these events. The demon spoke of a debt. What debt?"

"He was a gatekeeper of sorts. He didn't like Cass trespassing into the world of the dead. Apparently, there are rules for necromancers. I assumed when Cass died, her debt would die with her."

"Then why didn't you fight the will? Why did you let me go to strangers when you promised my mother you would take care of me?"

"What?" Brant frowned at his mother.

"My parents originally wanted your parents to adopt me, but then right before their deaths, they changed it. I got sent away with specific rules about my proximity to this town. They didn't want me here. If the debt was erased, why did I have to leave?"

Genie's eyes wandered up to the ceiling, and her head wobbled. "It was for the best."

"They had to suspect something was going to happen to them for them to change the will so drastically, so suddenly. Did they know what was coming? Why didn't they leave the house?"

"It was too late!" Genie yelled at me. "Don't you understand? It's not the house. The house was fertilizer, but your mother was always the seed. By the time we realized how much danger she was in, he was already inside her, getting stronger and branching out. He was too strong for either of us to suppress. There was nothing we could have done differently."

"If it was never about the house, then why did my mother send me halfway across the country to protect me from it?"

Genie frowned, tears forming in her eyes. "She didn't send you away to protect you from the house. She sent you away to protect *us* from *you*."

My eyes and mouth gaped, neither able to close. I wasn't quite sure I had heard her correctly.

Genie stared back at me, sad and apologetic. Brant was caught somewhere between confusion and anger. I was glad to see he didn't have a clue what his mother was talking about either.

"Mom!" Lane's voice traveled through the house as the front door slammed. "What's for lunch?" He popped around the corner and saw all of us. "Hey, nobody invited me to the party," he said cheerfully, oblivious to the tense moment he had walked in on.

"Hello, Lane," Genie greeted him, seeming almost relieved for the interruption.

"Mom, what are you doing..." Lane took the bottle from her grip and wrapped his arm around her waist. "...not sharing with me?" He took a swig from the bottle and gave her a kiss on the cheek. "Will you make your favorite son something to eat? I'm starving." Lane pulled away and headed toward me. "Hey, beautiful." He plopped down beside me and scooted his chair closer. "Did you come over to play?"

"Lane, this isn't a good time," Brant insisted. I caught his eye as Lane put his arm over my shoulders. He didn't like what he was seeing, but he wouldn't stop it.

"Hey, I sympathize, but my stomach knows no boundaries."

"Mother." Brant looked at his mother, begging for support.

She took a deep breath and smiled sweetly at him. "How about some grilled cheese and tomato soup? For old time's sake."

Brant rolled his eyes and walked off while Genie started to prepare a familiar childhood feast. I rested my head on Lane's shoulder. It wasn't the type of consoling I needed at that moment, but I was happy to have someone to lean on.

Half an hour later, I stared down at a bowl of tomato soup and a grilled cheese sandwich. It was certainly a flashback, but nothing like I had just experienced. We were outside eating at Genie's small patio set. It was much too hot for soup, but the lemonade was going down well enough. It could have been snowing outside, and I still don't think I would have been hungry. There were a thousand questions rolling around in my head, and the one person who had answers was stuck on pause to play her mother's role for Lane.

"I thought about what you said." Lane leaned across the corner of the small patio table, pulling me in closer to collude. "And I think you can't possibly know what we have in common yet." He reached under the table and rested his hand on my knee. "Not without spending some time together."

Brant was to my left at the table. He wasn't partaking in the meal since he had already eaten his lunch. I looked over to see what he thought of this display. He was looking at me, no doubt curious about *my* reaction. I looked at Genie across from me. She was only offering me surreptitious glances. She probably didn't want to get involved in either of her sons' love lives, or perhaps she didn't want me with either of them. I didn't know how to handle the situation to my left, my right, and especially not in front of me.

I retrieved Lane's hand and gave it a squeeze before placing it on his own leg. "We can discuss this later." He mistook my lean as an invitation and gave me a kiss on the lips. Startled and embarrassed, I rapped my hand on the underside of the table as I pulled away. I nearly toppled two lemonades.

Lane laughed at me. "Easy, girl. Save the bucking for later."

I gaped at Lane and shook my head.

"Lane!" Brant scolded.

"I'm just joking. Tori gets my humor, don't ya?" He gave my shoulder a dull slap.

"I'm not in a joking mood. What I'm really in the mood for is a story." I stared across the table at Genie. "A story that doesn't have any lies or exaggerations."

"Well, what's the fun in that?" Lane asked, barely recognizing that Genie and I were about to have a showdown.

"Lane is exactly right. Stories like that are no fun at all," Genie said.

"The tragedies never are, but that doesn't mean there isn't an important lesson to be learned from them."

"Did I miss something?" Lane asked, looking between us.

"You mean like the last twenty years?" Brant asked snidely. "I'll give you a hint: you're a selfish, ignorant brat."

"What the hell got up your butt?" Lane squawked.

"What happened, Genie?" I asked firmly, ignoring the budding man-fight next to me. Lane and Brant simmered and sat back to listen. "I came back here for one reason: to find out what happened to my parents. To understand why and how they died."

"Do you really want to know?"

"I don't *want* to know; I *need* to know!"

"Fine," Genie whispered. "The answer you want...The answer I have been trying to hide from you since that day..." She sighed. "You did it. *You* killed your parents."

The Pool

The silence stretched out between us. At one point I had started shaking my head, but there were no words to match it. Brant looked ashen, and Lane looked dumbfounded. Genie, on the other hand, looked as if her admission had lifted a weight from her shoulders.

"I don't understand," Lane whispered. "I thought Tori's parents died in that fire."

"They did," Genie answered, rubbing his arm.

"Did she accidentally start the fire or something?"

I looked at Genie, hoping against hope the answer could be that simple, but I knew it wasn't. I knew the fire chief had mentioned heat upwards of 2800 degrees. That was no matchbook accident.

"No, sweetheart, it's a little more complicated than that."

"That's why you said everyone needed protection from me?"

Genie glanced at Lane, her precious forever baby boy, naïve to the point of being stupid, or at least in heavy denial. "Lane, why don't you head inside and play your video games?"

Lane looked at me and then at his brother. Brant was giving him no grief, but I could tell there was some jealousy in his eyes. Lane had the luxury of being protected from his mother's nefarious pastime. Brant, however, seemed to have gotten thrown under the bus.

When Lane turned back to look at Genie, his resolve had hardened, and he leaned back in his chair. "I'm not a child, Mother," he said without the usual tone of playfulness or sarcasm in his voice. "If there's something I need to know about Tori, I'd rather know now."

"Well, wonders never cease," Brant mumbled under his breath, legitimately surprised by Lane's gumption. Apparently, his brother was ready to accept the truth. There was no telling whether he would be able to handle it, though. Even I was still getting used to the idea, and I was a necromancer.

"When your mother first moved here," Genie began, "she was happy. Her powers..." Genie glanced at Lane, but he didn't flinch at the phrasing. "...weren't much of an issue. She would occasionally meet a specter or a spook, but she was aware of her powers before she came into that house, so the increase in activity was more of a nuisance than alarming. As I said, her interactions took place in dreams, so they never truly interfered with her life.

"She and I met at one of those dreaded bake sales the school puts on. We got to talking and became fast friends. It didn't take long for us to discover each other's secrets. I immediately sensed an odd flavor to her presence, and she felt something she described as a low hum coming from me. That's when we started the playdates." Genie glanced at Lane nervously, but to his credit he wasn't objecting to her phrasing or scoffing at the ridiculous nature of her choice of hobby.

"We used that time to explore our power. We also did a lot of drinking." Genie chuckled to herself as if remembering a very specific instance of drunkenness. It took her a moment to find her words again. "The necromancer's primary skill is to commune with the dead, but that ability can be used to determine one's future. The dead have a clear view of the world around us and they provide a great deal of assistance in determining which paths to take and which to avoid. Between my abilities and Cass's, we were able to predict the future of just about anyone we could get a lock of hair from, or a unique personal belonging.

"I'd be lying if I said I weren't addicted to our sessions." Genie frowned at Brant. "So much so that I'm afraid I may have neglected my children. It was a time in my life when I was able to express myself fully and completely without judgment or ridicule. I did let it go too far, though, but there was hardly any choice to make."

"What happened? When did it go wrong?" I asked.

"One of our neighbors was having a Fourth of July party. We attended along with Cass and her family. They had a swimming pool. That was a big deal in those days. We all felt very fortunate to be invited, and the kids were ecstatic about swimming with their friends. The pool was packed. There wasn't an inch of space that didn't have a body or a beach ball. There was yelling and laughing—and that was just the adults. The kids were screeching and shouting."

Genie stopped talking. Her eyes glazed over as if she remembered that day all too clearly. She eventually looked up at me and shook her head. "No one can claim to be the perfect parent. With so much ruckus, it was easy to lose track of a child. By the time we realized something was wrong, you had already been underwater for several minutes."

I gaped at Genie. "Me?"

"We pulled you out of the pool, but you weren't breathing."

The moment was surreal, as if she were telling me about somebody else's life. I was trying to remember swimming, water, but I had no recollection of this event. Maybe that was for the best.

"We started performing CPR."

Brant abruptly stood from the table and walked away as if he couldn't stand to hear this story. He went inside and closed the patio door behind him. I quickly calculated that he had to have been at least 12 years old when it happened. That meant he should have remembered it clearly. It surprised me that he hadn't mentioned it. Not that it was a pleasant remembrance, but certainly a crucial one.

Genie glanced after her son but continued with her story. "The paramedics were on their way, but to a mother, a minute seems like an eternity. Cass and I were beside ourselves. I was doing my best to console her, even though I was almost as hysterical as she was. We knew what your chances were. Half drunk and half high, I knew there was nothing anyone could do to save you.

I put my hands in hers, and when our eyes met, something happened. Weeks and months of practicing spells, predicting futures, and playing with fire had attuned us to each other's energies. At that moment, I knew what she was thinking, and she knew what I was thinking. There were no earthly means of saving you, but there was a chance magical means could. While our husbands shared the duty of performing CPR, we performed a spell.

"I don't even know what the people at the party thought of us, standing on the edge of the pool, staring at one another, while we murmured in unison. We told them later we had been praying, but I'm not sure if everyone believed that.

"That spell was the most powerful one we had ever performed. To this day, I can't imagine doing anything like it. I think the only reason we were capable of it was because of our emotional state and our proximity to a potential rising soul. I wish I could say it was God that brought you back to us," Genie said to me. "Unfortunately, that's not what happened. We didn't have permission to do what we did."

"What does that mean?" I asked.

"We stole your soul from the grip of death and forced you back into your body. We saved you, but we also pissed someone off by doing it."

The Blame

I knew Genie wasn't anywhere near done with her story, but I needed a break, and by the looks of Lane's pallor, he needed an opportunity to escape. I grabbed my bowl of soup I had barely touched and the remnants of my grilled cheese sandwich and took them inside. I heard Lane asking his mother questions as I closed the door behind me. I wasn't sure she was going to answer them all, but it was nice to know Lane was ready to ask them.

I saw Brant sitting alone in the living room, so I dropped off my dishes and joined him. I sat down in the chair across from him and rocked in the glider chair. He looked as if someone had stolen his puppy. I wasn't sure what to say since I didn't understand the reason behind his turbulent emotions. All at once, his eyes watered and several tears poured down his cheeks. I leaned forward, ready to offer my sympathy for whatever he was feeling, but he spoke before I could.

"It was me," he said, nearly losing control of his voice.

"What was you?" I asked.

He refused to look at me, even though his body was rocking with stuttering breaths. "It was my fault," he breathed out. His face turned red as he tried to keep himself from wailing.

"If this is about Lane, don't worry. I'm not—"

"I pushed you into the water," he said, straining to speak each word to keep it understandable. The explanation dawned on me as I thought about the pool party. "I didn't know you couldn't swim. I pushed you into the deep end, and you didn't come back up." Brant leaned forward, taking several breaths, trying to stop his own hyperventilating. "You got lost in the water. I couldn't see you. I didn't know what to do. It was so loud, and everyone was drunk and confused. I tried to find my mom, but I took too long. You drowned because of me." Brant looked up at me, eyes red from tears and wide with fresh memories cutting at his heart. "This is all my fault. All of it. I was a jealous little shit, and I bullied you. That's why they had to save you. That's why all this started to happen. Your mother and father are dead because of *me*. Because of what *I* did that day."

I paused to consider what he was saying. My feelings for Brant were already tangled up with feelings of resentment. He had been a mean little kid who had hurt my feelings and made me feel bad about myself. And now he was adding three deaths to his resume of destruction. He was probably right that all of this was his fault. It was the butterfly effect in action. If he hadn't been such a jerk, I wouldn't have drowned, Genie and Cass wouldn't have trespassed into the netherworld, and my parents wouldn't have paid the price for it.

He had been the catalyst of the life I was currently living.

"I shouldn't have fucking touched you," he castigated himself. "I wish I could go back in time and punch myself in the face." Brant spat the words through clenched teeth. "I wish I could..." I could see the determination in his eyes as he gained the courage to say what he really felt. "...kill that little shit."

It was an odd emotion to see on a man—a murderous intent that, by all rationales, was also a suicidal intent. He had been too young at the time to understand what his actions could do, but now as an adult he knew all too well. Suddenly, our relationship made more sense to me. Not only had Lane fueled his vacillating interest but also his belief that he didn't deserve me. He had said as much, but I hadn't understood what he'd meant until now. Brant had bullied me to the point of almost getting me killed. Barring the intervention of our mothers, Brant *had* killed me.

And yet...

I looked over Brant's tormented face—red with anguish, wet with tears, his jaw clenching so hard to maintain some control of it all. His hands shook, and his breathing stuttered. He was miserable. His past behavior haunted him as deeply and darkly as any demon could.

"You were just a child," I said finally. "You didn't know—"

"I knew what was happening. I should've jumped in after you. I should've screamed for help. I just stood there for nearly a minute while you sank down." Brant nearly crumpled as another wave of emotion hit him. "Fucking stupid little boy!"

I couldn't take it anymore. I moved from my chair and pushed between his arms, forcing him to give me space on his lap. At first he seemed to want to push me away, but once I was in a comfortable spot on his leg, he wrapped his arms around me tight and pressed his face into my chest.

"Stop it, okay?" I scolded him. "I know you weren't actually trying to kill me. You weren't a little psychopath killing cats. It was an accident. You were just a little boy."

Brant shook his head, refusing to release.

"Yes, you were, Brant. You have to let go of this guilt. You've been holding onto it for all these years, and I'm telling you, it wasn't your fault."

"It was!" He looked up at me, still refusing to release himself from the prison of his shame.

I looked down at him, somewhat irritated that he wasn't letting me console him. Instead of fighting his logic, I nodded in agreement. "Okay, it's your fault I almost drowned." His face pinched, as if my admitting it was even worse than his admitting it. "And I forgive you," I added.

The pain on his face relaxed into shock, and he shook his head. "You can't."

"Yes, I can, and I just did. I forgive you, and I forgive that little boy you used to be." He shook his head. "Imagine how much he must have been hurting for him to want to hurt someone else. You must have been feeling ignored by your mother—dismissed even. If you want to trace the blame back, then we can put it all back on our mothers. They stuck us in this living room together while they sat out on the patio drinking." I shrugged. "There you have it. Let's blame our mothers. Everyone else does."

Brant stared up at me as if all my words had been in some foreign language. When he finally said something, it wasn't what I'd expected. "I think I'm in love with you."

I took a deep breath, unprepared for the profession of love.

"But I don't deserve you. I don't even deserve your forgiveness, let alone...you." His attention shifted to my chest. I had been holding his face endearingly against me while he'd bared his heart, but now he seemed to be very aware of my breasts pressing against him. "You should hate me," he whispered.

"I don't hate you. I—"

Before I could offer any reciprocal admission of love, he shifted his lips across my chest, grazing the tender flesh beneath a thin layer of cotton and satin. The subtle, albeit intimate, contact sent a shockwave through my body, alerting my senses and silencing my words.

He peered up at me. There was worry in his eyes even as his lips became more brazen. He kissed my breast where my nipple had already sprung to attention. I swallowed hard as another shiver ran through my body. His confidence seemed to increase as he watched me. He no longer looked nervous. He looked to be his assertive self again. He parted his lips and flicked his tongue over the same sensitive spot. I gasped and nearly doubled over from the referred pleasure.

I heard the patio door open and suddenly remembered where I was. I scrambled to get off Brant's lap to avoid being caught in such a compromising position. Dizzy with burgeoning desire, I tripped over my own feet. Brant reached out to catch me, but he was still struggling to get out of the chair himself. I inelegantly landed face first on the carpet.

When Lane walked in, he saw me on the floor and Brant climbing out of the chair. His confusion about the scene was there and gone. He put his hands on his hips and glared at his brother. "How long have you known about all this stuff?"

"This *stuff* has been going on for years." Brant reached down for me, and I took his hand to help me up. "Just because you and Dad chose to ignore it didn't make it go away."

"So, you believe all of it?"

Brant sighed and shook his head. "Yes, and so do you."

"I don't believe Mom brought Tori back from the dead. That was CPR and good luck. This is just more of Mom's delusions of grandeur." He glanced back at the patio door to make sure Genie hadn't sneaked in behind him yet. "Mom is a bored housewife, looking for something to make her feel special. She's exaggerating the truth."

"You sound like Dad."

"Dad is a smart man," Lane said defensively.

"Stop lying to yourself, Lane. I know you were scared shitless after the seance Mom did that Halloween; you just didn't want to believe it was real. You *want* Mom to be a bored housewife. You *want* her to be eccentric and neurotic because you can't imagine a world where your mommy has more important jobs than to kiss your boo-boos and feed your ego. Face it, Lane, Mom is a witch! And in case you are still too blind to see it, she is a pretty badass one."

"Well, thank you, Brant," Genie said as she joined us in the living room.

Brant clenched his jaw and turned away from everyone. He probably hadn't intended to compliment his mother, lest he encourage her bad behavior. Lane, on the other hand, seemed to be panicking. He looked at all of us for an answer that no one would give him. He wanted a way out. He wanted to go back under his rock, but he couldn't. He was in the daylight to stay now. When his anxiety peaked, he only had one thing to say: "This sucks!"

"Lane, don't get too excited," Genie chided him. "If you want to forget everything you heard today, I can put a tiny little forgetful spell on you."

Lane looked between his mother and Brant. "Is she serious?"

Brant nodded. "It's actually a lot like hypnosis."

Lane scoffed. "Ma, you can't just make me forget."

"I can, I have, and I will again unless you can prove to me you are capable of handling the truth." Genie sat down in one of the chairs and leveled a deafening mom stare at him. It was the look I had seen her give Brant many times, but this was the first time I had seen Lane on the receiving end.

"You've done it before?" Lane asked cautiously. She didn't answer but instead perked an eyebrow. She was testing him, daring him to have a tantrum—or perhaps at this age, it would be a breakdown.

"Fine." Lane sat down in the chair I had recently vacated. We all watched him, staring miserably at his lap. When he looked back up, he met each of our gazes before scoffing. "I'm fine. I'm still just digesting or whatever."

Brant took a seat again, and even though I really wanted to sit on his lap again, I chose the chair next to his. I hadn't noticed before, but the chairs were positioned around a coffee table that had a large pentagon-shaped doily beneath its glass. I smirked at the little detail. Genie's proclivities had always been in plain sight, but only those willing to see them would have noticed.

After a short silence, Genie spoke. "Now, where were we? Oh, yes, I was about to tell you that when we brought you back from death, you weren't alone."

The Parasite

"It came back on me?" I asked. "I brought it into this world?"

"Yes, the darkness returned with you."

"So, wait, *Tori* was a demon?" Lane asked more bluntly than I preferred.

Demon was the best name Genie could think of to describe the unwelcome guest that had piggybacked on my soul when it was returned to my body. I cringed, wishing there were a better explanation. One that didn't make me sound like a creature from hell. Of course, it was all euphemisms at this point. Heaven, hell, angels, demons; even the soul was just a name for whatever life force resided inside of us. Who knew what other forces were at work in the world of the dead? Perhaps it had been an evil spirit that had returned with me. One that longed to have its body back.

"That's not what she's saying," Brant defended. "It's not as if Tori went to hell. She just had a ghost hijack her body."

I was happy to hear Brant had the same theory I did. I looked at Genie to see if she agreed with that.

"It wasn't as if Tori was possessed. It was more that our meddling with nature caused a breach between the world of the living and the world of the dead. We pried open the door, but we couldn't shut it all the way. Cass and I were already trespassers by using our magic to predict futures, but that was the equivalent of peeking through keyholes. When we brought Tori back, we became thieves. Someone or something didn't like that. He—the entity that haunted your mother—took advantage of her necromancy to communicate with her."

"He spoke to her?" Lane asked. "Like The Exorcist or The Shining?"

I didn't appreciate Lane's questions, especially since he was making everything seem like a joke. This wasn't funny at all. My mother had been tormented by this thing because she'd saved me. My parents had ultimately died because I had lived.

Brant reached over and took my hand. I looked at him and saw his concern. The word *empath* suddenly popped back into my head. I wondered whether he could sense my frustration. Not that it probably wasn't obvious on my face.

He stroked his thumb along my knuckles, and I felt the knot in my stomach ease. As awful as the revelations had been so far, I was happy he was being more affectionate towards me. I really needed someone to help me get through this, and I wanted it to be him.

"It started out like the other communications. Just dreams. Normally the conversations were civil, but this entity was making demands of her. Demands that no sane human could give in to. "

"What did he want?" I asked. "Why was he so persistent?"

"He wanted you." Genie gave me a moment to process that. "We had robbed him of your soul, and he was demanding it back. He had been tormenting your mother for nearly a year, demanding of her to kill you. When she didn't give in to the demand, he tormented her physically. That's when she started waking up with bruises and cuts. That's also when I began to suspect her husband was abusing her. She tried to hide the severity from me, but she finally broke down and told me the truth.

"That's when I realized we were both to blame for what was happening to her. I tried to help her. We did several protection spells on both of our families. We did manage to suppress him, but then Cass started to lose time. That's also when the rumors of her adultery started to circulate. She denied it, and I believed her. It wasn't until that night at the party, the party you witnessed, that I realized. Not only was she having affairs, but she was having them against her will."

"Whoa, so you're saying Cass was being roofied by a ghost?" Lane asked.

"Not exactly, sweetheart. This entity was using her existing connection to the netherworld to take control of her. He used her body to cheat on her husband. He was doing it as a punishment, to humiliate her and to bully her into doing what he wanted."

"So, if this thing came back with Tori," Lane said, "why didn't it make her kill herself or something?"

"I'm not entirely sure. It could have been because it was too difficult. Tori's abilities were not fully developed at that time. Her link to the afterlife was not as strong as Cass's."

"Link?" Lane looked me over. "What do you mean?"

"Tori is a type of witch, like me. She, like her mother, is a necromancer."

"Eww," Lane said flatly. "That's gross."

"It's not what you're thinking," Brant said.

"Why would you do that?" Lane asked me, appalled.

"That's necrophilia, you moron!" Brant scolded Lane. "Tori can communicate with the dead."

"Oh." Lane relaxed back in his chair, but gave me another once-over to see if I was visually different to him.

"When Cass confessed she was losing time and having unintentional affairs, we decided the best answer was yet another dose of magic. Our first spell had blocked off his ability to communicate with her in her dreams. We were certain another spell would block him from controlling her body. Unfortunately, he found another path." Genie looked at me somberly.

"Me?" I asked.

Genie pinched her lips together and slowly shook her head. "We cut off his connection to your mother, so he had no choice but to move on to the only available link to this world—premature as it was."

"The cuts and bruises? That was him?"

"Yes, but it was more than that. Your powers may have been underdeveloped, but he was strong enough to open you up. He started possessing you."

A shiver ran through my body as if I could feel something inside me at that moment. I wondered what my eight-year-old self might have said or done while I was under his control. Maybe it was a very good thing I didn't have those memories.

"We tried to banish him entirely, but we couldn't get him out of you—no matter what we tried. That's when

Cass knew there was no way to beat this thing. That's when she surrendered, as it were. We removed the first protection spell from her, which allowed him back into her dreams—but by that time he was stronger. He broke through the second suppression spell and continued to control her. He destroyed her life as a punishment for her thievery. She did everything possible to try to appease him, short of giving him what he really wanted. She even offered her own life in return, but apparently it wasn't enough."

"What happened that day? The day of the fire?"

Genie shook her head. "I wasn't there, but I know she planned on telling Mark what had happened. He was like my husband. He understood she was special; he just didn't know how special. I doubt she would have convinced him of anything in one night."

"If you weren't there, how do you know I killed them?"

Genie grimaced. Her eyes were pinned to mine, and her lip quivered as she opened her mouth to speak. "Because you told me you would."

The Mistake

Lane, Brant, and I sat in the kitchen on the three bar stools. We had traded our lemonade for something stronger. Emotions were high, and the day was getting away from us. Rex would be home soon, and I knew Genie wouldn't talk in front of him. She was already beyond her tolerance by jading Lane.

"It was him though, right? When he was inside me, he threatened to murder them?" I asked. "It wasn't really me."

"Of course not, sweetheart." Genie reached out and touched my hand, not to hold it so much as touch it. "You loved your parents, plain as day at midnight."

"Is he still in there? Inside of me?"

"No," Genie answered, but she drew away from me so fast that the ice cubes in her bourbon clanked.

"What is it?"

Genie laughed. "It all seems so stupid now. We were desperate to shake off that monster. Your mother was being ripped apart by this thing. Emotionally, she was at her wit's end. So, we tried one more time to dig ourselves out of our hole." Genie took a breath. "We decided to push him out. It was the first time we had attempted to attack him directly. We were able to get him out of her, but not out of the realm. The door was shut or not open enough. We couldn't reverse what we had started. When we realized he was holding on too tightly, we changed tactics again—a choice I now regret deeply."

"What did you do?" I asked.

"We bound his energy to this realm instead. Specifically, we bound him to the house. To your house."

"That thing is attached to my home?"

"Yes, it was the only way to get him off your mother and you."

"So, the house is evil?"

"The house is his cage."

"And I moved in with its prisoner." I didn't care that I sounded snide. Genie had known the house was dangerous, and she'd said nothing to me. Brant had insisted more vehemently that I move out than she ever had. She was making the same mistakes with me as she had with Cass. Then again, maybe that was intentional. Was Genie using the house as an excuse to practice her magic with a new necromancer? Was her obsession that out of control?

Genie ignored my unspoken accusation of neglect. "We realized the mistake we had made. There was no way any of you could stay there. Your mother tried to convince your father to move, but he wasn't having any of it. It became an ongoing battle between them. Compounded by the rumors of adultery, Cass's marriage was falling apart. She was desperate to fix everything, and so was I. I even tried on my own to repair the damage. I thought if I could appease him somehow...but he insisted the only way to reconcile with him was to kill the child."

Lane's head snapped up. "Kill the child?" He stared at his mother, brow dipped deep. "That night around Halloween...That's what you were doing. You were contacting him, weren't you?"

"Yes. I needed a coven of sorts to communicate with him without your mother. Your friends got the message wrong. It was only one child he was asking for." Genie glanced at me sheepishly.

"*Can* he kill me?" I asked.

"No." Genie swirled her bourbon. "I don't understand the rules, but one thing has always been clear to Cass and me. The entity cannot do the killing. Death has to be by human hands or by human error." Genie paused, licking her lips nervously. "And you can't be replaced by another." She took a long drink of her liquor before continuing. "I thought after your mother died it would be over, but obviously not. The debt seems to be as much about reparations. It's a punishment for my and your mother's arrogance to interfere."

"But if he wasn't satisfied with their deaths, then why hasn't he emerged until now?"

"I'm honestly not sure. I assumed your presence in the house awakened him, or maybe your power inadvertently summoned him."

"Can't she just move out of the house?" Lane asked.

"It's not about the house," Genie said, perturbed. "That thing is awake again. Do you think it will go back to sleep the moment Tori leaves? That we will all get to live happily ever after."

I glanced at Brant, who also seemed perplexed by his mother's sudden anxiety. "What aren't you telling us?" Genie took another drink of her liquor.

"Mom, what is it?"

She sighed and shook her head. "You aren't the only one being affected by his reemergence, sweetheart." Genie's face wilted. "I've been having nightmares."

"I'm sorry, I didn't realize." I now understood her reluctance to simply ship me back across the country. Regardless of where I was, she would still have an angry demon to deal with.

"It's not your fault, and I don't care about me. I deserve whatever retribution I get, but if he can get deep enough to influence my actions, I wouldn't want my family to be hurt." Genie glanced at Brandt. "I'm also concerned about Brandt."

"What do you mean?" I asked.

"I'm concerned his abilities might make him susceptible to influence as well."

I looked at Brant, who looked down at his lap rather than at me. I had never considered that he could get tangled in this mess. If that demon was strong enough to get inside of me when my powers were still undeveloped, what was to stop him from finding a pathway into someone with psychic ability? I couldn't let Brandt get hurt because of me. "So, the only way to truly be rid of him is for me to die?"

Genie looked at me, her eyes fluttering over me. She didn't seem to want to speak the words.

"We'll find another way," Brant insisted.

"Yeah," Lane added. "We aren't gonna let this freak get you."

Genie smiled and nodded, but it was a thin smile. I caught her eye, and I saw the truth. She and my mother had already thought of everything to fight this thing, and they had lost. I should never have returned to this place. I should have heeded all the warnings about the house.

"I'll do some research," Genie said brightly. "There's always an ancient spell for this sort of thing—banishing demons or bad juju."

"Is there any way to find out for sure what it is?"

Genie shrugged. "I'm afraid that's your department, honey. The dead don't talk to me without a Ouija board, and even then it's usually a short conversation."

"Maybe you could show me how to—"

"Hello! Hello!" Rex called from the front foyer. The door slammed right after.

Genie waved her hand across all of us and made a shushing sound. "In here, honey."

Rex turned the corner and looked at all of us in the kitchen, half tipsy with fake smiles plastered on our faces. "So, this is where you two slackers went after your lunch breaks." Rex gave his wife a kiss. "I thought we only had two kids." He counted our heads with his finger.

"Oh, I think there was a third one in there somewhere."

"I also recall that they had moved out. Or had I been imagining that?"

"Hey, as long as the liquor is stocked." Lane raised his glass. "We will be here."

"Is everyone staying for dinner?" Rex glanced back at the stove for food. "Or is there dinner?"

"We were just leaving." Brant stood up, motioning for our exit. Lane and I stood and waved our goodbyes.

"Sorry, hun, we got caught up in talking and I forgot about dinner," I heard Genie say as we rounded the corner.

The three of us piled out the door, and Lane grabbed my hand. "I can take you home, Tori." He tugged me along as he walked backward to his car.

"It's okay, I can drive," I said, jingling my keys.

"I don't care what Mom says about the house. She's not going back there." Brant said as he headed to his car. "Until we can figure out a way to remove that thing, she'll stay with me." Brant opened his passenger side door and leaned against it, waiting for me to get in. It was news to me that I wasn't going home, but given the information that had been divulged, I was happy never to sleep in that house again.

Lane stopped and dropped my hand. "Your place? Why not my place?"

"You mean your studio apartment with a bed/couch?"

Lane shrugged. "There's room for two."

Brant chuckled and looked at me. I took a subtle step in his direction, so he knew I would rather stay at his place. He moved away from his car and closed the distance to his brother. He swung his arm over his shoulder and gave him a squeeze. "Yeah, so, I hate to jerk you around. I know I kind of instigated this and encouraged it, but this thing with you and Tori is gonna have to be over."

"What the hell, man? That isn't fair. You tapped out."

"I know, but I'm gonna have to enforce the bro code."

"Enforce my ass." Lane shoved his brother away. Brant shoved him back, and before I knew it they were wrestling around like children, give or take some extra pain. I wondered whether either of them wanted my opinion on the subject, but without a whistle, I would have no luck breaking up the match. Since Lane's car was blocking me in, I leaned against my car and waited for them to finish.

They bickered and flung insults at each other as their shoes scraped around on the driveway. After a few minutes, they were both sweaty and panting, but neither one had actually pinned the other. Brant eventually got Lane in a headlock and ran his knuckles over his head until he screamed for mercy. "We good?" Brant asked.

"Yeah, fuck, we're good." Brant let him go, and Lane yanked away from him. He looked pissed and slightly embarrassed to be whooped by his brother, but he shook it off like it didn't matter. "It's not like I expected to end up with her, anyway. My dreams never lie." Lane dusted himself off and headed to his car.

"Wait, what?" Brant smacked his arm.

Lane turned back and shrugged. "Tori." He motioned to me. "I had a dream about her wedding day." I stepped away from the car, intrigued by this.

"Yeah?" Brant asked breathlessly. "What about it?"

"Sometimes I get those promenades Mom talks about. The dreams that tell you the future."

"Premonitions."

"Yeah, those. I get 'em once in a while, and they always come true. I never told you because I didn't think you would believe me." Lane motioned to the house. "But hell, after all that, I must be a freakin' psychic."

"What happened in the dream?" Brant took a step closer, licking his lips.

"Oh, I was walking up to a priest with Tori."

"You were marrying her in the dream?"

Lane shook his head. "Nah, I thought that at first, but we never made it to the altar. I just leave her there. I figured since her dad is gone, maybe I volunteered to walk her down. Like, give her away. What do you say, Tori?"

Lane called over to me. "If things work out for you and this asshole, do you want me to give you away at your wedding?"

I glanced at Brant, who had a strange expression of shock on his face. I nodded to Lane. "That sounds good, Lane."

Lane smiled, but it didn't reach his eyes. "Well, whatever." He kicked a rock at his feet. "I guess you could end up with somebody worse." Lane took the opportunity to slug his brother in the chest while he was still perplexed by what he had said. Brant snapped awake and attempted to hit him back, but Lane was already running away. "Later, losers." He jumped into his car and drove away, hitting breakneck speed when he reached the main road.

"Is that normally how breakups go?" I asked.

Brant looked at me and nodded. "Yeah, when you aren't meant to be, that's exactly how they go. Come on." He nodded toward his open passenger door.

"What about my car?" I asked.

"Just leave it. No sense in wasting the gas." He came over and ushered me into his car. "We'll probably be right back here tomorrow night anyway," he mumbled and shut the door. He jogged around to the driver's side, jumped in and started the engine. "I need to make a quick stop before we head to my place. Do you need anything from your house? I think your bag is still at my place." He put the car in reverse and navigated his way down the driveway and back to the street.

"No, I should be good," I said. "Are you okay?" I asked since he still looked like he had seen a ghost.

"I'm good." He finally remembered to fasten his seat belt after he shifted into drive. "I'm really good," he said and took off at a speed I would have expected from Lane.

The Husband-To-Be

After a quick stop for gas, Brant drove me to his house. Our entire conversation on the trip had consisted of me babbling about his mother's information. I was subtly trying to imply she had betrayed me by not telling me the truth sooner, but Brant was oblivious. He was focused on driving and only occasionally grunted in agreement.

When we reached the house, he slipped off his seat belt and grabbed a small paper bag from his door compartment—something he had purchased inside the gas station. He jumped out and ran around to open my door before I had even removed my belt.

"What's that?" I nodded at the bag as I got out.

"Nothing," he mumbled. He shut the car door and led the way into the house.

Once inside, I snagged the bag away from him. He immediately tried to take it back, but I ran around the island playing keep-away with him. "Tori, give it back," he scolded me, but I knew he was worried.

I laughed. "It's Ex-Lax or something, isn't it?" I joked. "Hemorrhoid cream." I opened the bag and peeked in.

"Don't," he objected as I drew the small box from the bag.

My face flushed as I looked over the box of condoms. I looked up at Brant, who looked thoroughly dejected. "Is this for me—for us...tonight?"

"I realized I was out. That's all."

I smiled at his reluctance to admit what he really wanted. "Would you still have bought these if Lane hadn't changed your interpretation of your premonition?"

Brant shook his head and let out a soft chuckle. "Lane didn't change my interpretation." He leveled a stern, almost scolding look at me. "Tori, I knew I was going to marry you from the first moment I laid eyes on you at the furniture store. I've been fighting it ever since, lying to myself and even you to avoid it...because I don't deserve you."

"Brant—" I started to object.

"But I'm willing to earn that right." Brant took a nervous breath. "Every day and for the rest of my life if necessary."

"Um, you aren't actually proposing right now, are you?"

"No." Brant cleared his throat. "I'm just saying...for future reference."

"Good, because I didn't get a premonition. According to my clock, our relationship is still back on second date status."

"Second date?" Brant frowned. "As much as we have been through in the last few weeks, we should at least be up to the third date."

"You're only saying that because the third date means sex."

"Doesn't matter, we had sex on our second date."

"That wasn't a date; it was an emergency, and even if it was, that only means we have to have one more sex-free date before we can use these condoms." I tossed the box onto the island.

"Oh, bullshit." Brant's eyes danced over me. "Why don't you sit on my lap and tell me that lie?" Memories of that afternoon's mouth-teasing put my heart into a faster rhythm.

Brant's eyes lit with interest. He seemed to recognize the change in my mood. He smirked at me and grabbed the box of condoms off the island. He moved to me and took my free hand. He paused there for a moment, as if offering me a chance to object if I really wanted to, but I didn't. I was bluffing about the no-sex date, anyway.

Brant led me out of the room. We didn't stop in the living room. Instead, we meandered through the back hallway to his bedroom. Once we were past the threshold, he leaned in to kiss me.

"Wait a minute." I dodged his kiss. "Why did you act surprised when Lane told you about the premonition?"

"Because my brother is psychic. Now I'm going to have to start listening to his advice."

Brant pulled me over to the bed and sat down. He pulled me onto his lap, and we were right back where we had been that afternoon. It occurred to me that he had professed his love to me already and I hadn't said it back yet.

"Take your shirt off," he ordered. Thoughts of conversation went out of my mind, and I slipped the cotton fabric over my head, revealing my bra. He slipped a finger into the nylon material and pushed it down, revealing one of my breasts. Rather than kiss it as I'd expected, he blew onto it. The cool wisp of air against my bare skin made me shiver and ache in anticipation. He did the same with the other breast, releasing it and letting his chilled breath harden the nipple.

He raised his hand to my breast and caressed it. His eyes watched me carefully as if gauging my reaction to the stimulation. He slowly circled my nipple with his thumb, making it tense. My breathing quickened, and I gripped his back.

He moved his hand away and continued to tease me with his lips. When I thought I might start ripping my clothes off, I felt his hand press between my thighs, offering a full accompaniment to my pleasure.

For the first time in weeks, I stopped thinking about ghosts, demons, and witches. I gave in to the moment without regret or concern.

For the rest of the night, all I thought about was Brant Hart.

The Next Morning

I woke to lips on mine. It took me a moment to reciprocate and another moment to realize those lips weren't in bed next to me. My eyes fluttered open, and I landed my sleepy gaze on Brant's smile. He was fully dressed, sitting on the edge of the bed beside me. I smiled back at him and stretched. He shifted back, letting me contort as needed before leaning back in for another kiss.

"I have to go to work. You have free rein of the house. Eat what you want. Watch what you want. Read what you want. Okay?"

"Okay," I responded groggily.

"Do you want to have supper in town tonight?"

"Mmm." I nodded.

"I'll be home after three."

"Mmm," I groaned again. "What? No." I snapped back into reality and rubbed my eyes. "I don't have my car."

"I'll come back and pick you up after work."

"No, I need it," I grumbled, thinking how stupid it had been to "save gas" last night if we were only going to waste the same gas with an unnecessary second trip today. "I need to go see Ed." Brant frowned, obviously disturbed by any mention of my former crush. "I need to cancel the house renovation. I need to cancel everything. Shit. He's gonna kill me." I buried my face in my hands. "What's worse is I can't in good conscience sell it. Anything I've put into it is now down the toilet."

"We'll get it figured out," Brant said. I noted the "we" portion of his statement, but didn't object. He was apparently one step away from marriage already. I would just have to catch up. He leaned down and kissed me again. "I can drop you off at your car before I go to work, but you gotta shake a leg. If I blow off another day's work, Dad is liable to put an ad out for a new son."

Thirty minutes later, I gave Brant another kiss goodbye before waving him down the driveway. I leaned against my car and stared after him, starry-eyed. I wasn't sure if it was too early to be in love, but I definitely was in the dreamy phase. It might have had something to do with a second night of admirably generous lovemaking, but I wasn't sure. I would have to do more research on the topic, just to be sure.

I turned my attention to the Harts' door. It was a little early for a visit, but I had a few criticisms that I wanted to get off my chest, namely Genie's lack of honesty and the danger she had put me in under the guise of denial and avoidance. I could see why Brant had turned his nose up at her pursuit of magic long ago. She seemed to cultivate more trouble than she prevented. I could hardly blame my mother for not wanting to let me die, but clearly the two of them had been adding fire to an already heated situation.

I rang the bell on the front door and considered my future. Would I be forced to leave Harold? Would Brant come with me? How far did I have to go to avoid the reach of the entity imprisoned in my house—if I even could avoid his reach?

Or was there a way to stop him so I didn't have to leave?

If I were more powerful than my mother, then perhaps...

Perhaps I was falling victim to the same egotism that had put my life in debt to begin with.

When Genie didn't answer, I got in my car and drove away. My intent was to go see Ed about the house, but that wasn't what I did. Despite Brant's insistence that I not return to my house, I did anyway.

I made the excuse that I needed to pick up my birth control, which I hadn't remembered to pack the other day. With more lovemaking in my future, I wanted to keep my backup prophylactic on schedule. However, when I reached the house, I knew I had other things in mind beyond my medication.

The Plan

I looked at the predator cleverly disguised with brick feet and wood bones. As I stared at my house, the memory of my parents' death overwhelmed me. Searing flames and torrid screams bled over into the few staggered memories I had, making it nearly impossible to get a clear view of what had happened that day and every day before it.

The only vivid memory I had recovered from that time was from an echo. As dangerous as it was to play the part of a necromancer in a house filled with an embodiment of evil, I couldn't resist trying to activate another vision. This place was the only connection I had to my parents, and I didn't want to lose it. Not yet.

I stepped onto the front porch. I braced my hands around my face to peek inside the window next to the door. Through the curtains, I had a view of the staircase, but it was empty. No looming shadow ready to shove me down the steps if I tried to ascend.

I moved to the picture window and gazed in at the front room that held my father's piano, and the living room beyond. I even squinted to see all the way back to my cleared-out dining room. There was no one there. I wasn't sure what I'd expected to see. Everything looked the same as when I had left. The only light on the main floor was a glowing amber mica lamp in the living room. I must have forgotten to shut it off.

I tapped my finger on the glass almost mockingly. "Are you in there?" I asked no one in particular—or someone very particular.

There was, of course, no response.

I sighed and looked back at my car. I knew I needed to leave, but the temptation to get more information was overwhelming. It had occurred to me that whatever resided in this place might have been drawing me in, luring me with my own desire to speak with my parents.

This was the part of the horror movie where every dim-witted victim goes into the haunted house instead of going home.

Sign me up for the role of victim number one.

I twisted the knob on the front door and pushed it wide open. The usual smell of stale dusty air hit me first, followed by the heat of an unairconditioned space. I took my first tentative steps inside and waited for the door to slam shut behind me, but it didn't.

"Hello!" I shouted as loudly as I could. "I'm here. If any ghosts or demons would like to talk to me, I would be happy to listen." I took a breath and headed upstairs. I glanced back at the door, making sure it was still open. I wanted a quick escape...just in case.

When I reached my bedroom, I found my birth control and stuck it in my back pocket. On my way out, the view of the garage out the window caught my attention. The door was open, and a car was parked inside. I couldn't see enough of it to recognize whose it was.

I looked around the backyard to see if anyone was roaming the property, but there was no one. However, I noticed a row of rocks in the yard. The white stones varied in size, and the spacing was far from perfect, but they were obviously the beginning of a circle.

I moved into the bedroom down from mine and looked out that window. The row of stones continued, as I'd suspected they would. Someone had put a circle of stones around my house. The question was why?

I headed downstairs and witnessed my rock dropper finishing up the last stones in front of my porch. "Mrs. Hart?" I asked.

Genie plopped the last stone into place, and a warble like heat off a fire shimmered along the rock path. She looked back at me, giving me a thin smile. "Hello, Tori."

"What are you doing?" I leaned against the doorframe.

She looked down at the rock barrier she had created. "Oh, just a little protection spell."

I should have known Genie would be more than eager to use her arsenal of magic. She was no doubt frothing at the thought of getting a second round with my debt collector. "Where did you find so many rocks?" I asked.

"Oh, I have a friend who does landscaping for a living. On occasion, I borrow some ingredients for spells." Genie gingerly climbed the steps and stopped in front of me. She folded her arms over the book she had brought with her. "How are you?"

I shrugged. "Fine, I guess."

"I thought you might be a little sore with me."

I nodded. Had she been at home when I'd picked up my car, she might have gotten a full dose of my soreness, but my thoughts had since turned to more pressing matters. "I was a little disappointed you hadn't been honest with me from the beginning."

"I didn't want you to blame yourself. Besides, some memories are best left buried." The mirthful ring in her voice was gone, making her sound dismal and defeated.

"Mrs. Hart, are you okay? You look like you've been crying." I motioned to her smeared mascara and dewy red cheeks.

She nodded. "I didn't sleep last night. I was so worried about this place and you." Her eyes bloomed with fresh tears. "I don't want this thing to come back again. I don't want anyone to get hurt, but I don't know if we can avoid it this time."

"We'll get through this. I know we will."

Genie frowned. "The only way I can help you is to do more of the same, but I'm not strong enough on my own to make a difference." She looked at me expectantly, but I didn't respond. "I know magic started this. But magic will also end it."

"It didn't end it before."

"I've had years to grow my craft. I'm stronger now. And even if I weren't, you have far more power than your mother ever had."

"How do you even know that?"

"The things you've been able to do. The things you've been able to see. Plus, I can feel it. I know you don't want to make things worse, but sweetheart, your life is in danger either way. I don't want to put you in this position, especially when it puts you in opposition to Brant. But if we don't do something, he will get inside you again. He'll destroy your life and the lives of everyone you love." Genie looked at me fearfully. "You don't want that, do you?"

For a moment I stared at her. I knew she was fighting for my cooperation on behalf of her own self-interest, but it didn't matter. She was right. I couldn't risk hurting anyone because I didn't want to dabble in the dark arts with my potential future mother-in-law.

"What do we need to do?"

The Other Side

The moment I agreed to merge our powers, Genie whisked past me into the house. "In here," she called from the living room when I didn't immediately follow her. I rounded the corner and found Genie sitting cross-legged on the wood floor. She was already setting out a picnic of magical tools on a decorative scarf. The book she had been carrying was open in the center of it all.

"Are we going to cast another protection spell?" I asked.

She looked up at me and nodded. "Something like that. Please sit." She motioned to the floor across from her smorgasbord of witchcraft.

I sat down and mimicked her position in case it was an important aspect of the merge.

"This particular ritual is going to be a bit more intense than our last collaboration, so I don't want you to be alarmed if you feel any pain."

"Pain?" I grimaced.

"I know." Genie frowned at me. "I wish there were another way to do it, but there isn't."

"Are we going to push him back into his realm?"

"No." Genie pinned me with her eyes. "We are going to *pull* him back into his realm."

I stared back at her, swallowing hard. "Doesn't that mean we have to be on his side?"

"Yes."

I frowned. "And where exactly is his side?"

Genie wrung her hands together. "Someplace that living people should not go."

I let out an exasperated breath. "This is dangerous, isn't it?"

"I'm not going to wait for him to—" Genie's lower lip quivered and new tears sprang from her eyes. "We have to do something before he fully awakens. Before he gets a hold of another mind. Before someone gets hurt." She was saying the words quietly, but the urgency in her tone was pleading. She was begging me to do the right thing, no matter what the cost to either of us.

"It's okay. I'm willing to take the risk." I reached my hands across the scarf, and Genie took them into hers. She nodded and mouthed "thank you" before looking down at her book. She began reading from it.

The initial litany seemed like a traditional Wiccan blessing. Something about water, earth, wind, and fire. Genie released one of her hands to dribble water onto the scarf from her water bottle. She then sprinkled dirt from a small jar she had brought along. She leaned down and blew a breath, scattering the dirt further. Finally, she lit a tiny votive candle with a lighter from her pocket.

Upon the final element, I felt something take hold. The warble of the protection spell outside was nothing compared to the shimmering curtain that fell around us. Something in the air felt tangible and bright, though it only lasted a moment, and then everything changed.

The darkness fell over us, turning white to black, and black to gray. The air went cold and smelled musty. I looked around at the walls, feeling the pressure of an unseen force weighing down on me.

Behind me, I heard the heavy breathing of an asthmatic old man. I turned my head slowly and looked at the overweight intruder who had caused me to call the police to my house. Every instinct in my body demanded I run, but the man wasn't doing anything to harm me. He wasn't even awake. He was simply leaning back in an oversized recliner I didn't own, taking a nap.

"It's okay. We've crossed into the veil. This is as far as we will go," Genie said.

I turned to look at her, but she too looked strange to me. Her features were shadowed as everything in the house was, but through her skin, I could see her skeleton. A vague outline of her skull pierced her facial features, making it hard to look at her without thinking about a dead body.

"It's cold here," I said, to hear my own voice. From somewhere in the distance, I heard a little girl laughing. I rationalized it was one of the other specters that had died on the property, but that didn't make the sound any less creepy.

"I know," Genie said. "Come. Let's take a look around." She stood up and helped me off the floor. She released my hand, and we walked back to the foyer. I peeked out the open front door, but what I saw frightened me more than what was inside.

The blackest night had arrived, but instead of the moon and stars, it had brought monsters and demons. Standing on the rim of the rock circle were snarling beasts, crouched faceless creatures, and the disembodied dead.

Moans, growls, and screams penetrated the wall, but only as whispers. The longer I looked, the larger the crowd of onlookers got. They were piling up on the edge, just waiting for a chance to get inside. "We shouldn't be here," I whispered.

"Come on." Genie grabbed my hand and ushered me away from the door and up the stairs. "He's in the attic."

"Attic?" My mind frantically tried to think of any reason not to go to the attic. It was already the scariest place in the house, save the basement. I didn't want to add to the extra thumps this dark side had put into my heart.

Despite the drag in my footsteps, Genie opened the hatch to the attic and pulled down the ladder. She climbed up and tugged me along with her. When we rose to the highest level of the house, another few degrees were sapped from the air. I could no longer hear the rasping breath of the man downstairs or the screams from outside. However, those noises were replaced by a creaking and clicking that echoed on and off from the room. I searched the room for the cause, but all I could see was boxes and odds and ends, none of which belonged to me.

"Hello?" I asked the darkness since Genie hadn't spoken yet.

"Hello, Tori." A throaty voice spoke to me, and I shuffled back, nearly falling through the hole I had come up through.

"Who are you? Where are you?" I wheeled around again, trying to find the source of the man or monster behind the words.

A series of clicks sounded ahead of us, and there was a movement in the shadows. I stared at it, trying to place the shape as it shifted upward. It was tall. I detected the hooded robe as it emerged slightly from the darkness. Though it was no more visible than before, I could at least recognize the shape of a man in its physique.

"I've done as you've asked," Genie said. "Now will you forgive my debt?"

I looked at her. I was surprised she was able to face this creature without a tremble of fear.

"If you had done as I asked to begin with, none of this would have happened," the cloaked figure said in a scolding tone.

"We didn't know!" Genie screamed at him. I imagined she had screamed this same thing at him many times before.

"Foolish girls," he grumbled. "Why did you ever think you could win a war with me?" He moved forward, out of the shadows. He revealed no face, but the movement caused a ruckus on the floor beneath him. I looked at the skirts of his robe and saw a thick, heavy chain dragging beneath them. The chain's origin disappeared into the darkness he had emerged from. "You should have brought me the child from the very beginning."

"What?" I looked between Genie and the darkness within the hood. "What's going on? Why are we here?" I moved away from Genie, but the figure reached out for me. A hand without flesh grabbed my wrist. Knobby bones dug into my skin with an unbreakable grip. I shrieked and tried to pull away, but it had snared me. "What *are* you?" I screamed at him.

He turned to look at me. "I am the guardian of this realm. Keeper of the dead."

"You're...?" I looked at Genie. She gave me a miserable frown before answering my question.

"Death?"

"I am the reaper of souls, and I have come to collect yours."

"No!" Somewhere between yanking my arm for dear life and kicking at the grim reaper, I found myself on the floor, face down, coughing on dust and cobwebs. I pushed against the palm at my back to look at Genie. "You did this! You brought me to him? Why!"

She wasn't crying anymore, but I could tell she was not happy about this decision. "I'm sorry, Tori."

"Let us finish this. Release me, witch," Death demanded.

Genie reached into her pocket and pulled out a key. It was bound to a lock of hair with a piece of string. She held it up and slowly unraveled it. When the string released, the lock of hair fell to the ground along with a splinter of wood I suspected had come from this very attic.

Death groaned as the shackle around his ankle dropped away. Genie stepped back fearfully as his image distorted. The bones that had recently grabbed my wrist grew flesh, though only enough to cover them. He hunched forward as something projected from his shoulders beneath the cloak, making him look hunchbacked. He used his free hand to lift back his hood, revealing a sickly, gaunt face and jet-black hair. He smiled at Genie. "There. That feels better."

"My debt? Is it cleared?"

"Yes. Now go before I find a new reason to punish you."

Genie wasted no time. She climbed down the attic ladder, only glancing at me momentarily before disappearing below the floor.

"Genie!" I screamed after her. "Don't do this!"

"It's already done, little one," Death said above me. "You were dead long before today. We just hadn't met yet."

The Prison

I searched the house for an escape, but the front door only brought me face to face with more unsavory beings. Their snarls and growls spilled in through the open door, but so far they were still on the other side of the barrier of stones.

I moved down the hall to the kitchen, where draped plastic hid my view of the demolition. I stopped when I saw movement on the other side. I heard a man yelling about loyalty and honor, followed by a woman pleading. I barely had time to register the telltale clicking of a trigger before the gun went off. I jumped at the ear-shattering noise and ran away from the murder scene playing out in my kitchen.

A giggle echoed around me, and Anna ran past me from the stairs to the front room. "Anna," I called after her. "How do I get out of here?" I followed her into the living room and found her standing over a body on the floor. The heavy man in the lounge chair was still asleep, adding his nauseating gurgles to the eerie sounds all around me.

"You'll be one of us soon," Anna said with a broad smile on her face.

I looked at the body beneath her a little closer. It was me. I was slumped over on the floor, seemingly passed out.

I rushed to myself and shook my body, but there was no longer anyone inside it to awaken.

Creaks and cracks resounded through the house as heavy footsteps descended the staircase in the other room. Anna looked up and frowned. "He's coming," she whispered.

"How do I get out of here?" I asked.

Anna shrugged and pointed to the body before me. I looked down again and saw myself, but this time I was a child. I was sopping wet and turning blue.

I looked back at the encroaching darkness foreshadowing the reaper's entrance.

"Damn it!" I picked my younger self up and carried her through the plastic curtain separating the dining room from the living room. I could hear the kitchen argument commence again as I neared the wall I had previously broken out. In this place, however, it was whole again, covered in the wallpaper from years past.

The squabble between the farmer and his wife had consisted of his angry accusations of infidelity and her denials, but this time I heard her accuse her husband of lacking virility. I waited for the gunshot, then peeked around the wall. The dead man on the floor with a gunshot wound to the forehead was the least of my worries, but his wife did concern me since she was still holding the gun. Was this just an echo? Could she actually hurt me here?

The wife suddenly turned to me, looking at me, eye to eye. There was no mistaking that she was seeing me. This was not an echo. Her hands shook, and her eyes widened with fury. "He had it coming," she insisted with a venomous tone.

She lifted the gun at an awkward angle, aimed it at her chest, and fired. I jumped away from the spraying blood and watched her body crumple to the floor, where she wheezed and coughed.

I heard a splintering crack and looked at the wall behind the woman. There was a tiny hole in the plaster from the last gunshot. I watched it grow. Feather-thin cracks spread from it like roots. Flakes of paint fell away, followed by chunks of the plaster. Between the lathe, fingers popped through, clawing at the slats like prison bars. A face appeared behind the exposed wood, eyes wide, mouth gasping for breath. "Help me!" the woman screamed. I realized it was the farmer's wife—trapped inside the wall.

She was no longer on the floor. Nor was the body of her husband. They had been replaced by the heavyset man with the gravelly asthma. He was standing behind me. I turned to face him, and he grabbed my shoulders. He pressed his enormous weight down on me, keeping me from running. "I can't breathe!" he rasped at me.

"I can't breathe!" the farmer's wife screamed as blood dripped from her mouth.

"I can't breathe," my younger self whispered from my arms. Though she still appeared to be unconscious, water dribbled from the corner of her mouth.

In unison, they all screamed, rasped, and whispered their ailing symptoms. "I can't breathe!"

Fear and dread that only a glance into hell can provide forced motion into my feet. I made it to the stairs before the hands of Death could capture me. His clawed fingers yanked a few strands of hair from my head as I passed him, but I was otherwise unharmed and, for the moment, still free.

I saw Anna standing by the ladder leading to the attic. She looked at me inquisitively. "You can't outrun him. He will eventually catch you."

"Help me! There has to be a way out of here. You've crossed over the veil before. How do you do it?"

"I didn't do it," she said defensively. "You did."

My eyes flickered over hers, and then I understood what she meant. I had summoned her to me. Not consciously or intentionally, but if I was the necromancer, then I was the one bringing the ghosts through. I may not have had magic, but I had some kind of power. Now all I had to do was use that power to cross myself over.

Clicks of old joints and creaks of bone on bone sounded behind me, and I jumped up the ladder, precariously balancing the child in my arms. Though I was certain it would do no good, I raised the ladder and shut the door. I looked around and found a toolbox among the junk. I yanked it open and found a hammer and nails. In quick succession, I hammered nails through the door's housing, into the frame, making it nearly impossible to open—at least by anyone of human strength.

I looked around again and found the string and lock of hair on the floor where they had dropped. I ripped out some of my own hair and gathered it with the hair that had dropped on the floor. I used the string to bind them together, tightly wrapping my hair to what I assumed was my mother's hair. If there were any way to get answers about my abilities, I assumed it would lie with her. And if I was right, this was where my mother was—trapped in this godforsaken place along with the creature that brought her here.

"Are you ready to see the truth?" A voice hissed from the shadows. I peered through the darkness, seeing only the vague rivulets of red and pink through burned flesh.

"Yes," I whispered back.

"Then close your eyes."

The Drowning

My first vision was of water. I was floating, unable to breathe or move. Then I was coughing and staring up at two men who were petting my face and head. I recognized my father, and my heart rejoiced. He was crying and kissing my little hands. Mr. Hart was the other man. He folded his hands together and repeated, "Thank you, God," until my mother burst past him. She was hysterical, nearly screaming her relief as she hugged me.

I realized I was not conjuring my mother's memories, but my own. That lock of hair was mine. I had bound myself to myself. These were *my* memories.

Over my mother's shoulder, I could see Genie smiling. The odd expression on her face was not relief, though. It was pride. Her newfound skill of defying Death exhilarated her. Little did she know it was a far more dangerous hobby than fortune-telling.

The Friend

I felt a tug on my hair and looked up at the little boy sitting beside me playing with Legos. I knew it was Lane. In defense of my hair, I smacked his little shoulder with my tiny hand. He looked up from his toys, shocked. His little face scrunched up tight, and little tears sprang to his eyes. I heard a laugh from behind me. I looked back and saw Brant. He was covering his mouth, thoroughly pleased with his private joke.

Lane's crying should have brought the attention of his mother, but it didn't. Neither Genie nor Cass emerged from around the kitchen to check on us. I stood up and walked to the kitchen, but the two cups of coffee on the bar counter were growing cold.

I went to the patio door and saw them outside talking. Judging from the hand gestures, they were doing more than talking. I slid open the door to hear their words.

"He's not going to let up, Genie," my mother said. "I stole my daughter from him, and now he is punishing me for it."

"I know."

"What am I going to do? He is destroying my life. Everywhere I go, men are looking at me like a platter of meat. I don't know who I've slept with or who just wants to sleep with me. I'm becoming the town whore, and I don't even remember any of it. Mark is going to find out eventually, and then what? How do I explain this?"

"Maybe you could tell him the truth?"

Cass scoffed. "Just like you are honest with your husband."

"I don't hide my craft."

"Is that right? Did you tell him we brought Tori back from the dead?"

"Of course not. He would have me committed, but Mark is more open-minded than Rex."

"I doubt he's open-minded about his marriage vows," Cass snapped.

"What do you want to do? Maybe we can put a spell on—"

"No! No more magic! That's what got us into this in the first place."

Genie frowned. "We can't give up, Cass. I know you're scared, but if we can bring a child back from the dead, surely we can close up this rift."

"The rift is open *because* we brought her back."

Genie put her hands in prayer against her mouth. "You aren't suggesting we give her back."

"No!" Cass screeched. "Of course not!" There was a long silence between them before my mother spoke again. "Maybe he will accept a different soul in return for the one that was stolen."

Genie's eyes widened, and she shook her head. "No. I won't let you sacrifice yourself. This was both of our doing. We will both pay the price. Whatever the cost, we will pay it, but no one is going to die." Genie grabbed her by the shoulders and shook her. "I am not going to let anything happen to you or your daughter. Just give me some time to think of a solution. Please." Genie pulled Cass into a hug, and she cried on her shoulder.

"You're a good friend, Genie."

Genie nodded and stroked her head.

The Debt

It was unusual to wake up in a bed next to Lane, but since we were still children, I assumed this was our usual naptime procedure. I left the bed and tiptoed down the hallway to spy on the fun I assumed my mother and Genie were having while I was sleeping.

The half-wall allowed me to sneak up on the living room unnoticed. I could easily peek through the decorative wood spindles at the activity in the center of the room without being discovered.

To make room for a circle of pens and pencils, they had moved the coffee table from the center of the room. At the epicenter was my mother. She was on all fours, writhing and frothing at the mouth. She was growling and snorting like an animal. At first, I wanted to laugh. The deep, dark secret in my mother's life was that she liked to pretend to be a wild animal.

Then her head snapped to one side, and her jaw ratcheted open with a loud crack. "How dare you summon me!" The voice from her mouth was not her own. She sounded like a man—an angry old man. "You are tangling with power that is not your own, witch!"

Genie circled the incarnation with a watchful eye. When she stopped, she raised her hands in a lazy surrender. "I have not brought you here to fight you. I have brought you here to negotiate on Cass's behalf."

"I do not negotiate."

"We didn't understand what we were doing that day. We only wanted to save a little girl."

"The child was meant to come to me. She was destined to pass through the veil."

"And she will, when she is old and gray."

"No."

"What does time matter to you?"

"The power of the soul matters."

"I don't understand."

"It must be a child."

"You want Tori's soul because she is a child?"

"That is the debt. The payment for my loss is the soul of a child. My patience grows thin. Decide your sacrifice, or I will decide for you."

"What do you mean, decide?"

Cass stood and looked at Genie eye to eye across the expanse of her magical barrier. "I require a child's soul to fill the vacancy. I do not care which one." Genie shook her head. "Tori is who you owe." Genie's face crumpled with fear. "But Lane or Brant will satisfy the debt."

Tears sprang to her eyes, and she started panting. "Never! I will never let you take my children!"

"Then choose as you please, but I must have the soul of an offspring to pay your debt."

"There has to be another way!"

"Nothing you can do will prevent me from getting what is owed to me. I am forever. I am always. I am the only power that has ever or will ever matter. Nothing and no one can escape death."

The Binding

I heard a gentle humming behind me. My hair was being brushed in a soothing and loving manner. I looked back and saw Genie prepping my hair for a second braid. I touched the left one, admiring the way the tight plait felt to my fingers.

Genie clicked her tongue. "Looks like someone has gotten gum in their hair. I wonder how that got there," she asked as she reached around and popped the bubble I was blooming with my bubble gum. I giggled and pulled away to protect my next bubble from being prematurely popped. "Hold still; I'll get it."

She tugged on my hair, and I felt and heard the familiar snip of scissors.

"There, all better. You won't even notice it missing."

I smiled up at Genie as she winked at me. I noticed the length of hair between her fingers. She folded it up and placed it in her pocket before continuing to braid my hair.

The Threat

The argument I heard outside my bedroom was not the usual ruckus of drunken partygoers. This was something different. I pulled myself out of bed and peeked under my door to see what was going on.

Down the hall, I could see my parents standing face to face at the top of the stairs. They tried to keep their voices below the din of music and conversation downstairs, so they hissed every word they spoke.

"How could you do this to me, Cass?" My father motioned to their bedroom.

"It's not me!" she hissed.

"For fuck's sake, I caught you in the act. You can't deny this."

"I'm not denying what you saw, just who was in control."

"I've heard the rumors! I didn't want to believe them, but it's true, isn't it? It's all true."

"Please, Mark, I beg you to listen to me. I was not in control of myself. There is something inside of me making me do this."

"Don't! You can't keep making excuses for your behavior. You have been out of control since...since the pool." My father seemed to deduce the connection as he spoke it.

"Yes, because something happened to me that day."

"You almost lost your daughter."

"Yes, and everything since then is a direct response to that."

"So, your daughter almost dying gives you an excuse to fuck Ted in our bedroom?" Mark asked with barely contained volume.

"I'm not choosing to do this. I'm being controlled by a force."

"Oh, really? And is this force making you hit your child too?"

"What?" Cass shrank back. "What are you talking about?"

"I know what you did to Tori yesterday. I saw the burn on her arm."

Cass shook her head. "She burned it on my curling iron."

"Is that what you want to believe?" Mark asked.

"I didn't see her do it. She told me that's what happened. I put ice on it right away. She's fine."

"That's not what she told me."

There was a long pause as Cass's mouth hung open. "What did she—?"

"She told me you grabbed her and pressed it to her arm."

Cass lurched and held her stomach like she was about to be sick. "Oh, God. Oh, please God, no!"

"She didn't want me to tell you," Mark said. Cass looked up at him, questioning the statement. "Tori said it wasn't your fault. She said it was 'Mean Mommy' that did it."

"Mean Mommy?"

"Yeah, she said sometimes Mean Mommy hurts her and yells at her."

"No." Cass sank to the floor. "I didn't know. I swear to God, Mark, I don't remember. I don't remember hurting her. I don't remember the affairs. I would never do that to either of you." Cass reached for Mark, but he backed away.

"Do you want to know what Mean Mommy says to her while she's hurting her?"

Cass froze, staring at Mark, waiting for the awful truth.

"She says..." Mark choked on the words as his anger turned to anguish. "*The child must die.*"

Cass's gaze fell to the floor as she took in that information. "He's trying to get to her through me. He's getting stronger. He's using my connection to—"

"I can't listen to this bullshit!" Mark waved her away. "I don't know what's going on with you, but it stops now. You want to fuck other men? Go ahead. But you ever touch my little girl again...I'll kill you." Mark turned to go downstairs. "What the fuck are you looking at?" he hollered down to someone as he descended the staircase. A moment later, I heard the front door slam.

The Betrayal

"I know what you did!" Cass yelled from downstairs. I sneaked down to watch the argument unfold from the obscurity of the stair balusters. My mother and Genie were inside the living room, standing apart as they yelled at each other. "I can feel it! He's here! He's in this house with us!"

"I had to!" Genie yelled back.

"You had to! You had to put my child at even more risk?"

"You don't understand, Cass. He was threatening to take one of my children in her place. I had to protect them."

"By putting mine on the chopping block?"

"It was her soul that we stole. I'm sorry it happened, but it was your child lying dead on the side of that pool, not mine."

"Only because your son pushed her into the deep end! Maybe *he* should be the one to pay the debt!"

"It was an accident!"

"Oh, bullshit, that brat has been picking on her since the first day he met her."

"That doesn't mean he deserves to die."

"You're right. All of this is *your* fault. My daughter nearly drowning. My being tormented by a vengeful monster. My marriage falling apart. All this pain started because *you* couldn't be bothered to discipline that little shit."

Genie slapped my mother, and Cass slapped her back. For a moment they just looked at each other, eyes virulent on both sides.

"I'm sorry you have to go through this again, Cass, but I will not allow my sons to die in place of your daughter."

"And what can you do to stop it?" Cass propped her hands on her hips. When Genie's face expressed her shock, Cass laughed at her. "You don't think I know? All this power we have together. Everything we've been doing since the beginning. It's me, Genie! It's all me. I'm the one with the power here."

"I have power!"

"Oh, yes, I can't wait to see who you'll recruit to get your fix now. Brant doesn't seem to like playing Mommy's magic game anymore. How about Lane? Maybe he'll be able to tap into the ether world between snack time and nap time."

Genie stared at her, eyes turning cold even as the rest of her expression deadened. "I am stronger than you think, Cass. Maybe not in magic, but in resolve. That's why I bound him and Tori to this house. This is between them now. If he wants a soul, then he can take the one he originally came for. And if you want to stop it, then you'll need to find a way that doesn't put my children at risk." Genie moved past Cass toward the front door. I slipped back on the stairs to stay hidden.

Genie stopped at the door and looked back. "I didn't want things to end this way. I still don't. I'll do what I can to help. If there is anything left to do."

The Escape

"We can't just leave!" Mark called after my mother as she frantically packed my things into a bag. I was watching from the bed, though I doubted either of them even remembered I was there.

"Yes, we can. And we will. It's the only way to protect Tori."

"From what?"

"From this thing inside of me!"

"The only thing inside of you is a mental break!" Mark yelled back at her.

"Fine! Call it whatever you want, but I know you've seen it. I know you've seen the face that looks back at you in the mirror." Mark's expression sobered, and he took a step back. "Did you think that was me? Did the face staring back at you remind you of your loving wife? Or did you see the monster inside of me peeking out?"

"I don't understand."

Cass moved to him and touched his face, even though it made him flinch. "You don't have to understand, just do as I say. That thing inside me is tied to this house and to Tori. I am going to get her as far away from this place as I can, and I am going to make sure she never comes back. All I need you to do is pack a bag for us and get her in the car so we can get the hell out of this house and this town before anything bad happens to her."

Mark stared at her, fear creeping into his dumbfounded expression as he tried to comprehend the urgency she was putting into her words. He glanced at me and nodded. He put on a fake smile and moved toward me. "Okay, kiddo, time for a trip. You wanna help Daddy pack?"

I nodded, and he picked me up. We headed into the master bedroom, and he frantically threw clothes into a suitcase. He didn't seem to care what went in as long as it was tops and bottoms, male and female. With over half the clothes still in the closet, he closed the suitcase and latched it. He picked it up by the handle and ushered me into his arms.

I clasped onto him like a monkey, and he left the bedroom. Just as his feet started to tromp down the stairs, a horrific cry pealed through the air. I looked over his shoulder at Cass racing down the hall. "You can't take her!" she wailed.

Mean Mommy, as I had designated her, leaped onto my father as he turned to look at her. We fell back, toppling over one another as we rolled down the flight, bumping and skidding against the stair treads one by one. We all landed at the bottom slightly stunned.

Cass awakened and grabbed me. I screamed as her nails pinched into my arm. My father awoke and wrestled to peel her off me. When I was free, I scrambled away, taking refuge under the piano in the front room.

"I will have what's mine!" Cass screamed with the voice of the great beyond. Power rippled off her like a wave of heat. I felt it in my throat, robbing me of air. I panted, grasping at my neck, though there were no hands strangling me.

"Daddy!" I croaked a scream before coughing up water.

Mark looked over at me as he struggled to hold Cass. He frowned at my obvious and unnatural peril. He turned his shock to the woman snarling above him.

"She belongs to the dead."

Mark seemed to glean the true nature of the threat before him. Instead of cowering before the awesome strength of Death itself, he narrowed his eyes and tensed his jaw to glare at it. "The fuck she does!" Mark threw his fist hard into my mother's chin. Her head ratcheted back. Her eyes rolled and then she flopped down against his chest. My suffering was instantly relieved, and I could breathe again.

He maneuvered from under her and flopped her limp body over his shoulder. He left behind the suitcase and reached out for my hand. "Come on, honey. Mom's sick. We need to get her out of here before she gets sicker." I reluctantly came out of hiding and took his hand.

He pulled me along, down the hallway toward the back door. I could barely keep up with him. He shoved open the creaky screen door with such force that it banged against the house. It sounded like a gunshot to my ears.

Sunlight blinded me, and for a moment I saw fire in my vision. It passed, and I jumped off the small cement stoop to keep up with my father's pace.

The screen door slammed shut behind us. I looked back and saw it banging rhythmically as it settled into the doorframe.

Thump. Thump. Thump.

The noise echoed in my head, demanding my attention. I looked toward my father. My mother was unconscious, lying limp over his shoulder, but her eyes snapped open and looked directly at me. "He's coming," she whispered to me.

We were still racing for the car, but we weren't making any progress. Time was standing still. The only movement was of that damn screen door.

Thump. Thump. Thump.

I looked back at my mother; her now-charred face stared back at me. "He's here!"

A crash sounded behind me, and the house shattered into splinters of wood. Darkness surrounded me, and the reaper charged forward. I was in the attic again. He had broken through the door.

He leaped onto me, and his bony fingers ripped into my soft flesh. He held me down against the floor, pressing me deeper until my chest couldn't lift for a breath. I turned to look at my body—my younger self. She roused and coughed up water.

"Mother!" I yelled at the darkness in the corner where I had seen her before.

The blackened form shifted. "You must save yourself," she rasped.

"How?" I yelled with my last useful air.

"You must use your power." I shook my head, no longer able to move air past my vocal cords. "You are a necromancer like me. You can breach the veil between worlds. You are more powerful than you know. You must tap into the deepest part of your gift and use it to fight your attacker."

"How?" I mouthed more than spoke.

"You've done it once before. You must do it again," she said. "Remember," she whispered, and the world shifted again.

The Sacrifice

Dark to light. Light to dark. And back again.

The screen door had stopped banging, but my heart's thumping had taken its place in my ears. I was in the car now. We should have been driving away, but my mother was awake.

I registered her fingers piercing my skin, her tight grip on my neck. She was screaming at me, demanding my soul. My father was a blur beside her. He was trying to pull her off me, but she was unnaturally strong.

His screams were pleas for my mother to release me and to wake up. To protect me, he had taken to outright punching her again. Her face turned bloodier with each impact. The purple swelling in her right eye did little more than obscure her vision.

I felt a tightness in my throat cutting off my air. The vision flickered again.

Light to dark.

The reaper was over me, pressing me down. I felt a pressure inside me, different from the pain of exsanguination. It was building, like anger, waiting to explode out of me.

"There," my mother whispered from out of the darkness. "You found it."

The light returned, and my mother's face loomed over me in the car as she strangled me. "Use it," she whispered through the face of my Mean Mommy even as she was trying to kill me.

Darkness returned, and I felt the power surging up inside of me. Something was wrong. I didn't want to use this power. I knew what it was. I knew what it would cost me.

I shook my head, gripping the two locks of hair in my hand—hair that had bound me to myself. Bound me to my younger self. Bound me to another time.

This was not an echo.

"No!" I screamed in the light and the dark.

"It's okay," my mother whispered from the shadows. I turned and saw her emerge, but now she was whole again, her beautiful face no longer marred with the evidence of her cruel death. She leaned down and brushed a tear from my cheek. "It's what has to happen."

"No, I can't do this! I won't do this!"

"You cannot escape death." The hooded face above me spoke. "Not without a price."

"It's too much!"

"It's already done, sweetheart," my father spoke from the light. He turned from his struggles with my mother and looked at me with a serene smile. "Your mother and I have already made our choice." The darkness returned, and I was back on the attic floor. My father had joined my mother and was leaning over me on the other side. "You have to start this here, so you can finish it in the past."

"I did it?" I cried. "I killed you?"

Mark pushed back my hair and leaned down to kiss my forehead. "That doesn't matter now. All that matters is that a debt must be paid, and we..." Mark reached across to Cass. She took his hand, and they both looked down at me lovingly. "We paid that debt."

"But I love you!" I yelled, feeling the pain I should have felt then. Years of memories had returned, leaving me with the despair of knowing how much I had lost. Knowing what I truly should have missed.

"We love you," my father said. "That's why you must do this."

"Do it for us, Tori," my mother said. "Let us die, knowing that you will live."

I screamed in agony from the hole being ripped in my heart. The heartache overwhelmed me, and the world between the veil and the past merged. A torrent of power surged all around me, consuming the two worlds in fire. It charred the human flesh of my parents and ripped away the inhuman flesh of the reaper, revealing his bony hands and skull.

The only sounds I could hear were my own screams...and then I only heard my cries.

The Remembrance

I lay on the floor crying for hours. I was back in the world of the living in my own body and in my own time, but I was not the same as when I had left. My memories had come flooding back—the bits and pieces that made little to no sense, now connected thread by thread to the fabric of my life. The death of my parents, which had once held no emotional weight, was now an overwhelming pressure on my heart. The shame of my actions and the grief of their loss inundated my thoughts. With every renewed memory of parental love, I wallowed in anguish for what I had lost. It was fourteen years too late, but the tears were as ardent as they should have been the day it happened.

I wanted to take it all back and undo what I had done, but I couldn't. Even if I could take back my choice, the fire was already fourteen years in the past. All it took was my permission to complete the sacrifice.

I hadn't made the choice as a child. I couldn't have made that decision then. What little girl would willingly sacrifice her parents?

But an adult—an adult with few memories of them—could think logically. I could understand the purpose of their death, even if I didn't want to be their executioner.

I could still feel the two locks of hair gripped in my hand: the binding that had allowed me to connect with myself in the past. I unraveled the string and released both of us. The hair dropped to the floor.

I looked around my home, which was filled with bright streams of dusty light. The only thing different about it was the little girl sitting on the piano bench, swinging her legs as she watched me.

"Is it over?" I asked.

"Yup," Anna answered. "Are you sad?"

"Yup," I answered, wiping away another set of tears. "Now what?" I asked her.

She shrugged.

"Is the house empty, or are the other ghosts still here?" I asked, hoping that the more aggressive ghosts had only been here on Death's coattails.

Anna shrugged again, giving me a sour face, like I was taxing her patience.

I laughed at her despite my morose mood. "You know, you aren't a very helpful ghost."

She scrunched her face up tight. "My daddy says that fortune-tellers are for people who don't have hands and feet of their own."

I nodded, assuming that was Anna's way of saying I was going to have to figure things out for myself. "Your daddy must have been a smart man."

I pulled myself off the floor and looked around my home. I wasn't sure I could sense evil the way Genie claimed to be able to, but there was something different about the house. Without the threat of death looming over me, it was just lumber and plaster again.

With the memories of my past stitched back into place, I had far more attachment to it than before. Despite its murderous history, this house had also been filled with love.

I wasn't sure my renovations would shed the home's stigma for being haunted, but I suspected I would still try. It was high time for me to put some proper roots down, and give or take the occasional run-ins with nosy gossips and wicked witches, Harold was a nice place to live.

I grabbed my keys and headed to the front door. Before I left, I looked back at Anna. "I'm not sure how it works where you're from, but if you happen to see them, would you tell them something for me?" Anna shrugged and nodded as if she had no intention of remembering what I was asking of her. "Tell them I love them."

She snorted out a laugh. "They already know that, stupid."

I chuckled at her blunt response. "Good. Will you be hanging around?"

Anna poked at the piano, making up a makeshift melody with three keys. "That's up to you," she said, reminding me that her presence here was more up to me than it was her.

"Okay, I'll see you later, kid." I headed out the front door and froze on the front porch. The rocks surrounding my property reminded me I had unfinished business with Mrs. Hart.

Her actions were necessary, of course. Being trapped in the veil allowed me to pay my debt to Death. My memories had returned, and I had solved a 14-year-old mystery. My questions finally had answers.

Still, my future mother-in-law had effectively just tried to kill me. That wasn't an affront that could go unanswered. We had a very awkward conversation in our future.

I tromped down the front steps and kicked a few rocks out of the so-called protective circle before I headed to my car.

The Warning

"I was kind of hoping to have a romantic dinner by ourselves tonight," Brant said as we approached his mother's door.

"I know. I'm sorry, but Genie and I have something to discuss."

We rang the doorbell, and Lane opened the door. He looked us over and laughed. "Why do you ring the doorbell at your parent's house, moron?" he asked Brant.

"Because privacy is appropriate for everyone, including parents."

"Whatever. Hey, Tori, I was about to start a game. You wanna race?"

"I'd love to, but I need to talk to your mom first. Can Brant fill in for me?"

"I don't know." Lane turned his narrowed eyes on his brother. "Can my brother demean himself by playing a child's game?"

Brant chuckled and nodded. "You mean, can I lower myself to your level of immaturity?"

"Yeah."

"Of course." Brant jumped through the door, and they started smacking each other and wrestling like children.

I laughed at them and maneuvered around the melee to get to the kitchen. "Hey, Tori, she's grilling in the backyard." Mr. Hart pointed to the patio door. "Hey, you boys stop that," he griped at his adult children.

I slipped through the patio doors and headed toward the grill where Genie was toiling to make dinner. "Honey, did you remember the thermometer? I can never tell when the chicken is done." When I didn't answer, she turned around.

She caught sight of my face and gasped. She dropped her tongs and backed into the grill. She yelped as she burned her back and shifted forward again. "Tori." She looked at me fearfully and then toward the house. I knew what she was thinking about. She was thinking about the risk to her sons while I was still alive. She licked her lips as they quivered in terror. "I..."

"It's over," I said.

She paused and looked at me, baffled. "What?"

"It's over. The debt has been paid."

"It has?" She frowned. "How?" she asked as if I might have kidnapped a small child to do it.

"My parents paid the debt."

"They...But they were already... He was..."

"It's hard to explain, but what needed to be done was finished today. I finished it."

Genie's eyes flickered over mine. "You finished it?"

"Yes. Both my parents had to die, so I could live."

Genie released a breath and looked at the floor. "I didn't want to do what I did. I was afraid for Lane and Brant."

"I know. I know everything. I know you were put in an impossible situation. I know saving me nearly cost you one of your own children."

Genie took a stuttering breath, tears blooming in her eyes. "I never meant you harm. I do love you, but..." She looked toward the house.

"It's okay. I really do understand. A mother must protect her own. That's what my mother did."

Genie frowned. "So, the fire that day...? Did Cass...?"

"No. It was me. I was the killer all along."

Genie's face fell with that realization. "Oh, Tori. I don't know what to say."

"You don't have to say anything. I have the answers I needed. They just weren't the answers I wanted." Genie reached for me, but I stepped away from her. She frowned. "I need a little more time. I suspect you and I have a long journey ahead of us." I nodded toward the house. "Brant and I are officially dating."

Genie smiled. "Good."

"I have one condition for this happily ever after, though."

"What's that?"

"The magic. It has to be done."

She frowned and shook her head. "What do you mean?" She gave me a fake smile.

"You know what I mean. It's too dangerous, and you were more than a little addicted to the power you got from my mother—and me."

"Don't be silly, it's only a hobby now."

"Herbalism is a hobby. Crystals are a hobby. Tapping into the energies of the afterlife is meddling with things you don't understand. And I won't let you do it any longer."

"But think of what we could achieve! You are so much stronger than your mother."

"Yes, I am," I said resolutely. "That's why I'm not asking you to stop." The grill behind her flared up with a sudden burst of flame. She jumped and looked at it. When she looked back at me, she was frightened again. "I'm *telling* you to stop."

I walked back to the patio door and opened it before turning back to face her with a cheerful smile. "Smells great, Mrs. Hart. I can't wait to sink my teeth into some home cookin'."

I headed inside and found the boys playing a vicious game of car racing. Part of their strategy seemed to be punching each other to throw the other person off. I disrupted some of the violence and sat down on Brant's lap. "Everything okay?" he asked.

"It's perfect," I said and pulled his hair.

"Ouch," he complained. "What was that for?"

"I'm starting to get some of my memories back, and I recall that I owe you *many* hair pulls."

"Is that so?" he asked seductively. "Can I at least choose when and where my punishment takes place?"

I laughed, and he pulled me into a kiss.

"Hey, no making out; we're playing a game here," Lane whined.

"Dinner's ready," Genie called from the kitchen.

"Come on, boys," Mr. Hart ordered. "Let's not keep the food waiting."

Lane and Mr. Hart headed out to the patio for dinner, but Brant and I stayed back a moment longer to finish our kiss.

FELICIA JEDLICKA

SUCCESSORS

Book 1
THE WARDEN

THE WARDEN
Successors

Somewhere in depths of the arctic circle lies a prison that holds as many secrets as it does monsters.

Thrust into the secret world of supernatural criminal containment, Ethan and Cori do their best to serve the prison's warden and acclimate to life as they now know it. While Ethan thrives under Danato's effort to mold him into the next warden, Cori's independent nature rebels against the intemperate man at every turn.

As the plus one in the warden's effort to expand his personnel, Cori finds that the honor of her servitude to this enigmatic man will involve a lot of shit-shoveling. And that's not a metaphor. Benefiting from the freedom of her janitorial duties, she recruits a lovestruck werewolf to escape her captivity. Though a death sentence according to the prison rules, Danato is reluctant to be responsible for the death of yet another woman he has grown to care for.

After another of life's poetic misfortunes brings Cori back to the prison, she finds herself at square one. Newly motivated by despair, she is determined to make the best of her situation, just like Ethan. Unfortunately, her lofty pursuit to steal the wardenship steps on more than a few toes. While Cori has been living a normal life, Ethan has blossomed into a man worthy of leading the prison. His resentment of Cori's twice-over betrayal leaves him vulnerable to the many creatures in the prison that can't be contained behind bars. Cori and Ethan will soon learn how lesser demons deal with broken hearts.

Thank you so much for reading. I hope you enjoyed the ride and if you aren't getting off here, I encourage you to sign up for my newsletter so I can return your generosity with new release updates and special offers.

Sign-Up

You can also find me on Facebook or visit my website. Keep reading!

Website

Facebook

Author

FELICIA JEDLICKA writes immersive fantasy and science fiction that blends strange worlds with deeply human characters. Known for crafting character-driven stories with escalating stakes, Felicia weaves complex relationships, moral dilemmas, and epic confrontations into every book.

Whether it's a book about a top-secret prison, witches performing exorcisms, or the unraveling of galactic alliances, Felicia's work centers on the people at the heart of the chaos. Her prose is straightforward and infused with a sharp, elegant wit that pushes her story forward without stealing the stage.

When not writing, she can usually be found playing video games with her husband, cooking delicious meals from her garden, or hanging with her girls at her weekly girls' night.

www.ingramcontent.com/pod-product-compliance
Lightning Source LLC
Chambersburg PA
CBHW021240190726

48289CB00005B/1411